FORMATION

FORMATION

THE GHOST SQUADRON BOOK 1

SARAH NOFFKE

MICHAEL ANDERLE

FORMATION TEAM

**JIT Beta Readers -
From all of us, our deepest gratitude!**

Kelly ODonnell
Tim Bischoff
Keith Verret
Micky Cocker
Daniel Weigert
Larry Omans
Kimberly Boyer
Sarah Weir
James Caplan
John Raisor
AbH Belxjander Draconis Serechai

*If we missed anyone, **please** let us know!*

For Lydia. My greatest treasure in the universe.
-Sarah

To Family, Friends and
Those Who Love
To Read.
May We All Enjoy Grace
To Live the Life We Are
Called.
- Michael

Five Trees Bar. Trill Mining Colony, Lorialis System.

T'turk played with his drink. His four shipmates were rowdy and occasionally bumped him, so he had to be careful not to spill his drink. He looked around Five Trees, the only damned bar worth visiting, in his opinion, for five systems.

That wasn't saying much, of course, since the only people living out this far from the Etheric Empire's territory were pirates, miners, and smugglers. Bastards, all of them.

"My kind of people," he muttered to himself, smiling as his shipmate Fr'ling caught the eye of one of the girls.

Fr'ling wouldn't be leaving this space station with much money. Hell, neither would the other three. By the time the night ended, they'd each spend most of their earnings.

Nursing his drink, he looked around the establishment, blinking with his yellow eyes. There were a lot of Kezzin in the bar tonight, including himself. Their red skin gave off a familiar glow in the artificial light. T'turk's homeworld wasn't far from here, so it was common to see his people on many of the stations in the neighboring systems. He liked it that way. The rest of the galaxy was far too crowded with non-Kezzin species, like humans and the other Etheric Empire scum. He couldn't stand any of them.

It was unfortunate, then, that he saw a man sitting on a stool with his face planted on the table. A human male who didn't belong here.

T'turk smirked. Perhaps he'd have a little fun today, after all.

"Hey, you," grunted T'turk as he got up from his table and walking to where the man was sitting. "Human."

The man had his face on the table—probably passed out from too much alcohol. "Look at this guy," said T'turk. "Typical human. Can't even handle his drink."

The man moaned, shifting a little.

T'turk leaned over him and examined his equipment, hoping to find some money or possibly a key to a ship. The bastard wasn't holding much except for a gray bag on the seat next to him. T'turk reached for it.

"Don't," said the human, slowly looking at him.

T'turk could never tell one human from the next. They all looked like a bunch of slugs to him, ugly and spongy. This one was no different.

"What are you trying to hide, human? Got yourself a secret stash?"

The man said nothing.

T'turk laughed. "That's what I thought. Too bad you

were stupid enough to come in here." He reached for the bag.

A hand grabbed his wrist, surprising him. "I said don't."

T'turk paused, glancing at the man again. "Do you have a death wish, meat sack? Back off before I kick your ass."

"No can do," replied the stranger. "That's my stuff. I need it more than you do."

"It's mine now, unless you want a bullet in your empty head." T'turk shook his wrist free, then took the bag and began emptying it. A pad fell out, hitting the counter, along with a handful of unopened soda cans, one of which rolled and hit the floor, breaking and hissing.

T'turk stared at the contents of the bag, confused. "What's all this trash?"

The stranger looked at the soda on the floor as it sprayed chaotically. "Mother fucker," he muttered.

T'turk threw the empty bag down by his feet. "You better have something on you, human! I'll rip you a new one right now. You know how many of your kind I've killed just this week? You're all a bunch of mushy pieces of—"

"You killed humans?" interrupted the stranger, raising his brow.

"Over a dozen in four days!" bragged T'turk. "Ain't that right, boys?"

His crew cheered. "We raided a ship on its way to Nexus Colony," announced Fr'ling. "Killed half and saved the rest for later."

T'turk grinned, revealing a set of razor sharp teeth. "That's why we're here celebrating.

The human let out a sigh. "All I wanted was a drink and

some food, but you just had to go and bring that up like a fucking jackass."

"What's he saying, T'turk?" asked Fr'ling. "Tell him to speak up! It's hard to hear humans. They're too tiny."

T'turk laughed. "He's scared. He knows he's about to die."

The door to the Five Trees opened, and in walked another human. A woman, perhaps, but T'turk couldn't be certain. They all looked the same to him, ugly and pathetic.

She took a seat at the bar beside the male, motioning to the barkeep. "Whiskey," she requested, turning away from T'turk.

"You," he said, puffing his chest at the female. "You're interrupting us."

She didn't answer.

T'turk was about to raise his fist to the woman, when the male got to his feet. "Let's leave the lady out of it. This is between you and me."

"Between us?" grinned T'turk. "Finally."

The man turned to the female. "Hey, wanna do me a favor?"

She shrugged. "Depends."

"Just watch my drink while I take care of this idiot, would ya?" He slid his glass over to her. "I'm Eddie, by the way."

"Whatever," the female answered, still not bothering to look.

The human male turned back to face T'turk. "All right, then, big fella," grinned the little man. "Let's see what you can do."

The bartender set the glass of whiskey on the table, and Julianna thanked him for it. "Bring me another three, would you?"

"Certainly," he said in an agreeable tone.

She tossed the shot back in one straight motion, letting it slide down her throat with ease, ignoring the burn. It was hard to find the good stuff this far out into the galaxy, here on the rim, but she'd take the worst whiskey in the universe over the alien sludge they called alcohol here. These people wouldn't know a good drink if it cracked them over the side of their—

A glass went flying across the bar, hitting one of the patrons between his eyes. The alien fell straight to the floor, which caused his friend to panic. From the other direction, she heard the sound of someone getting beaten, followed by a scream.

"Here you are," said the bartender, delivering the rest of her drinks.

She looked down at the three shots of whiskey, and nodded. "That'll do."

The barkeep turned and left her alone. At the same time, a splatter of blood landed on the seat where Eddie had been sitting.

Julianna took the first of the three shots and slammed the tiny glass on the counter. The whiskey burned her lips and went down hard, putting a fire in her belly.

At that same moment, an alien by the name of Fr'ling spiraled into two of the barstools nearby. She felt the vibration in her legs as his red, scale-covered head met the metal support.

She took another shot.

"Whoa," said a husky voice near the bathroom. He was a military man in every sense of the word, except he wasn't wearing a uniform. Instead, like Julianna, he wore a set of ordinary-looking civilian clothes. It was an attempt to blend in and draw less attention. Uniforms weren't common out here on the fringe, after all, and they didn't need anyone asking questions. Even still, despite the outfit, the man had a hard time hiding who he truly was—a hardened, long-term military veteran with centuries under his belt. Like Julianna, this man had witnessed the birth of the Empire. He'd seen the deaths of countless enemies, even slain a few himself. Hell, depending on who you asked, this individual *was* the Empire. At the very least, he was the one at the top.

His name was Lance Reynolds, a living legend. A man they told stories about. He was the father of the great Queen herself.

And he had just taken a piss in the bathroom of a back-alley bar in the middle of nowhere. "What did I miss?" asked the General. He zipped up his fly, then walked over to the bar and looked at her.

"Just a bunch of idiots, sir."

"Is that our boy? Looks like he's taking quite the beating," observed Lance.

She shrugged. "He was asking for it." She glanced down at her last drink.

"We should probably do something," Lance suggested.

Julianna pursed her lips, then nodded. "Yes, sir."

She picked up the glass with three fingers and flung the awful whiskey back. "Ah," she sighed, forcing it down. "Tastes like shit."

One of the aliens let out a cry from behind them. Julianna swiveled in her seat to see what was going on, half-expecting to find her target dead.

Instead, she saw two aliens holding him by the arms. He had them locked together, all three of them unable to move.

Julianna got to her feet and cleared her throat. She looked directly at the three fighters as they pressed against one another. "That's enough!"

Her voice boomed through the bar like thunder, and everyone who was still conscious turned to look in her direction.

Edward had his fist raised, and there was blood on his knuckles, but he didn't move. "Oh boy," he grinned. "That's some kind of voice."

"Quiet, human," ordered T'turk, who had his arms around Edward's neck and chest, keeping him in place. "Or you'll be next."

Edward snickered. "Get in line for the bad ass kicking."

"You think I'm playing with you?" asked the alien. "I'll rip you apart like a—"

Before the word could leave T'turk's mouth, Eddie slipped through his arms and ducked beneath him. He dug his fist straight into the alien's ribcage. Julianna heard a bone crack. Eddie's foot came up, bashing the second alien in the waist, stifling him.

Julianna looked at Lance. "Do you mind?"

The General chortled. "Have fun, you two."

She returned her gaze to the alien captain, the one who had bragged about how he had taken the lives of all those humans and how he'd tortured them, and Julianna leapt forward. She dashed so quickly that she was almost a blur, her fist hitting the thick-chested alien in the neck, breaking his windpipe. Before he could realize what was happening, she fell to her side and brought her foot up, kicking him in the face, sending him to the floor. He fell like a brick wall, shaking the very foundation of the place.

Edward grinned at the sight before him, but rather than gawk and stare, he turned toward the only alien remaining.

"No, wait!" begged the thin, red-skinned Kezzin.

But Edward wasn't listening. He punched him in the jaw, sending a splatter of orange blood into the air. Eddie jammed both palms into the alien's chest, sending the pirate two meters back and into the wall, instantly knocking him unconscious as he slid into a puddle of spilled beer.

Julianna stood over T'turk as he struggled to gasp for air. The alien clutched his throat. "H-How?"

Julianna towered over him with Eddie by her side. "You're surprised?" she asked the pirate. "You didn't expect humans to wipe the floor with you?"

"That's why you lost," muttered Eddie.

Julianna took a step back, and turned to the man she had traveled so far to see. "Edward Teach, is it?"

He took a napkin from the nearby table and wiped the blood from his fingers. "And you are?"

"Julianna Fregin. I've come a long way to meet you."

He twisted his lips, curiously. "That so? Are you from a collections agency? I owe you some money? If this is about the ship I crashed a few months ago, that wasn't my fault. I was sideswiped. It was a good old-fashioned hit-and-run."

"It's not about that, although I might have questions." Julianna glanced at General Reynolds. "Would you care to step in, sir?"

"Who's a '*sir*'?" asked Edward.

"That would be me," answered Lance, approaching from the edge of the bar. "General Lance Reynolds. Pleased to meet you, Captain Teach."

"Wait, wait, wait...You're Lance Reynolds?" asked Edward. He shook his head. "No fucking way. That's not—"

"Possible? I'll be the first to admit, I don't normally run off to this sector, but I decided to make a special exception today."

Eddie studied the General for a moment, analyzing his clothes, and leaning in to examine his face. "You don't look like the most powerful man in the galaxy. Are you two fucking with me right now? Is this a joke or something?"

"I'm undercover," said Lance. "You should know, since, based on your clothes, I'm guessing you are too."

"What's wrong with the way I'm dressed?" asked Eddie, looking down at his messy appearance. He wore a set of baggy clothes, which were now ripped in several places, and his thick, untended beard made him appear homeless.

"Is that a serious question?" asked Julianna. "You look like shit."

"Okay, okay," said Eddie, raising his hands. "But why would you come all this way just to see a guy like me? Did I piss off the wrong person in the Empire?"

"It's the Federation now, but no, nothing like that." Lance chuckled. "Quite the opposite, actually."

"Right, well, what is it then? What would make a guy like you come all the way out to the middle of bum-fucking-nowhere just to see me? I mean, if I don't owe you money and I didn't piss you off, there has to be a good reason."

"Because, Eddie," said Lance, smirking. "You had fifty-seven confirmed kills during your service. You saved countless lives, and your men respected the hell out of you. Sure, you fucked up sometimes. Got into a few scrapes here and there. Spoke out of turn. But you kept those kids alive through the worst of it, and any one of them would give their life for yours. That's what I found out when I went snooping. That's why I'm here. I've been searching far and wide for the right person to do a job, and your name keeps coming up. 'Edward Teach,' they kept saying. 'That's the guy you want.' Is that who you are, Captain? Are you the man they said you were?"

Edward stared at the General, this impossible figure from stories and myths. He was so composed, so relaxed, but there was a strength in his eyes. The kind that only people like Eddie knew. "I'm none of those things anymore."

"Bullshit," said Lance. "You're a goddamn soldier." He pointed to the aliens lying on the floor. "You didn't just pick a fight with them. You raised your fist and you *punished* them, Edward. That's what *we* do. They said they killed a dozen humans, and you taught them why they *shouldn't*. That's the kind of man I came to find. That's the kind of man I need. Someone who knows *what* justice is, and who isn't afraid to show it."

"I'm not sure what to say," Eddie admitted.

"Say you'll come with us and hear me out."

"Hear you out about what, sir?"

"A mission, son." Lance took a step forward, placing his hand on Edward's shoulder. "A mission to save the Etheric Federation."

2

Passenger Lounge Six, *QBS Atticus Finch,* **Lorialis System.**

Eddie sat on the QBS Atticus Finch with his hands at his sides watching the home of the Trill Mining Co. and the Five Trees bar get smaller and smaller as they departed the system.

As the ship activated its gate drive, it prepared to transit, the planet became an instant blur, fading into the void like a pebble into the sea. It had been several years since Eddie had been aboard an Etheric ship like this one. He'd been out of the service for almost a full decade, never spending much time on any of the core planets, and typically hitching rides on cargo ships. It was simply too difficult to be around these types of vessels and not be actively involved.

Even now, the memories flooded him, reminders of a better time, back when he was still useful.

Not the wandering exile he'd since become.

What could General Reynolds possibly need a man like Eddie for? Didn't he have enough soldiers at his disposal to do the job? What could one guy with a drinking habit and a bad haircut do that no other person could?

He scoffed, rolling his eyes. *Don't be an idiot, Eddie. Your hair is fucking phenomenal.*

Eddie had hitched a ride on this cruiser all because a man claiming to be the head of the Federation had asked him to.

Maybe this was all a giant mistake, but Eddie didn't think so. He had a feeling that everything the old man had told him was true—that humanity was under attack and it needed to be protected. After traveling across the outer rim of the galaxy for the last decade, Eddie could tell there was a stink in the air, a certain level of unrest building against the original Empire and the rest of the core planets. Pirates and smugglers had appeared in larger numbers; raiders were becoming more prone to attack. The people were afraid, and no one understood why.

But something told him that General Reynolds knew the answer to that question, and, right now, Eddie was willing to follow him to find out. Even if it was all bullshit, the truth was worth taking a chance on. It was worth uncovering, if only for his own curiosity's sake.

The lights of the passing stars whipped by in a mesmerizing display, relaxing Eddie as he sank into his seat. He watched them fade in and out like falling raindrops, disappearing back into the darkness from which they came.

Docking Bay 17, Deck 25, Onyx Station, Paladin System.

"Follow me," instructed Julianna, standing on the loading bay of the *QBS Atticus Finch*. The ship had only just docked with what appeared to be *Onyx Station*.

Eddie stared at her with an auspicious eye. She was quite the babe, this Julianna woman; tall and slender, with gorgeous, obsidian hair. He could tell she was beautiful the first time he saw her, even in the dimly lit bar. But here, with proper light, she was almost angelic, like she'd been molded by the gods themselves.

Eddie had heard of genetically modified humans, but he'd never actually met one for himself. Such a thing was reserved for higher-ranking military personnel or proven combatants that the Empire viewed as invaluable. The process, what Eddie knew of it, involved a long hibernation period inside a specialized pod, and resulted in enhanced abilities such as speed, strength, and increased reflexes, among several others. It also had the added effect of making you far more attractive. At least, those were the rumors.

In Julianna's case, all of the above seemed to be true.

"Are you my escort?" asked Eddie, walking down the deck.

Julianna raised her brow. "We have a meeting with General Reynolds in five. Are you ready?"

"All work and no play, I see," he remarked.

"Our mission is of the utmost importance. You understand that, right? This isn't some pleasure cruise."

"Are you sure? Because I packed a few pairs of shorts and some sunscreen," he quipped.

"Try and fail to be clever later. We've got shit to do now."

"Let's hit it, boss," said Eddie, tossing his duffel over his shoulder.

She led him through the deck and onto the station's platform. Onyx Station was one of the largest in the Empire, with over six million residents across several species. Some people called it the 'Etheric melting pot'; others said it was nothing but a suffocating box. The few times Eddie had been here, he'd found it to be a mixed bag. He enjoyed the variety of people and experiences, and there was always a new restaurant to try, but he also enjoyed his privacy, and Onyx Station wasn't exactly built for solitude.

Still, it was worth a visit every now and then. He liked the hot dogs on the main deck; Bokey's Pups, he believed the establishment was called. And then there was the Main Street Diner, the closest thing to Earth food you could get out here: burgers, soup, steak, eggs and hash—even spaghetti.

Eddie had never been to Earth. Humanity had long since left it behind. Oh, sure, people still lived there, but he'd never see them. Not in his lifetime.

The galaxy was his home. It always had been.

Eddie was born on an Etheric ship and raised by patriotic parents who knew what they believed. The two of them had met in the military, both of them pilots, and fell in love between missions. For Eddie, being a pilot was in his blood. It was part of his soul.

He had always liked fighting. It relieved his stress, gave his life purpose, and he liked helping people. Moreover, he was good at it. For all of those reasons, being a soldier made sense to him. It was the *only* thing that did.

"Hurry up," prodded Julianna, turning to look at him as they walked through the deck.

He was trailing behind, unaware of the growing gap between them. "Slow down a bit. What's your hurry?"

"We have to meet with General Reynolds in less than two minutes. You're moving too slowly."

He double-timed it to catch up. When he was finally at her side, he gave her a sideways look. "Happy now?"

She didn't answer.

"You're kind of a downer, aren't you?"

"I just have a job to do, that's all," she stated.

"Doesn't mean you can't enjoy it." He grinned. "See? I'm having all kinds of fun."

They reached the elevators, and the doors suddenly opened, as though the machine had been waiting for them.

"Inside," she told him.

"That was…convenient."

"I'm simply never late," affirmed Julianna.

The doors closed and the elevator began its descent. "That so?" asked Eddie.

"I hope you can adjust to being a soldier again, Captain Teach. I understand it's been a while since you last wore the uniform."

"True, but you never really forget, do you?" he answered as the doors opened. "Even if you want to."

She glanced at him and nodded. "No, I guess you don't."

They stepped out, making their way through a long corridor with silver walls. Each side was lined with offices, though a single desk sat in each of them. It seemed both natural and strange that no one should be on this deck, based on what he knew about the meeting he was about to have.

They rounded the corner, and Julianna stopped. "With ten seconds to spare. In here," she directed, motioning to a closed door.

Eddie smiled. "You should know, my birthday isn't until next month. I hope there's no party inside. I'd still take some cake, though."

Julianna rolled her eyes, and Eddie opened the door, revealing another office—although this one was certainly not empty, nor was it small. Unlike the others, this room revealed a man waiting with a cigar in his mouth, sitting back with his feet up on the surface of the desk.

"Ah," said General Lance Reynolds, grinning his trade-mark smile, the same one featured on all the posters that were outside Federation recruitment centers. "Right on time, Captain Teach."

"Weren't you on the ship with us?" asked Eddie. "How'd you make it back here so fast?"

Lance tapped his cigar into an ashtray. "I took a shuttle before you docked. They make you wait too long when you bring a battleship in. I had shit to do."

"Perks of being the boss," mused Eddie.

"Pretty much," said Lance.

"Are the reports ready?" asked Julianna.

"Not yet," said Lance. "I need to review the latest intel

before I hand it off to you. I'm thinking tomorrow morning. We'll be able to get you both situated soon."

"Understood."

Eddie scratched his chin. "Sir, if you don't mind me saying so, I haven't agreed to anything yet. I'm only here because you asked me to listen."

The General chuckled. "Of course, you're right, but let's wait and talk about that tomorrow. I've got a presentation lined up that I think you'll want to see. In the meantime, why don't you two go and have some fun? You can show Julianna around the station."

"How do you know I've been here before?" asked Eddie.

"Do you really need to ask that question?"

Eddie smirked. Of course, General Reynolds, because of his intelligence chief, Nathan Lowell, probably already knew everything there was to know about him. His parents, favorite foods, ex-girlfriends, former residences. "Right."

"Anyway, you'll be happy for the extra downtime, if you decide to sign on for this job. Trust me. You too, Julianna."

"Yes, sir," she answered.

"Yeah, I get the feeling she could use a break," remarked Eddie, glancing back at Julianna, who was still standing at the door.

"I'm perfectly fine," she said.

"Still, go have a drink," suggested Lance. "Bond, for shit's sake. You're about to be partners."

"If you insist," said Julianna.

"I'll be happy to drink," grinned Eddie. "You covering the tab?"

"Why not?" asked Lance. "Enjoy yourself."

Eddie strolled into the hall to wait.

Julianna drew closer to the desk. "Sir, is this really necessary? It might be a better use of my time to assist you with the reports."

"Not this time, Commander Fregin. Try to enjoy yourself, for once." Lance puffed on his cigar and dabbed it one more time on the tray. "That's an order."

3

Desert Lounge, Deck 25, Onyx Station, Paladin System.

Eddie carried two beers in his hands, squeezing between two fat guys and a Yollin as he tried to make his way back over to Julianna in the corner.

"Excuse me, fellas," said Eddie, forcing his way through. When he finally reached his target, he let out a short sigh. "Damn, this place is packed."

"It is," remarked Julianna.

"I don't remember it being this crowded the last time I was here, but that was years ago."

"The station recently took on several hundred new jobs. Since the Federation is expanding, colonization has significantly increased in this region."

Eddie took a drink of his ale, gulping down a third of the glass. "Not bad," he said, wiping his mouth.

Julianna did the same. "I've had better."

"Well, sure. I didn't say it was great." He took another drink. "But it's better than Five Trees."

"That's the bar we found you in, right?" she asked.

"If you can call it that. It's mostly a front for smugglers and pirates."

"I knew that part," Julianna admitted.

"Oh?"

"I researched it on the way to pick you up. I also know why you were there."

He drank the last of his glass. "I doubt that."

"You went there looking to fight," she said simply.

He chuckled. "Not just any fight. I was there for a specific one."

"Was that the alien we took down?" she asked. "I believe his name was T'turk."

"That's the guy," confirmed Eddie. "Heard rumors of an alien frequenting that bar. People said he was the one who killed the crew of the Valiant. I'd had my eye on him for half the night, but I wasn't absolutely sure until he admitted to it. That's when I knew he deserved an ass kicking."

She nodded. "I read the report on the Valiant. Did you have a friend onboard?"

"No, I didn't know any of them," he said.

"Then, why would you take such a risk?"

"Because no one else was going to," said Eddie. His eyes drifted to the table, and he cleared his throat. "I need another drink."

Julianna paused, reaching for a pad, which she had strapped to her side. "Oh, is that so? Thank you, Pip."

Eddie glanced at her. "Did you just call me 'Pip'?"

"No, I apologize. I was talking to my E.I."

"You have an E.I.?" he asked.

She nodded. "He's extremely useful. You can meet him officially when you receive your new clearance, possibly tomorrow." She looked at the pad, and then tapped the screen. "Oh, he suggests we check out the bar below deck. It's called Wash-it-Down, but it's off the books. No government personnel allowed."

"They got any Blue Ale?" asked Eddie.

"Best rated on the station, Pip says."

Eddie leapt to his feet. "Let's do it."

Wash-it-Down, Deck 13, Onyx Station.

Wash-it-Down was far below the main sections of the station. According to Julianna, this floor was filled to the brim with unsavory types—criminals, thieves, smugglers, and just generally unpleasant fellows.

Eddie didn't mind it, and he wagered she didn't, either. They could handle whatever bullshit came their way.

Taking a seat in the hole-in-the-wall establishment, Eddie could see the decay in the walls. Leaks formed water spots in the ceiling. Every step they took on the floor was sticky and gross. Oh, and it smelled like absolute shit.

"Not a bad spot," remarked Eddie. "I like it."

"Let's try the drinks first," said Julianna.

They ordered two Blue Ales and a shot of whiskey. Julianna took a drink of the beer, and then flung back the shot in a single motion.

She grinned. "That's better."

Eddie did the same. The beer, unlike the stuff he'd had upstairs, had some thickness to it. It didn't taste manufactured or fake. On the contrary, it was the fullest drink he'd had in weeks. "Damn. That's good shit."

"It seems Pip was right," said Julianna. "Let's have another round." Eddie watched his new coworker place their order.

As she did, a set of aliens entered and took a seat in the back. They were Trids, a shark-like humanoid species, built for both water and land. Their skin had to be constantly moisturized, so they'd often be seen rubbing their bodies with a special chemical to retain their wet appearance.

"What kind of name is Pip?" asked Eddie, referring to the E.I.

"A good one," said Julianna. "It was 'Assface' before that."

Eddie chuckled. "You changed it? What happened? Was the name too offensive to someone?"

"No one tells me what to name my E.I.," scoffed Julianna.

"Then, what was it?"

"A bet," she said, taking a gulp of her drink. "If he won, he got to choose his own callsign. If I won, I got to choose."

"I take it you chose 'Assface'."

"Yes, and I also chose 'Pip' a decade later. He hasn't won a bet yet."

"How often do you guys make bets?"

"Every ten years."

Eddie blinked. "Ten years?" he asked, looking her up and down. "When did you get him? When you were five years old?"

"I'm older than I look," she allowed.

"How old?"

"Don't worry about it," she said dismissively, chugging the rest of her drink. "Besides, it's rude to ask."

"So you and Pip have been together for a while apparently."

"Yeah, but before him I was paired with Ricky Bobby. He was an A.I. and my role as pilot wasn't the best for his future. He went on to do other things. End of story," Julianna said, her eyes distant, like remembering a long ago memory.

Eddie didn't think that was the end of the story, but he wasn't going to press. Julianna, from what he could tell was a doer, not a paper pusher, but somehow she looked burned out from the front line. Maybe that's why she had agreed to be commander.

The bartender brought another round out to them, and Eddie smacked his lips and took the glass. "Just in time. This stuff is delicious."

"Bartender!" yelled one of the Trids. "What's a guy gotta do to get some falibia?"

"We don't have that here," replied the barkeep, a rather short-looking human with brown hair and glasses. "Sorry."

"You don't have falibia?" asked the Trid. He was suddenly on his feet and marching to the front.

"We don't get many requests, so there's never been a need."

"Well, I'm requesting it now," demanded the Trid.

"I'll place an order tomorrow. Shipments arrive every two weeks."

"I want some right now!"

"I appreciate your eagerness, but it's not possible."

"If you don't get me some in the next ten minutes, I'll

kick your ass," said the Trid. He started to lean across the bar.

The short man reached beneath the table and, in less than a second, retrieved a small pistol and aimed it at the Trid's forehead. "I wouldn't do that, sir."

The Trid blinked at the gun in front of him. "Uh."

"Can I help you with anything else?" asked the barkeep.

"No…" muttered the Trid.

The bartender lowered the gun. "Let me know if you change your mind."

As the Trid returned to his seat, Eddie chuckled. "I like this place."

"I can't imagine why, aside from the drinks," said Julianna.

"Don't you ever just want to unwind? Watch a show, get into a fight? You know, cut loose?"

"That's not really my thing," she said.

"You should try it. It's cathartic, especially with guys like that," he emphasized, thumbing the Trid in the back of the bar. "Assholes that think they can throw their weight around, treat the rest of us like shit."

"I don't need to lash out to feel better. I don't fight because it feels good, I do it because it matters."

Eddie motioned for another round, but this time he asked for double shots. When the drinks arrived, both he and Julianna drank them down like they were actually thirsty.

He burped, smacking his chest. "It sounds like you haven't had any fun in a while."

"If you mean I haven't kicked someone's ass for no reason, then sure."

"All I'm saying is that sometimes you just need to let loose, you know? Give in to your instincts. Do something that—"

"Hey," interrupted the same Trid as before. "Do you two work for the Federation?"

Eddie glanced at the alien. "Nope. Sorry." He turned back to Julianna. "I'm just saying, you should lose the cold, rigid persona you're putting on."

"I don't need you to tell me what I need to do," countered Julianna.

The Trid stood beside Eddie. "I think you're lying, human. Tell me the truth or I'll—"

"I don't know, Jules. You're not giving me any confidence," said Eddie.

"Fuck your confidence," said Julianna. "And don't call me 'Jules'."

"Why not?" he asked. " 'Jules' is a pretty name."

"I don't want a pretty name. I want my name," she barked.

The alien stepped closer and towered over them with his hammerhead eyes and reflective skin. He smelled like fish, gross and intolerable. "You people are pissing me off."

"You know what I think?" Eddie pressed his new partner. "I think you're too scared to let it out. I think you've spent so much time building up this serious-badass thing that you just can't show the real you. You're afraid that if you do, it'll make you look too human."

"Keep talking shit, and I'll show you how human I can get," she replied, anger burning in her eyes. She was going to explode at any moment. Eddie could see it.

He leaned forward. "I don't think you've got it in you."

The Trid smacked his chest. "I said, look at me, you piece of shit humans!"

Julianna gritted her teeth and snarled. "Enough!" she yelled and, together with Eddie, turned and delivered a right hook directly into the Trid's face. Both she and Eddie landed a blow at the same time, punching the alien in a single motion, and sending him directly to the floor. He fell onto the table behind him, suddenly unconscious.

The two Trids in the back of the bar sprang to their feet.

Eddie glanced at Julianna. "See? Didn't that feel better?"

"Shut up," she answered, but there was no anger in her voice. She looked rather satisfied with herself. "Let's take care of those two and get the hell out of here."

The two remaining Trids tossed a table out of their way and came at them. One of the aliens opened his massive jaw, trying to rip his teeth into Julianna, but she leapt into the air and, using one of the chairs as leverage, dug her foot into the Trid's face, knocking him away.

Eddie grabbed hold of the second one's nose, keeping the creature back, and kicked it in the stomach, forcing it to regurgitate its recent drink. Alcohol and bile spilled onto the floor between them, and Eddie stepped back. "Ew, what the fuck?" he asked, disgusted. "Come on, man. That's just nasty."

The Trid charged at him, but Eddie dodged, stepping aside like a bullfighter and letting the alien smash into the wall, denting it.

A gunshot rang out from behind the bar. Everyone stopped fighting and looked at the little bartender holding his pistol into the air. "I'd appreciate it if you all could calm down now. Thank you."

The Trids raised their hands.

"Sorry about that," apologized Julianna.

"We'll pay the bill and tip you," offered Eddie.

The barkeep smiled, warmly. "Well, that would be mighty fine of you folks."

The Trids gathered their still-unconscious friend off the floor and carried him out of the bar while Julianna paid the barkeep with an Etheric Federation credit card.

"We should come back here sometime," Eddie suggested as the two of them left the bar.

Julianna nodded. "I can get behind that."

"Ready for another bar? I think there's one on Deck eight, too."

She smiled. "You read my mind."

General Lance Reynolds' Office, Onyx Station, Paladin System.

"Is that you, Nathan? Comms are fucked sideways for some reason," the General growled, looking at the box on his desk.

"How's that? I adjusted the signal a bit," said Nathan Lowell, the head of Etheric Federation Intelligence and the creator of the Bad Company—a military organization that some might call mercenaries, though they only took jobs that they could get behind...jobs that, after they were done, didn't prevent them from looking at themselves in the mirror.

"Sounds good. Now, care to tell me what sparked a call

from the spymaster-in-chief?" Lance Reynolds laughed at his old friend.

"That sounds so twentieth century, Lance. I wanted to bring you up to speed on what we're doing in the Gamalux sector."

"Never heard of it," the General admitted, stuffing the butt of his old stogie into his mouth and chewing on it. He considered activating the galactic map to find the location, but decided against it.

"It's so secret even I don't know where it is," Nathan replied in a hushed voice.

General Reynolds looked at his computer as he ground his teeth against the cigar, enjoying the flavor of the tightly wrapped leaves. "You're fucking with me."

"I am, but I wouldn't be me if I didn't," Nathan replied before turning serious. "We have some thirty teams deployed throughout the various systems, and very few of them know about any of the others. Most think they're the only ones out there fighting the good fight for the Empress and the Federation."

"I know you want it that way. Plausible deniability and all that, but you want to keep Julianna in the dark? She already knows a little bit about some of the other teams. But Eddie? Kid doesn't know shit yet, and you want to keep it that way?"

"We don't know what we're going to come across out there. There could be telepaths, parasites, creatures that take over our souls. Ignorance will be the weapon we need that could save us all."

"Hard to argue with that. We've both seen some shit in our time way out here in the dark. I'll follow your recommendation and keep them on a need-to-know basis—let them think they're going at this alone. I guess they are, in a way, since all the other teams are so spread out."

"It's not entirely inaccurate," Nathan agreed.

"What can I count on from the Bad Company?"

"Nothing. We don't have assets anywhere near you. You are on your own in that region."

Lance shook his head. "You're a real piece of work, Nathan."

Something about this plan irked the General. Information was power, and he was going to deprive his team of that? It didn't seem right.

"You expect me to keep them in the dark forever?" he asked.

"It's the best solution," Nathan stated firmly. "You know all about dissemination of knowledge, about keeping things compartmentalized. Just don't tell them what they don't know... only what they can confirm."

"So we keep a lid on this, let them do the job."

"They'll work better thinking there's no backup, no cavalry to save them—and frankly, there might not be. Trust me, Lance, when the pressure is on, they'll deliver. These are the best of the best. You hired me to know it, and I'm telling you it's the truth."

"I'll be goat-fucked if I understand the way your brain works sometimes."

"And don't you forget it. Nice chatting with you, Lance, as always. Too bad there won't be a record of any of our conversations." The comm box went dead.

"ArchAngel, what do you think about that?" the General asked.

"Think about what, General?" the A.I. asked.

"The conversation I just had with Nathan Lowell."

"What conversation?" ArchAngel asked.

Lance chuckled as he shook his head. He stuffed the stogie back in his mouth and mumbled about how much he needed a drink.

4

Cargo Bay 06, Onyx Station, Paladin System.

Eddie's head was pounding from the night before. He really shouldn't have had so much to drink...or maybe he hadn't had enough. It was difficult to say, based on his experience.

"You look like shit," remarked General Reynolds.

"Well, you said to go drink. That's what I did." Eddie flinched from the artificial light overhead.

Lance smirked. "Here," he said, handing Eddie a small, white pill. "Swallow that."

"Is this where you poison me? It took you long enough."

"It's for your head. Tripinol. You'll feel great in five minutes."

Eddie shrugged and swallowed the pill dry. "If you say so."

The door to the cargo bay opened, and Julianna entered, walking with her head up and shoulders back. She seemed energized and focused.

Lance glanced at his watch, an ancient and rarely seen device from old-Earth. "Right on time."

"Thank you, sir," Julianna said. She looked at Eddie. "I'm surprised you're here so early."

"I called him myself," said Lance.

"I could have gotten him," suggested Julianna.

Lance held up a hand. "Doesn't matter. It was faster this way. No middle man." He paused. "Er...middle woman."

"Will you two stop talking about me like I'm a six-year-old?" asked Eddie.

Julianna smiled. "Stop acting like one, then."

"That goes for both of you," corrected Lance. "Don't think I didn't hear about your little brawl." He shook his head. "Honestly, kids. Two bar fights in two days?"

"They started it," Eddie said, grinning.

"Don't do it again," ordered Lance. He took out a small device from his pocket, some kind of remote control, and tapped a button. When he did, the floor behind him opened, sliding into itself, and a strange-looking ship lifted up from below.

Eddie watched as the ship settled into place. The design was strange, almost resembling one of the old Black Eagle fighters, but still very different.

The thought of the Black Eagle brought Eddie back suddenly. Back when he'd been a pilot he'd had an implant. However, he took a pulse beam to the head during the war. Most were amazed it hadn't killed him, but it did fry his chip and he was too close to being a civilian to get a new one. Eddie complained that he didn't want them messing around in his head anymore. It was that disconnection from the Federation that made him think he could just walk away and start a different life. He wasn't sure he'd been right. Once a pilot, always a pilot, right? Once a part of the Federation, always, he now thought.

The ship before him had thicker plating and was far bulkier. *Is this some sort of transport vehicle?*

"We call it the Q-Ship," explained Lance.

"The Q-what ship?" asked Eddie.

"Q-Ship," the General repeated. "It's experimental, but this is the first in the Alpha line. We'll have more in the near future, but I thought you'd like a chance at flying one."

"I don't have any training for that," Eddie admitted.

"The controls are exactly like the Black Eagle, so you should be able to acclimate easily enough. In any case, our E.I. will be there to assist you during your training. I suggest you defer to him if you need help."

Eddie looked at Julianna. "Does he mean Pip?"

She nodded, taking out her pad. "Pip, can you say hello?"

"Greetings, Edward Teach," said a voice. It seemed to come from everywhere. "My name is Pip." The voice was soft and easy-going.

"Hey, Pip," he replied.

"I am pleased to meet you, Captain Teach."

"Is that technically possible?" asked Eddie. "Can he actually be 'pleased'?"

"It's a standard greeting. Don't think too much about it," Julianna suggested.

"Are you ready to begin?" asked Pip.

Eddie looked up and around him. "To begin what?"

"Training, of course," responded Lance, motioning to the Q-Ship. "You've got some catching up to do."

"He'll probably need a few months to pick things up," Julianna teased.

"I'll have this puppy purring in an hour. Just you two wait."

"Puppies don't purr," stated the General.

"They bark," supplied Julianna.

"Give me a break! I've never seen a dog. I don't know."

"You've never seen a cat or a dog?" Lance asked incredulously.

"Only once and it was online. And it didn't make any kind of sound," explained Eddie.

"Well, now you know what to expect if you see one in the Federation," said Lance. "Now get your ass in the bird and stretch your wings. You'll need the practice if you're going to take down your first target. But we'll talk when you get back. For now, let's have ourselves a test flight."

Eddie cracked his knuckles and grinned. He approached the Q-ship. "Sounds like a plan. Let me show you guys how it's done."

He realized his hangover was gone, much to his surprise, and he'd soon be back in a cockpit. His circumstances were looking up.

Six Hundred Kilometers Outside the Asteroid Belt, Paladin System.

"That's far enough, Pip," said Julianna over the comm. "Captain, are you ready to take over the controls?"

"I thought you'd never ask. The last ten minutes felt like a boring tour."

"We couldn't risk you colliding with any incoming or

outgoing ships during your training lesson. Pip is here to help you avoid any distress."

"I'm also quite adept at personal shopping," informed Pip.

"That's good to know." Eddie smiled and gripped the handle in front of him.

Surrounding the ship was a vast stretch of nearly empty space. The station was so far behind him that he couldn't see it anymore, and the asteroid belt was some distance ahead, the large rocks blocking the starlight as they hovered.

Eddie pushed the handle forward, and the thrusters accelerated. He tilted left, and the ship began to turn. He tilted right, and it went the other way.

The controls were remarkably similar to what he remembered from flying his old Black Eagle.

With the flick of his wrists, he did a barrel roll, spinning to the right until he'd done a complete rotation. It was easy enough to do in space, surrounded by nothing but good, wide-open training areas.

"Let's see here," he murmured, looking over the rest of the controls. One of the buttons had a symbol on it that he recognized as the booster. "Not ready for that yet," he decided.

"Captain, let me know if you need any assistance," offered Pip.

"Just hang back and let me do my thing, Pippy."

"'Pippy'?" echoed the E.I.

Eddie squeezed the grip and pressed it forward, igniting his thrusters and moving ahead. He performed a double roll, then an aileron roll for good measure.

As he continued, he noticed the asteroid belt was approaching. Or rather, he was approaching it.

"Sir, you may want to avoid the belt for now," advised Pip.

"Don't be a baby," said Eddie. "Didn't your mother ever tell you, it's better to run first and crawl later?"

"I don't believe that's how the saying goes."

Eddie twisted the ship around the first asteroid, which was double the size of his craft. He squeezed between two more, which was as large as houses. In the midst of the field, he weaved and turned, barely missing several of the boulders.

Eddie felt a rush flow through him, and the controls began to feel tighter, more responsive. He reached for the triggers behind the wheel—small buttons, one for each finger. With a distant asteroid in his sights, he fired, releasing a string of bullets and piercing the stone, breaking it apart and shattering it into pieces.

He was finally home—here in this cockpit, surrounded by the deadly void. This was where he belonged, with wings at his sides and bullets between his hands.

"What else do we have on this thing?" he asked, looking over the buttons. "Hey, what's this red button do?"

"Don't fuck with that," cautioned Julianna over the comm.

Eddie's finger hovered over it. "But it's so…enticing."

"Don't you do it, Edward!"

"Must…touch… button…"

"If you do, you'll plow straight into one of those asteroids, you idiot."

Eddie froze, his finger a few centimeters from the button. "Huh?"

"It produces a gravitic field and launches the ship through a gate. You hit that button, and you'll be halfway to the next star system in ten seconds flat."

Eddie blinked. "This ship has gate capability?"

"That's right," she confirmed.

"How's that possible? I've only ever seen that on Empire battleships and other big ships. Aren't gate drives the size of a fucking building?"

"Most of them are, but we've got a special model. Good for exactly one jump in case of emergencies."

"One jump?" asked Eddie, staring at the special button that he could never touch.

"And the same rules apply as with any other gate engine. If you activate it too close to an object, such as that asteroid in front of you—"

Eddie raised his head and looked at the giant wall of stone towering over him. In his fascination with the button, he had apparently not noticed it.

"—you'll end up like a bug on a windshield," continued Julianna. "Activate it too close to a planet, and you'll—"

"Destroy the planet," finished Eddie. "You don't have to tell me that part. "

"Good. I'm glad you managed to retain *some* of your training."

Not that it ever mattered before. He'd never had to deal with his own gate drive. They only taught him that stuff because he was a pilot and it was required reading.

"Okay, so the button is off the table. Got it."

He snagged the controls again and turned the ship around. "Anything else, professor?"

"Pip, can you show him how to use the cannons?" asked Julianna.

"Certainly," answered Pip.

"I have cannons? Oh, boy. What decade is it anyway?"

"We're a rogue operation and can't have Federation weapons. Get ready for some old school guns."

"Hey if it fires and explodes, then I'm happy."

"There's a switch to your right. Do you see it?" asked Pip. "I am blinking the light."

"I've got it. Same place we had it on the Black Eagles."

"Correct. The difference here is that the Q-Ships use a much higher yield of explosive. Specifically—"

"Enough to kill a small moon," interrupted Julianna.

"Holy shit," breathed Eddie.

He pulled the ship back and took aim at the largest asteroid he could find.

"Now we're talking!" exclaimed Eddie, getting ready to fire.

"Hold on," Julianna's voice stopped him. "Do you have any idea what'll happen if you blow up an asteroid that size?"

Eddie looked at the massive asteroid, and then at all the smaller ones surrounding it, realizing he could cause a chain reaction.

"Oops." He scratched the back of his head. "Good call."

"Don't worry," she said. "I'm sure there will be plenty of opportunities to use these guns in the future."

He grinned. "Now you're speaking my language."

5

General Lance Reynolds' Office, Onyx Station, Paladin System.

"Welcome back, Captain," said Lance.

"Thanks for the joyride," said Eddie.

Lance nodded. "Have a seat, would you? There's something we need to discuss. Oh, before we get started, I watched your training exercise. You did well, Captain, but you'll need to be even better. Understand?"

Eddie nodded, then pulled up a chair and sat across from the General. "I do, sir."

"Good, because the next few weeks will be extreme. Julianna is going to put you through the wringer. The two of you will fly in the morning, then spar in the afternoon, every single goddamn day. I need you at your peak, son; I can't stress that enough."

Julianna had been standing at the back of the room. She now shut the door and joined the two men, taking the remaining seat.

"It won't be easy, but I'm confident he'll adjust," she opined.

"Fighting and flying for two straight weeks?" asked Eddie. "Sounds like heaven to me."

"That's what I like to hear," said Lance. He waved his hand, motioning for Julianna to toss him her pad. She did, and he caught it effortlessly. With a flick and a swipe, he pulled up an image.

He turned the pad around, revealing a document containing various redacted sections. "We have intel that one of our colonies is being attacked by a rogue group of Kezzin pirates. You'll no doubt remember the species as the same one you ran into at the bar where we met."

Eddie nodded. "Tall and red. Sure, I remember."

"They're largely isolationists, only initiating fights within their own territory. In the past, if we stayed out of their space, they wouldn't bother us. It seems that has started to change."

"You mean how T'turk was raiding human ships?" asked Eddie.

"Exactly so," responded Lance. "But there's more to it."

Julianna looked at Eddie and elaborated on the General's point. "We believe there's a network overseeing these attacks. A hierarchy of pirates, as it were."

"You're saying they're all part of the same group?"

"Correct," she said.

Lance tapped the pad again. "We didn't have the intel until yesterday, so I wasn't entirely sure about it when I recruited you, but we now believe they're all answering to the same individual—a Kezzin by the name of the Ox King."

"The *what?*" Eddie asked for the second time that day. "The 'Ox King'?"

Lance nodded. "Funny name, I know."

"Does he look like a cow or something?"

"Oh, so you know what a cow is?" asked Julianna, smiling.

"Cows are on tons of farming worlds," said Eddie.

"I just wasn't sure, since you've never seen a cat or heard a dog bark."

Eddie glared at her. "Just wait until I find out all the things *you* don't know."

"Good luck," she said, twisting her lips into a smile. "I know *everything.*"

"Anyway," continued Lance. "No, he doesn't look like a bovine. Not even remotely."

"Why is he called the Ox King, then?"

" 'Ox' is a word in their language that means…" Lance swiped his pad a few times, searching. "Ah, here we go. It translates to 'the courageous one, surrounded by enemies, who never flinches or yields'."

"That's a long definition," observed Eddie.

"And his actual title is 'King of the Ox', so you can see how it gets complicated."

"Okay, so he's not an ox or a cow. Got it."

"Still alien, though," remarked Lance. He turned the pad around, showing Eddie a picture. Like T'turk had been, Ox King also had scaled, red skin, yellow eyes, and sharp teeth. The real difference came in their body size. Where T'turk had only been a little larger than Eddie, Ox was significantly bigger. His stats said he was over two meters tall and weighed 170 kilos.

"Definitely alien," confirmed Eddie.

"Ox and his cronies are working to squeeze out all the human settlements in this region, killing whomever they find. They pillage every Federation ship they encounter, which has caused a serious decline in settlement volunteers," Lance explained.

"You mentioned that the Kezzin were isolationists, but that they are moving beyond their own territory now?"

"That's right," said Lance. "They've become uncharacteristically invasive. The Federation has colonies near the Kezzin border, but not inside it. For whatever reason, Ox and others like him seem to be intent on striking first in a non-existent war. Perhaps they believe our two sides cannot coexist, or perhaps there is another reason we don't know about."

"Where do I fit into all of this?" asked Eddie. He'd been wondering this ever since Lance and Julianna first approached him, back in that bar, but the answer still wasn't clear.

"Due to the current politics involved in the Federation, a military response is not possible. Not a sanctioned strike, anyway."

"What does *that* mean?"

"Humanity assured its allies that we would only use our remaining forces to defend our borders, not invade or attack other species. You have to understand, Eddie, the Empire no longer exists, not in the way you knew it. We're a united Federation now. Our agenda is to have peace among worlds. But you and I both know that sometimes peace isn't the answer. Sometimes, in order to keep people safe, you have to get your hands dirty. That's why I brought you in, because you've always understood how messy war can be. Ox is invading colonies along the border. He's killing our people. I could authorize a strike against his stronghold and take him out openly with a small fleet, but all that would do is bring unwanted attention and make us look like the aggressors. I don't want that."

"He's a pirate, though, isn't he? What's so bad about taking him out publicly?"

"He's hiding somewhere inside the Kezzin Empire. The Kezzin are already xenophobic and in the middle of a complicated political situation. You can see how things might get complicated if we invade their territory, I'm sure."

"You want it taken care of quietly, is that it?" asked Eddie. "If we go in on our own, no one will know the Federation is responsible. They'll think we're working independently."

"Exactly so," confirmed Lance. "What's more, I need to know who is pulling that bastard's strings. There's more to this story than just the Ox King. Of that, I have no doubt. We'll need to get in, learn what's going on, and get out, all so we can go after the guy at the top. If anyone discovers the Federation is behind your operation, we could lose our chance at finding the true culprit. The people responsible could slip away and start their shit somewhere else. I can't have that."

"I see," said Eddie.

"The squad we're putting together will be a hidden arm of the Federation. The tip of the unseen spear, so to speak. You, along with Julianna, will be leading this team. That's why you're here."

"Are you up to the task?" asked Julianna, looking at Eddie. "It's a lot of responsibility."

Eddie stared at the General, a serious look on his face. "If what you're telling me is true, then Ox is the guy responsible for killing all those people."

"That's right," answered Lance.

"In that case, count me in, sir." Eddie rose to his feet and extended his hand. "When do we start?" asked Eddie.

"Right away." Lance took his hand and shook it. "You're going to have your work cut out for you, soldier."

Eddie raised his eyebrow. "Oh?"

"Did you notice how large the Q-Ship was when you were flying it?"

"Yeah, it was big enough to fit half a dozen people. Maybe a few more."

"Exactly," responded Lance. "This team is going to be big. You two are just the beginning. There are going to be more soldiers to fight the good fight, and you two are going to find them. But not yet—not until you're ready. Not until we've taken care of Ox."

"So, what's our first course of action?"

"I've got intel that says Ox is aiming to take out a human colony on Praxus III in two weeks' time."

"Two weeks?" asked Eddie. "Is that why you wanted me to train around the clock with Julianna?"

"That's correct, Captain. Do you think you can bring yourself up to speed by then?"

Eddie gave the General a sideways grin. "Sir, leave it to me. With Julianna and a Q-Ship on my side, I could probably take down a small armada."

"Well said, Captain," Lance affirmed with a chuckle. "Let's make those assholes pay."

Cargo Hold 02, *QBS Atticus Finch*, en route to Alabaster System.

Eddie and Julianna stood together in the cargo bay, having just received their mission brief. The training had gone quicker than anyone could have anticipated.

The Ox King would possibly attack Praxus III in two weeks' time, according to a recent intelligence report.

Less than two weeks to stop a well funded, highly motivated terrorist organization, Eddie thought. *Shouldn't be a problem.*

Intelligence indicated that the pirate's crew had recently been spotted in the Alabaster system, not far from Praxus III. It was a good place to start.

After gathering their gear and securing the Q-Ship onboard the *QBS Atticus Finch*, they set a course for Alabaster. They'd arrive out of the gate near the most distant planet in the system, giving Eddie and Julianna the best chance to sneak in.

The Q-Ship was built with stealth in mind, its cloaking technology was second to none. They believed that it would be sufficient to get them close to the pirates without being detected. They could gather intel, then regroup to plan their real attack.

"We'll be arriving soon," said Julianna, once the two of them had their gear out on the deck. "I hope you're prepared."

"I'm ready," said Eddie.

"We're only going to investigate. Try not to kill anything, if you can help it. Keep it in your pants."

"If we get attacked, I make no promises."

"I assumed as much." Julianna twisted her mouth back and forth as she studied the pilot, knowing exactly what he'd do once the shooting started. "Just follow my lead, and things won't get messy."

"You know, considering we're both supposed to be in charge of this team, you sure do enjoy giving me orders."

"We don't have a team *yet*," said Julianna, winking.

The *QBS Atticus Finch* arrived within the hour, taking position behind the system's gas giant, Alabaster VI. Eddie climbed aboard the Q-Ship and strapped himself in. To his surprise, Julianna was standing on the other side of the bay.

"Hey, are you coming?" he called.

She turned to look at him. "We're not taking that one."

"Huh?"

"Come over here," she told him.

He climbed out of the ship and jogged to the other end of the bay. "What's going on? I thought we were leaving."

"We are, but not in that one."

"Then, what? I don't see any other ships."

She withdrew her pad and tapped the screen. "Pip, bring out the Alpha-class Q-Ship."

"Right away, ma'am," said Pip.

The floor opened beside the first ship, and a second one rose from beneath. It was older-looking, and seemingly thrown together. Wires and tubes ran along its sides, and the paint was scratched.

"What the fuck is this thing?" asked Eddie.

"Our new ride," replied Julianna as they approached it.

"You can't be serious."

"Just because it's ugly doesn't mean it's not good," she countered.

"Did you get that from a fortune cookie?"

"Why don't you try the ship out before you judge it?" she asked.

He cocked his brow. "If this is our ship, why did you let me practice in the other one?"

She laughed. "Because we couldn't risk you blowing this one up. It's one of a kind and state-of-the-art."

Eddie was skeptical, but climbed into the ship. He strapped in while Julianna took a seat beside him.

"If this hunk of junk blows up with me in it, I'm coming for you," he told her.

"Just hit the ignition and let's go," she said, giving him the stink-eye.

He did, and the engines ignited instantly. He pushed the stick forward, and the Q-Ship took off through the cargo bay shield, sending them into open space.

Eddie's head pressed back into his chair as the ship accelerated. "Holy shit!" he exclaimed.

He flew them a few hundred kilometers away from the *QBS Atticus Finch,* then let the ship settle before pressing forward again.

"Take your time to adjust. We want to make sure we're ready."

"You know, since you're familiar with this ship, you might want to take the controls."

"I will if I have to," she promised, tapping the stick in front of her. "We're copilots. Don't forget that."

They headed straight for the planet beyond the nearby gas giant. It was encircled by a large ring and orbited by several moons. Eddie took the ship around the planet, getting his bearings.

For whatever reason, the controls in this ship were far tighter and more refined than the one he'd trained in. These felt more natural to him, and he was somehow in touch with the way the vessel moved. The design was immaculate.

Eddie glanced over the controls. "Where's the cloak? I didn't get a chance to mess with it in the last ship."

Julianna tapped a button between their seats—a small green one, inconspicuously placed. "Here."

Eddie saw the wings quickly become transparent. However, the inside of the ship seemed to stay the same. "Did it work?"

"The cloak is generated about twenty centimeters outside of the ship, so anyone outside of that bubble will only see empty space."

"In other words, we can move in, fly around a bit, and hang out without worrying about anyone spotting us."

She nodded. "Right."

Eddie gripped the controls, which had an old leathery feel to them. "What say we check that pirate base out, then?"

"Does that mean you're all done playing?"

"I never said that," remarked Eddie with a grin.

As Eddie brought the ship further into the system, Julianna proceeded with a detailed scan looking for nearby movements. She quickly discovered several ships near the second planet's moon. "Looks like a base of some kind," she said, studying the data.

"Anything on the planet itself?" asked Eddie.

"Not that I can tell. It appears to be an ocean world. No land to speak of. The moon seems to be habitable, however, with an oxygenated atmosphere, although I believe it's artificial."

"Someone terraformed it?"

"Looks that way," she said.

"Maybe we can blow the terra-generator while we're there," he suggested, referencing the device that kept an artificial atmosphere intact, once it was terraformed.

"Let's not get too eager," said Julianna. "We're here for intelligence gathering."

"Fine, fine." Eddie shook his head as he tried to come to grips with a mission of stealth and observation. He liked the action.

He *preferred* action.

The Q-Ship, now cloaked and approaching the second planet, began to slow. The moon was bustling with activity, with a dozen Kezzin ships surrounding the base. There didn't appear to be many defenses, except for a single cannon, mounted near the entrance to the base.

Eddie just needed the word, and he'd blow that base to hell. "Are you sure we can't try out these cannons?"

"Pretty sure," Julianna replied, glaring. "A nice conversation with a compliant Ox King would be optimal, see if he's dancing to someone else's tune."

"If we blow it up and that doesn't end it, we'll just get to go blow *something else* up. I don't see the issue. If you haven't figured it out yet, *I like blowing shit up.*"

"Intel, dumbass!" Julianna barked. "Next time, we might not get a heads up, and then we don't catch them *before* they attack. Innocent people will die, and we're the protectors of *jack shit*. No free beer, no passing Go, no continued service. Back to the cesspool for you. Is that what you want?"

Eddie didn't have a good answer, so he kept it simple. "No."

Sadly, justice would have to wait.

The Q-Ship approached the moon base and hovered over the top of the largest structure. "Scanning the area," reported Julianna. "This shouldn't take long."

"No one can see us, right?" asked Eddie. "Take your time."

"There's always a chance," she reminded him. "You never know what the enemy might have up their sleeve. We cloak the ship and stay for as short a time as possible, give the fucksticks as little *opportunity* as possible to see us."

Eddie observed the ground beneath them, watching as several dozen people, guns on their backs, walked together along a large street. Each of them were Kezzin pirates, clad in armor, shouting as they marched, like they were preparing for war.

He wondered how many of them actually hated humans and the other races comprising the Federation. Were they all xenophobic like that or were some simply in this because they had to be?

Eddie knew full well that not every Kezzin was like that, but these were soldiers, here for a single cause, to wipe out Federation settlements. Would they really do something so vile if they didn't fully believe in it?

A large ship sat in the dock a short distance from where the Q-Ship hovered. It looked to be a cargo vessel, with several Kezzin soldiers piling crates into its hold. Was that one of the ships set to hit the colony? It didn't look like the sort of ship one would expect for a combat mission. Then again, neither had this Q-Ship.

Eddie turned away and faced Julianna. "Anything yet?"

"I'm detecting a lot of shit down there," she said, looking over her readout. "I'm also picking up some chatter on the outgoing line."

"What kind of chatter?" asked Eddie.

"The translation software is processing it now. Hold on." She tapped her finger on her knee, biting the inside of her lip. "Any second now."

"For having such advanced tech, this shit sure does take a while sometimes."

"Here we go," said Julianna, finally. She read over the display. "Oh, fuck."

"What is it?"

"They're getting ready to leave in a few hours. We don't have very long."

Eddie glanced back at the larger ship. Its doors were rising, concealing its cargo, and several dozen men were boarding via the side entrance. At the same time, a few smaller fighters were lifting off their landing platforms. "Oh, fuck," he repeated.

"We don't have time to return to General Reynolds. We have to take care of this now," said Julianna.

"By ourselves?" asked Eddie, slowly smiling at the implication.

"It's either that, or we signal the *Atticus Finch* and

request they head to the colony to cut the pirates off before they can attack."

"But if we do that, it defeats the purpose of our mission," Eddie pointed out. "They'll know the Federation's onto them. Open a channel to General Reynolds and ask him what to do."

"General Reynolds left this up to us. If we are going to prove we can lead then we have to make the decision. That's what he'd want. Not us calling him up every time we have a question. This is our call."

"Our call?" he asked, blinking. "Fucking hell."

Julianna stared at him, waiting for a real answer.

It had been ten years since Eddie had given an order. He'd almost forgotten how. *If I make the wrong call, thousands might die. Hell, we might get shot. Either way, I can't just stand by and wait like a helpless baby.*

He had to act.

"Let's do our jobs," he finally said. "We might get blown to pieces, but we have to take down those ships so they don't find their way to Praxus."

"You think a few fighters are enough to take down a Q-Ship?" asked Julianna, suddenly smiling, taking the controls. "Watch and learn."

Eddie released the sticks. "By all means, Commander."

Julianna turned the ship around and faced the rising fighters as they hovered off the ground. She flipped the switch to ready the guns. "Ready?" she asked, looking at Eddie.

"Light 'em up," he grinned.

She pressed her fingers to the triggers and unloaded the ship's armor-piercing rounds on the dozen fighters before them. The bullets seemed to appear out of thin air, with the Q-Ship cloaked, and they split apart the wings and engines of the other vessels. Several ships exploded at once, annihilating the pilots and sending flaming debris to the ground. Half of one ship landed, slid across the platform, and plowed straight into the large transport vessel. Several dozen troops attempted to mobilize, but couldn't seem to figure out where the attack was originating from.

Julianna continued firing and, with the flip of another switch, let loose a barrage of rockets that hit the hull of the transport ship, blasting it apart and spilling its guts—the same crates Eddie had seen the men loading previously.

Two fighters fired at them from the side—apparently realizing that there was a cloaked ship attacking them—and the shots hit the Q-Ship dead-on. To Eddie's surprise, the cockpit barely shook.

However ugly this thing might be, he realized, *it sure is handy in a fight.* He smiled to himself. *I **really** love this ship.*

Julianna switched her aim to the two attacking ships, utterly destroying them in a single motion. Both vessels ignited in flames, spiraling to the ground. One landed in a nearby field, while the other flew straight into the main building of the base, disappearing through the roof before an explosion rocked the complex.

Within thirty seconds, every ship in sight was obliterated, with scattered soldiers fleeing for their lives. Eddie had never seen such a one-sided defeat in all his life. He didn't know what to say.

With the ship still cloaked, Julianna set it down in front of the main building. "Our target is inside. Are you ready?"

"Should we just leave the ship here?" asked Eddie.

"Only authorized users can access it or drop the cloak. Anyone tries to touch it, they'll be electrocuted."

"Fancy," he smirked.

"Now would be the time to turn back," proposed Julianna. "If you aren't totally certain."

"I wouldn't have come all the way here if I wasn't sure," Eddie answered.

He popped the hatch and prepared to exit. Julianna handed him a rifle, which he took and secured at the ready.

"In that case, after you, Captain Teach."

He grinned at the sound of his designation. "Let's hit it."

6

Ox King's Foyer, Praxis III's Third Moon, Alabaster System.

Eddie busted through the door, immediately met by a rushing Kezzin soldier. Before the attacker could reach him, Eddie raised his rifle and blasted the alien through the chest. The alien was a corpse by the time it hit the floor.

"Good reflexes," commended Julianna.

Eddie examined the rifle in his hands. "Been a while, but guns and I are old friends."

"Come on, we need to move further in. We have to find the second control room. Scan shows that's where their database is."

"The target was a database?"

"Logs, records, access codes. We get our hands on that, we'll have more information than we can handle."

"I thought you meant our target was Ox, maybe we can snag him before we leave?" Eddie reminded her.

They raced through the foyer and into the nearest

corridor. The Kezzin inside were screaming that the base was under attack.

"Get to the ships!" one of them cried in a deep, scratchy voice. "Protect the King!"

"Who's doing this?!" yelled someone else.

"Must be the Krin. They've finally decided to make a move on us!"

Eddie crouched behind a wall, listening to the aliens ramble on about things they didn't understand. "Hey, you hearing this? They think we're the Krin. Wait...who are the Krin?"

"Another faction of Kezzin. They must be in another feud. Our intel said there were a handful of skirmishes between the two groups not too long ago," explained Julianna, whispering behind her hand.

"As long as they don't know it's us, I guess it doesn't matter."

A side door opened, and the two aliens ran out of the building, fleeing the scene. Eddie took the opportunity to push ahead, swinging around the corner and staying low as he ran.

"Up there," Julianna motioned toward the end of the hall.

Eddie approached the door and stood to the side with his back against the wall. He waited for Julianna to get into place beside him. He looked at her, waited for her confirmation, and then he opened the door. He remained against the wall and then twisted through the opening, his rifle pointed and ready.

As he entered, he spotted two pirate soldiers, both of them armed. They noticed him right away, but it took a second for them to react. In that moment, two shots hit them, one in each of their heads, a shot fired from each of the two humans' rifles.

Dead and dead.

Eddie didn't flinch. He simply continued moving, side-stepping the bodies as he and Julianna made their way through the hall.

They neared a stairwell further in, and a guard came running down. In a single, quick motion, Eddie lifted the gun and fired, clipping the pirate in the neck. He fell, tumbling down the stairs, only for Eddie to shoot him again—this time in the forehead.

He looked back at Julianna. She pointed upward.

Eddie nodded and began to climb.

At the top, Eddie shot two more armed soldiers who had come running at the sound of the nearby gunfire.

While he finished them with shots to the head, Julianna took aim at another Kezzin who appeared from within one of the nearby rooms. This one was armed with two hand-cannons, raised and ready.

The alien fired at the two humans, but they dived out of the way. As Julianna rolled to safety, she unleashed three shots from her gun, hitting the alien each time.

He staggered backward, stunned. Before he could move again, Eddie turned from behind a wall and shot him straight in the chest.

Done and done.

Julianna motioned for Eddie to move, and together they bolted through the hall, examining each of the rooms while moving as quickly as possible.

"Move, you idiots!" someone yelled from behind one of the open doors ahead of them.

Eddie and Julianna stopped before the entryway. Eddie took a deep breath and then stepped next to the opening. With his rifle extended, he turned into the room, scanned from left to right in a single motion, his rifle and eyes moving as one in case he saw something that needed to be shot.

He spotted three Kezzin standing together, frantically reaching for their guns. Behind them, another one stood atop a raised platform. He wore a more elaborate chest piece than the others, showing more medals and the insignia of a higher rank, demonstrating his superior station.

The three Kezzin attempted to take aim at Eddie as he entered the room, but before they could unload on him, he fired—hitting all three in the chest, one after the other.

The first hit the floor, dead, while the other two only staggered. Julianna stepped in and followed up with her own shots, striking the second and third Kezzin before they could bring their weapons to bear. Her well-aimed rounds hit both in the head, sending them to the floor to join the first.

"Bastards!" yelled the only remaining Kezzin. He was tall, thick, and muscular. His yellow eyes blinked as he stared at his opponents. "You think you can attack the Ox King in his own facility? Are you mad?!"

Eddie reloaded. "Are you Ox?" he asked. "About time we found your scaly ass."

Just then, the door on the other side of the room

opened, and in ran two additional soldiers. They sprinted straight for the two humans.

Julianna reacted instantly, grabbing hold of one of the guard's arms and using his momentum to throw him to the floor. The alien faceplanted, cracking his forehead, and screamed in pain.

Eddie charged his opponent and hit him in the chest with the butt of his rifle, then slashed the barrel across the alien's face, causing him to stagger. He hit him again, this time in the neck, crushing his windpipe. The soldier coughed and wheezed as he fell backward.

Julianna and Eddie both raised their rifles and shot each of their targets directly in the head to finish them.

With five Kezzin bodies strewn across the floor, the two human assailants turned to look at the Ox King standing above them on his platform.

"As I was saying," continued Eddie. "Glad we found you, Ox."

"You think that's impressive?" asked the Ox King. "I've fought and killed hundreds. You two are nothing compared to the strength of the Ox, and once I've ripped the pink flesh from your bones, I'll go after your families. I'll kill every—"

A blast struck the alien in the shoulder, leaving a crater in his flesh. Eddie turned to look at Julianna; her finger was resting on the trigger, and her rifle was raised.

"Enough monologuing," she said. "This isn't a Saturday morning cartoon."

Eddie grinned. "Now we're talking." He took his rifle and raised the barrel to the Ox King, who was holding his new wound and shaking where he stood. "You hear that, Oxy?"

"W-What kind of cowards would shoot an unarmed—"

Julianna shot him in the other shoulder. "Don't preach to us about honor. You wiped out two Federation colonies and ordered the deaths of countless humans." She took a step forward. "You're the coward, you piece of shit."

"You can either come with us or die where you stand," Eddie offered. "What's it gonna be?"

"I-I'll surrender!" stammered the King, his arms hanging impotently from his ruined shoulders.

"You try anything, and I can't promise my friend here won't blow your head off," explained Eddie.

Julianna scowled at the alien.

With her weapon aimed at the King, Eddie climbed the short staircase on the side of the room, which took him to the raised level only a meter off the bottom floor.

Eddie drew closer to Ox, his weapon ready and aimed. He could see blood dripping from the shoulder wounds. There was little reason to expect him to bleed out, given Kezzin biology and their penchant for quickly adjusting to a flesh wound. Any second now, the two holes in his shoulders would soon clot and stop bleeding.

"We just need to cuff you," said Eddie, reaching for a set of restraints he'd brought, hoping to use for this very purpose.

The King was motionless, standing and waiting, occasionally glancing at the rifle in Julianna's hands.

"Put your wrists out," Eddie ordered, stepping closer with the cuffs.

The alien did, and as Eddie drew near, the two watched

one another, their eyes fixed. This was almost over. If they could just get this asshole on the Q-Ship and off this moon, they'd be home free. Just a few more—

The alien's eye twitched, and he looked at the floor to his right. Eddie's eyes did the same, and he saw what appeared to be a weapon, resting in the bottom shelf.

Eddie clutched his rifle and dropped the cuffs. "Don't even think about it."

The alien froze, looking at the business end of a rifle, millimeters from his face.

"Pick up the cuffs," growled Eddie.

Ox stared back at him, not moving. He slowly looked down at the floor and the handcuffs, then again at the gun.

"Don't you fucking do it," said Eddie.

"What's he doing?" asked Julianna.

"There's a gun back here. He's debating whether to go for it."

"Hey!" barked Julianna. "Are you stupid? Do as you're fucking told!"

Ox blinked his yellow eyes as he looked at one rifle barrel to the other and back again. He slowly reached down for the cuffs. "I'm no fool," he answered. "See?"

"Good," replied Eddie. "Now, put them on."

Ox lifted the cuffs, holding them in one hand, and then dropped them. "Oops."

"I swear to God," said Eddie. "Don't you fucking do it, Ox."

"I'm not doing anything," he said, bending down to retrieve the cuffs.

"If you do, you'll end up with a bullet in that tiny brain of yours. You know that, right?"

Ox squatted and touched the cuffs again, thumbing them and inching them towards his leg. "Almost got it," said the alien. He began to lift them, but they fell once more, and he finally swept them up in his hand, beginning to stand.

Eddie felt himself relax. *Maybe this will all go smoothly after all.*

Ox looked at the cuffs in his hand, then back at Eddie.

"I'm telling you, Ox," said Eddie. "I can see the gears in your head turning right now and I'm telling you, don't you fucking do it."

Ox grinned. "Do what?"

"Goddammit, Ox," said Eddie. "Don't you fucking dare. Not if you want to make it out of—"

Before Eddie could finish the sentence, Ox dipped to the floor, tossing the cuffs at Eddie's face as he reached for the gun in the cabinet.

Eddie sidestepped the cuffs, and squeezed the trigger in one swift, immediate action, shooting the Ox King directly between his yellow eyes.

The alien's head exploded as his body dropped to the floor. He twitched in his death throes mere centimeters from the gun at the base of the shelf.

"Goddammit, Ox, I fucking warned you!" snapped Eddie. "What the hell is wrong with you?"

"Is he dead?" asked Julianna, who was blocked by Eddie's position from seeing the hole in the alien's forehead.

"What little brains he had are gone," confirmed Eddie with a sigh.

Julianna ran up the stairs to join him. She spotted the dead, still twitching alien where he lie. "Ouch."

"I knew what he was going to do. He knew that I knew it."

"Sometimes people are just stupid," she commented and pulled out her pad. "Pip, are you ready to do some hacking?"

"Of course," remarked Pip.

"Aren't you going to lecture me about how we lost the target?" asked Eddie.

"It's not your fault that he was a fool," she said simply, walking to the nearest terminal. She plugged her pad directly into the system, using a universal connector. "Sometimes you just can't fight stupidity."

"Initiating file transfer," confirmed Pip. "Thirty seconds remaining."

Eddie checked the Ox King's body and found a small pad, similar to Julianna's but less sophisticated. He tucked it away in his own pocket.

The King also had a stack of delios, the Kezzin currency. Based on what Eddie knew about the exchange rate, it was no small amount—still, he left it where he found it. His job wasn't to loot, but to gather intel and complete the mission.

"Got anything?" asked Julianna.

"Found a pad. It might have some data."

"Nice work," she said approvingly.

"Transfer complete," announced Pip.

Julianna removed the device from the terminal. "Looks like we're done here. Ready to fight our way back to the ship?"

"Should be easier without this asshole to weigh us down, so at least there's that."

Julianna smiled, cocking her rifle.

The doors to the facility flung open, and Eddie and Julianna came running out, guns at the ready.

A group of Kezzin was in the open field at the other end of the courtyard, unaware of the cloaked ship sitting less than ten meters from their position. They appeared to be strategizing—perhaps trying to figure out what their next move would be.

Maybe they'd split up and head in through opposite ends of the building, sweeping from the outside toward the center. Maybe they'd stay together and file their way in through the front, to come up behind the invading soldiers —whoever *they* were.

Maybe they'd just stand there and get shot, like the bunch of assholes they were.

At least, that was Eddie's plan for them.

He leapt down the central steps onto the stone platform, dropped to one knee, and took aim at the unsuspecting soldiers.

As he started firing, Julianna came up beside him and took out a small frag grenade. She spotted her target, removed the pin, and tossed it. The grenade flew in a long, high arc, finally landing in the bushes near the troops, who quickly realized their misfortune.

Two were sniped by Eddie's gunfire before they could clear the grenade's blast radius. The others panicked, unaware of what was happening, caught off guard by the sudden chaos. Just as one soldier began to take out his weapon, the grenade exploded, sending the bushes and each of the Kezzin pirates flying into the air.

Julianna and Eddie didn't bother waiting to see if any survived. Instead, they deactivated the cloak and opened the hatch, piling into the Q-Ship.

As Eddie was strapping himself in, he saw a horde of soldiers appear from beyond the nearby house. There were dozens of them, mostly armed, running as fast as they could toward them.

"Uh oh." He worked faster to buckle his seatbelt.

"You handle the guns and I'll start the engines," ordered Julianna.

"No problem there," Eddie remarked, gripping the controls.

One of the thugs at the front of the mob raised his weapon and started firing. As he did, many others followed suit, bombarding the ship with a wave of firepower.

It sounded like rain, falling on the roof of an old house.

Eddie leaned forward and squeezed his triggers.

The two machine guns on each side of the Q-Ship unleashed a spread of bullets into the small army, mowing them down like stalks of wheat in a field.

Before a quarter of the Kezzin had fallen, the rest ran for their lives, painfully aware of their own mortality against such a monumental threat.

The Q-Ship was the most advanced fighter aircraft ever conceived. It would not be taken down by handheld weapons, no matter how many Kezzin were using them.

"All done!" said Julianna, taking the controls. "Let's get out of here!"

The Q-Ship lifted off the ground, its cloak activating almost instantly, and began moving over the now-dispersed mob. *There's no use hunting each of them down,* Eddie knew. They would soon disappear, go to some unknown corner of the galaxy. For their own sakes, Eddie hoped they'd stay there.

As they lifted through the moon's atmosphere, an alert sounded on the dash. It beeped repeatedly, loud enough to give someone a headache.

"What the fuck is that?" asked Eddie, pointing at the red light.

"We're being targeted," reported Julianna. "The cannon near the base."

"Should we turn around and bomb it?" he asked.

"No need," she replied, giving him a slight grin. "Already taken care of."

"What are you talking about?"

"I believe I can explain," offered Pip, chiming in from Julianne's pad.

A holographic display sprouted up in front of Eddie. He saw the cannon in question turning and adjusting, taking aim.

"While I was inside the local network, I sabotaged the system to create an energy surge, should they decide to use the defense grid. If they fire it—"

The cannon suddenly exploded on the holo, the metal tearing itself in half. A fireball erupted from the massive gun, evaporating into the clouds above.

"Ah, there we are. The cannon will almost certainly explode," concluded Pip.

"Holy shit!" exclaimed Eddie. "Pip, you sly bastard."

"Thank you, sir. I aim to please."

The Q-Ship broke through the upper atmosphere, leaving orbit and heading back toward *The Atticus Finch*.

Eddie secured his rifle next to the bulkhead of the ship. He stared out the window into open space as they passed the large planet whose moon they had just invaded.

He took a long, steady breath. *Damn, it feels good to be back.*

7

Cargo Hold 02, *QBS Atticus Finch*, en route to Onyx Station.

"I hope you two brought me something nice," General Reynolds greeted them, arriving on the hangar deck a few moments after the Q-Ship had docked.

As soon as Eddie and Julianna pulled in, the *QBS Atticus Finch* formed a gate, getting right the hell out of there. It seemed what Lance had said about the Federation not wanting to be seen or recognized doing this sort of work was true.

Eddie took his helmet off. "Glad to see you too, sir."

"We brought some valuable intel," offered Julianna. "Unfortunately, Ox is dead. He refused to go quietly."

"I tried," Eddie said. "I really did."

"I'm sure you did," said Lance, raising one eyebrow as he smiled.

"I had Pip secure his logs. We should have plenty of information to keep us busy," said Julianna.

"That's good news," the General nodded. "Have your E.I. upload the contents to my system. Nothing on the main network. We want this staying where it is."

"Yes, sir," she said.

Eddie reached for the pad in his pocket. "Oh, sir, I also found this."

"What is it?" asked Lance.

"He had it on him when we took him down. Some kind of pad. I haven't looked at it yet." Eddie handed it to General Reynolds. "Hope it helps."

"I'm sure it will, Captain." He looked at each of them. "You've both done well today."

Julianna shook her head. "We did the job. Nothing more."

"She's so modest," Eddie chuckled. "But I'm not. That shit was hard!"

Lance chuckled. "Seems you've gotten your wings back, Captain. And your trigger finger."

"It's all coming back," agreed Eddie.

Lance nodded. "Get some rest. I need you two fresh tomorrow. This was just the first step. We've still got a lot to do, and not a ton of time in which to do it."

"What happens tomorrow?" asked Eddie.

"Recruitment, Captain. You need to fill out this team I've given you. Hell, you haven't even named it yet."

"Was I supposed to be doing that?" asked Eddie, a clueless look on his face.

"Someone has to, and as you can see," he held up the pad Eddie had given him, "I've got shit to do."

Guest Quarters, Deck 05, Onyx Station.

Eddie sat in his temporary quarters, watching a vid doc on Earth history. It showed images of a large bomb being rolled out onto a flight strip. The episode focused on a declassified United States government program from the 1960s called 'Project Pluto'.

According to the show, it was to be a giant nuclear-powered cruise missile, which would fly into the middle of the ocean and stay there for several years, waiting, in anticipation of World War III. Once activated, the missile would receive its orders and begin its supersonic flight, dropping thermonuclear bombs on the various targets. Upon completion, the missile would crash itself into a final site where it would then proceed to leak fallout from its fuel tanks, contaminating the surrounding area.

The engines were made and proved operational, according to the historical documentary, but the device was never fully completed, and was ultimately scrapped.

"Crazy," muttered Eddie, flipping to a cartoon of a duck fighting a mouse.

Someone pounded on his door. He turned in his bed. "Who is it?"

"Julianna. Open up."

He eased himself off the bed and went to the door, then hit the switch.

The door slid open, revealing Julianna. She was carrying a pad in her hand.

"Rise and shine," she said, handing the pad to him.

"What's this?" he asked.

When he turned it on, he was met with a *'Classified'* message and a request for his thumbprint. He touched the scan, and the screen faded to show an alien's face. Beneath it was a biography page with several redacted sections:

Name: A'Din "Hatch" Hatcherik

Species: Londil

Occupation: Mechanic, Engineer, Physicist, Pilot

Place of birth: Laden City, Planet Ronin, Behemoth System

Date of birth: AQ 35

Alias: Brody Chambers (Web Handle)

A'Din Hatcherik is well versed in mechanics, aerospace, and electrical engineering with specialties in astrodynamics, electrotechnology, avionics, robotics, statistical machine learning, and several other fields.

Hatcherik worked on the <REDACTED> for over two decades, accelerating its expected timeline of completion quite significantly, far exceeding expectations. Additionally, his work on <REDACTED> has assisted countless researchers with further developing other <REDACTED>, which have also led to the creation of more advanced <REDACTED>.

After an unexpected resignation from the Federation's foremost research and development center, Dr. Hatcherik was last seen in the Behemoth System. His current address is attached.

Eddie stared at the dossier, examining the picture of the one called A'Din Hatcherik. He was an alien, part of the Londil species. The Londil were large, tentacled creatures, almost like a deformed octopus. What possible reason could Julianna have for tossing this at him? "What am I looking at?"

"General Reynolds asked us to start recruiting," explained Julianna. "This is our first guy."

"Our guy?" asked Eddie, looking back down at the pad. "He's an alien. Not a guy."

"The Londil are part of the Federation, last I checked, and that's who we work for."

"I guess I just assumed we'd all be human. Not that I have anything against non-humans, or anything."

"Uh huh," said Julianna, giving him a skeptical look.

"What? I don't have anything against aliens. It's just that humans have been the targets of these raids, haven't they? Not just *Federation worlds*, but human ones."

"Nonetheless, you want to assemble the best possible team to handle these threats, right? This is where we start."

"Who exactly is this person?" asked Eddie.

"Can't you read?" Julianna grabbed the pad from his hand and pointed at the screen. "He's an expert engineer *and* a pilot. His research has led the way in multiple fields."

"Is that why half of his biography is redacted?"

"Exactly. This alien was the best kept secret in the Federation's R&D. Most of his inventions were shelved and he left in frustration after a historically short tenure. He wasn't given credit and asked to have his name and history with the department erased. He left shortly after the transition from the Empire to the Federation."

Eddie raised his eyes. "If he's so smart, why isn't he still with us? This file has him on Ronin, living in Laden City."

"He's retired, obviously."

"Then why bring him back in?"

"We brought *you* back in because finding the right talent is crucial."

"I do believe you just gave me a compliment." A roguish smile spread across Eddie's face.

Julianna ignored his comment, stuffed the pad inside her jacket, and leaned against the door. "You know that Q-Ship of yours?"

"Sure," said Eddie.

"He designed it," said Julianna.

"He worked on the team who made our ships?"

"No," corrected Julianna. "There was never a team. And he didn't make all of them. Just the one you're flying. The one you said looked like shit. It was the original, and also the best. Hatch made it himself, with his own tentacles, on his own time."

"No way," said Eddie. "That alien built my ship?" He paused for a second. "Did you just call him 'Hatch'?"

"Come on," she prompted, ignoring the question and tapping the button to open the door. "Let's go."

"No, wait a second. Answer the question."

"We don't have time to delve into that right now, Captain. Now, are you coming or not? The trip to Ronin will take a few hours. The faster we leave, the faster we'll get there." She walked through the door and started down the hall.

"Fine, but don't think I'm forgetting this," Eddie chased after her. "I never forget, just like a goldfish."

"There's something seriously wrong with your brain."

Eddie boarded the transport ship in docking bay 06, along with Julianna. He had an overnight pack containing two sets of clothes slung over his shoulder, a baseball cap on his head, and a pistol holstered at his side.

Not that Eddie didn't enjoy a good pat down, of course. He just didn't have the time. According to Julianna, Hatch-erik, or "Hatch," as she'd called him, was currently working out of an old garage on Ronin, but wasn't always there.

Apparently, he liked to travel back and forth between his village home outside the city and his new apartment on the east side. Thanks to a recent report attached to the dossier, however, they knew to start with the garage.

"Did you bring anything to do?" asked Julianna as the two of them took their seats, one in each of the two aisles.

As it happened, the entire ship was empty of passengers except for the two of them. Working for the most powerful man in the galaxy definitely had its benefits.

"It's a ten-hour flight, you know," she added.

"I thought I'd read a book," said Eddie.

Julianna paused, a stunned look on her face. "Come again?"

"A book," he repeated. "What, you don't think I can read?"

"I just didn't expect that answer," she admitted, her mouth slightly agape.

"Aren't you gonna ask what book it is?"

"I wasn't planning on it." She faced forward, folding her arms across her chest.

He reached into his pack and retrieved a pad. With a quick flick of his wrist and a few swipes, he pulled up Beetle Bailey Volume 1, a comic strip.

"Good old Bailey," grinned Eddie, showing the first few panels to Julianna. "It doesn't get better than this."

Her expression sank. "I should've known."

The ship detached from Onyx Station and, igniting thrusters, moved a safe distance away. After about ten minutes, once it was far from any orbiting objects or other ships, the pilot initiated a jump, propelling the vessel through a gate.

Once they were in flight, an attendant appeared in the aisle, carrying a pad of her own. "Can I get you anything, sir?"

"What?" asked Eddie, confused by the strange woman.

"Would you like a drink? Perhaps some distilled water or a refreshing juice from our catalogue? We also have desserts and pastries."

Eddie leaned forward, looking at Julianna. "Are you hearing this?"

"Just order something so she can get back to work." Julianna sighed as she shook her head.

Eddie paused, looking back at the woman. "What else do you have to drink?"

She tapped the pad and turned it around, revealing the full menu. "We have a wide selection for you to choose from, sir."

Eddie's eyes widened at the sight before him. "Yeah you do."

The lady smiled. "I'm glad you approve."

"I'll take two Blue Ales."

The flight attendant nodded.

"*And* two Tarsin vodkas," added Eddie with an eager grin.

Julianna looked at him before asking in a hushed voice, "You know we're on a mission, right?"

"So? We don't have anything to do until tomorrow. Plenty of time to sleep off a hangover. Come on, Jules, don't be a downer. Have some fun!" He turned the menu around. "Look, they even have whiskey."

"Whiskey?" she asked, raising her brow. "Uh, what kind?"

"Looks like Jameson Gold," Eddie replied, examining the list.

Julianna's eyes widened slightly. "They have Jameson?"

"Looks like it. Is it good?"

"It's one of the few high-end Earth blends to make it to the Federation. I thought it was all gone." She looked at the woman, who was patiently waiting for their orders. "Everything is comped by the Federation, is that correct?"

"Yes, ma'am," said the attendant.

"Do it, Jules. Come on, you know you want to," said Eddie, trying to egg her on.

"Okay, okay," she said. "Just one drink. No, wait—give me two. Yes, two."

"Right away," said the woman. She took the menu back, keyed in both of their orders, and returned to the rear of the ship.

A moment later, she returned with a tray full of drinks, and proceeded to hand them out. "Here you are," she said upon finishing. "Will there be anything else?"

"I saw you have steak," said Eddie. "I'll take that, but bring it out in twenty minutes. I want to be good and drunk first."

"Yes, sir," said the woman. "What about you, ma'am?"

Julianna took a sip of the whiskey and, for a moment,

her eyes rolled back. She looked like she was in heaven. "Oh, God."

"I'll return in a moment to check back with you," said the attendant, smiling.

Eddie reclined in his seat, relaxing his legs. He didn't mind long trips, particularly when there was free booze and steak.

If this is my new normal, I can certainly get used to the life-style. There's no doubt about that, he thought.

8

Docking Station 211. Laden City, Ronin. Behemoth System.

"Damn, it's bright out here," said Eddie, stumbling as he stepped off the platform and onto the central walkway.

Julianna grabbed his arm so he didn't fall. She was the perfect picture of poise even after drinking her weight in expensive whiskey. "I think you're drunk," she told him.

"And you're not?" he asked, his eyes half-closed.

"I'm slightly buzzed," she said.

"There's no way you could—" He paused, putting his hand over his mouth, then continuing. "—could just be buzzed. I watched you drink at least fifteen whiskeys."

"The nanocytes in my blood make it so I can't get drunk. Actually, I have to drink a ton to get a buzz," she explained.

"Damn, you sound like an expensive date," he said.

"We should get you to a hotel so you can sleep this off."

"Worth it. Did you see that steak? It was so fucking good. I haven't had meat like that in years."

"I can't argue that," she admitted. "The chocolate cake was amazing."

"Let's make sure we do that again on the trip back," he suggested.

They walked through the crowded arrival section of the spaceport and out into the street of the bustling Laden City.

Julianna waved down a taxi and stuffed Eddie into the back seat. "Nearest hotel that isn't shit, please," she told the driver, who happened to be human.

"That would be the Pristine," the man responded. "They cater more to us than the Londil. No need to worry about tentacle-friendly beds or anything like that."

Traffic was congested because of a recent raid, so they ended up sitting in the cab for longer than Eddie cared for. He fought the urge to vomit for a good ten minutes before they finally arrived. But once he was out and on his feet, the feeling subsided and he felt re-energized.

The hotel itself was massive. Eddie tried looking up when they were outside of it, but stopped himself immediately, as it made him sick again.

Julianna sat him down on one of the chairs inside. He melted into the cushions and closed his eyes. When he opened them, she was back, helping him to his feet. "Got the room," she said. "291. Let's go."

"Thanks, Mom," he said, grinning.

She escorted him upstairs and dumped him on the bed. "Get some rest and—" She checked the nearby fridge, pulling out a bottle of water. "—drink some of this so you don't get dehydrated. I'll be back in a little while."

Eddie wanted to ask where she was going, but the urge to sleep was quickly overtaking him. The cool pillow beneath his cheek relaxed him, inviting his mind to fade, and after a brief moment, it did, and he began to drift.

Julianna left the hotel and waved to the same cab that had dropped her off. She'd asked him to wait for her, and he had, probably because he knew humans were accustomed to leaving tips, while the Londil weren't.

"Take me to 1191 Orto Street," she said, climbing into the back of the car.

"Right away," said the driver, entering in the address to his GPS.

You're leaving Edward at the hotel?

Pip's words entered her mind, jarring her a little. He'd been uncharacteristically silent since she and Eddie landed on this planet. Perhaps he sensed it wasn't the best time to interrupt until she had Eddie safely in the room.

I have a few things I need to get done, Pip, that's all.

Like going to see A'Dil Hatcherik on your own?

I just don't see any reason to wait.

However, the plan was to go tomorrow. The Captain won't appreciate you leaving him behind.

Are you getting sassy with me?

I would never dream of such a thing, ma'am. I'm simply pointing out the likely statistical end of this scenario.

You know better than to try that math shit with me, Pip. Now, if you'll excuse me, I have a job to do.

The truth was, it was hard for Julianna to sit around when she could be getting stuff done. Harder still was this partnership with Eddie. She was used to being a lone wolf. However, Eddie had strengths that she didn't and vice versa. The General had been right to pair them together. Now she just had to get better about working with him.

Fifteen minutes later, the cab pulled up to a small garage overlooking the nearby bay.

"Here you go," said the cabbie. "Want me to wait?"

"No, thanks," she said, stepping out.

After paying the man, including giving him a generous tip, she walked toward the building, a small repair shop called Chambers Auto. It was a bit run-down, hardly the type of establishment one would expect to find someone like Hatch.

The building had multiple garages, each open and filled with a vehicle. Most were made for Londil drivers, but there were a few others, like the Shelby in the back, although it didn't look like it needed any repairs.

Julianna entered through the nearest opening and made her way to the human vehicle, ignoring the others. It was nestled in an obscured spot, behind several benches. As she walked closer, she could see it was raised a meter off the ground, with someone underneath, making sounds.

Sticking out of the passenger side, beneath the car, a single tentacle twitched back and forth, telling her that the mechanic was a Londil. "Hey, mister," said Julianna, standing in front of the Shelby. "How much is this car?"

"Not for sale," the alien beneath the vehicle grunted.

"But it has to be. Come on, how much?"

"Unless you've got two quarters of a million credits, you're out of luck."

Another tentacle appeared on the driver's side, clutching a screwdriver. It set it down and disappeared again.

"What if I paid that? Would you sell it *then*?"

"There ain't no way you've got that kind of cash. I don't care who you are."

"Maybe not, but I might know a guy."

"Look, I've heard all the jokes. I know you're not here to buy my car. Why don't you leave me alone and let me get back to work?"

"I will if you come out from there," she said.

The Londil beneath the car sighed, and four tentacles came out on both sides, dropping various tools on the ground before sliding back in. A second later, their owner rolled to the passenger side door, pushing himself up to stand. He was large and thick, but that was quite deceptive. Londil looked far bigger than they actually were, and could reduce their size whenever the need arose, much like the Earthborn pufferfish.

Presently, because he was rather pissed, this particular Londil appeared large and in charge, but Julianna knew better. "I really don't have time for this nonsense, kid," he said, a distinct annoyance in his voice. He scanned the garage, looking for the person who dared to call on him.

When his orange eyes stopped on Julianna, she smiled. "Hello, Hatch."

The alien's mouth dropped, and he quickly diminished in size, going from about three meters to his standard build of about one and a half meters. "Hot damn, if it isn't Julianna Fregin!"

"Good to see you too," she smiled, approaching him, hand extended.

He took it with one tentacle and shook it. "I'll be a barniby's cousin! I never thought I'd see you again. What the hell are you doing all the way out here?"

"I came to see you, of course," she explained. "Why else would I visit a shithole planet like Ronin."

"Hey, that's my home you're talking about," he said, seriously, but then laughed. "I guess it is kind of a shithole, though."

She released his hand. "I hope you don't mind me dropping by."

He raised four tentacles. "Like I'd complain about that."

"You might, once I tell you the reason."

"If it's on behalf of the Federation, you can tell them to fuck right off. I'm done with all that nonsense."

"I know, but this isn't for them," she told him. "It's for the Q-Ship."

"The Q-Ship?" he asked. "What about it? They gutted it and shut down the project. You know that."

"That's what they told you, Hatch, but—"

"I swear, if you're about to tell me they lied to me and I left over nothing, I'm gonna be pissed, Julie."

Julianna shook her head. "No, no, they definitely shut it down, but General Reynolds took the birds and repurposed them."

"Birds? As in, plural? I only made one. How many are we talking about now?" asked Hatch.

"Only two. Yours and a newer model."

"I bet that one runs like absolute shit compared to mine. Those idiots over in R&D could barely keep up with my designs."

"You're not wrong," she admitted. "That's part of why I'm here. We need you to—"

"There you are!" called a voice from behind them, near the front of the garage.

Julianna turned to see Eddie marching towards her. "Teach?"

"You drop me in a hotel room and head out to the middle of the city without me? That's pretty fucked up! We agreed to do this tomorrow."

"Who the hell is this?" asked Hatch, pointing at Eddie with one of his tentacles.

"My partner," she explained.

"Yeah, partner? You know what that means, right? Dammit Julianna, what the fuck were you thinking, leaving me behind? I had to call the front desk and ask for a hangover pill just to track you down. That thing had me pissing waterfalls for fifteen minutes! I'm gonna have to go again any second now."

"Bathroom's in the side office," informed Hatch.

"Not until I find out what's going on here," insisted Edward. "Is this our guy? Are you Hatcherkin?"

"It's Hatcherik," corrected Hatch.

"Yes, this is him," said Julianna, tossing her head in the direction of the alien. "I just figured I could do this alone. Hatch and I have history. You were drunk and I didn't want to freak him out. He and the Federation haven't always seen eye-to-eye."

"Ain't that the truth," muttered Hatch.

Edward scoffed. "So that means you get to ditch me? We're supposed to be a team, ain't we? I'm here to have your back."

"I'm sorry, Teach," she said. He was right. She should have just waited for him, not run off to find Hatch on her own. She wasn't used to having a partner, excluding Pip, of course.

I told you this wouldn't end well.

Dammit, not right now, Pip.

"Don't apologize," said Eddie. "It's fine, though. I get it. Just let me know next time you're gonna run off on your own."

She nodded, opening her mouth to say something, but then paused. "Wait a second, how did you find me?"

He pointed at her side pocket.

She looked down, then removed the pad. "What is it?" she asked, just before the realization hit her. "Did you put a fucking bug on my pad?"

Edward snickered. "You're not the only clever one in this outfit, Jules."

"Goddammit," she blurted out, turning the pad upside down to examine it. "Where the fuck is it? What did you do?"

"It's in the charger port. Honestly, you shouldn't leave your shit unattended when you use the bathroom."

"You did this on the ship?"

He grinned. "Don't be so surprised. Besides, it's a good thing I did, because now—" He paused, looking down at his crotch. "Hey, Hatch, where's that bathroom again?"

Hatch lifted his tentacle and pointed to the right-hand

side of the garage. "Over there. First door to the left. It's not human-friendly, though, just to warn you."

"No problem!" snapped Edward, running to the door. "Nice Shelby Cobra, by the way!"

Hatch made the equivalent Londil expression of amusement. "You said that guy is your partner?" he asked, glancing at Julianna.

"Yep. He's like an overgrown kid sometimes. Sorry in advance for your bathroom."

"No, don't apologize. I kinda like him." Hatch turned to look at the blue Shelby. "Anyone who knows what kind of car this is can't be too bad."

Julianna laughed. "Still the same Hatch, I see. Got your priorities in the right place."

Eddie watched Hatch as he put his tools away and lowered the circa 1964 (old Earth calendar) Shelby Cobra. "How the hell did you get your, uh, hands on a vehicle like this?"

"The Shelby?" asked Hatch. "I built it, of course."

"You what?" asked Eddie, thinking he must have misheard him.

"You can't get original ground transport vehicles from Earth, so I studied the database entry when I was working for the Federation—or the Empire, as it used to be called—and made one myself. It took about one solar cycle. Ten of your months."

"That's crazy. I've got a model book my dad gave me all about antique cars. I memorized them all when I was a kid."

Hatch laughed. "Ain't that something? Two Earth-auto lovers, meeting face-to-face. What are the chances?" He tapped Eddie's shoulder with his tentacle. "Pleased to meet ya, Edward Teach."

"Call me Eddie," he said, smiling.

"Eddie it is," agreed Hatch.

"If you two will excuse me, we're here for a reason," said Julianna.

"Oh, right. You want to recruit me into your gang," said Hatch.

"It's a team," she corrected. "But yes."

"I'll need the full story before I tell you to fuck off."

She smiled. "First, you'd have access to your Q-Ship again, so there's that."

"There is," he agreed. "What else? What are you up to, besides that?"

Eddie spoke up this time. "Our mission is to hunt down rising threats outside of Federation space."

"But there's treaties that prevent that kind of thing," said Hatch.

"Which is why our unit is off the books," said Julianna.

"Sounds like every job I ever did for the Empire," said Hatch.

"Look," Eddie began. "Right now, it's just the two of us, but you'd be the third. We're building this crew to handle serious problems that threaten the lives of every citizen in the Federation. It's important."

"It's also illegal. You have any idea what'll happen if you get found out? They'll disavow any knowledge of you. I've seen how big government works. If you actually succeed, you'll have risked your lives and no one will ever know what for or who you were."

"Who needs that kind of attention?" asked Eddie, scratching the back of his head. "I just want to give people a fighting chance against this universe, help them to help themselves."

Hatch chuckled. "Is that all? Then, go be a cop."

Eddie looked at Julianna, then again at Hatch. "Do you know what the two of us did a few days ago?"

"What?" asked the alien.

"There was a group of pirates who kept taking down Federation ships, civilian transports. They've killed over two hundred in the last eight months. Three days ago, we found them on a moon and stopped them. We rained hell on them and brought Armageddon. And we used your ship to do it. The one you built."

"The Q-Ship?" asked Hatch.

Eddie nodded. "It did everything we needed. Thanks to your work, lives were saved, Hatch. We stopped the Ox King and saved those colonies, and you helped us, even if you didn't know it."

Hatch's eyes dipped. "My ship, huh?"

"I do have a question though, about the Q-Ship. Why no railguns? Why no pucks?" asked Eddie.

"I didn't want to use any of their technology on this because then they could get into my special programming. I used what I thought the Q Ship needed, and I used only weapons and technology of my own design, nothing that could be traced back to the Federation," explained Hatch.

Eddie nodded, that all making perfect sense to him now.

"Hatch, we have a chance to do something real here," said Julianna. "General Reynolds is giving us all the resources and funding we need. He's even willing to give you back your ship. You'll be able to continue your work again. Think of what you can achieve."

Hatch made an expression, although Eddie couldn't tell what it meant. "Are you fucking with me, Julie?"

"Julie?" repeated Eddie.

She glared at him. "Don't." She returned to Hatch. "I wouldn't do that, Hatch. I promise. You know me. I might be an asshole, but I wouldn't lie to you about something like this."

"I guess that's true," muttered Hatch.

"So?" asked Eddie.

"So," echoed Hatch. "Let's say I do this, can I leave whenever I want? Do I have your assurances to drop the entire thing if I want to? If it smells funny?"

Julianna nodded. "You can do whatever you want, Hatch. I promise, I'll make sure you can."

"A shot at my bird again...some work that actually feels like it matters and getting top cover from a decent sort like the General," said Hatch. "Maybe I'll give you two a chance."

"But?" said Julianna.

Hatch puffed his cheeks, the Londil sign for amusement. "But, I want full access to any projects I used to be a part of. The full catalogue, as it were."

"Why?"

"Because I'm sure those idiots messed them all up," he explained.

"Can we authorize that on the spot?" asked Eddie, looking at Julianna.

She smiled. "Teach, you keep forgetting who we work for."

"Is that a yes?" asked Hatch.

"It is," agreed Julianna. "Come help us punish the bad guys and you'll get all your old toys back."

Hatch's cheeks puffed. "If that ain't a way to seal a deal then I don't know what is."

9

General Lance Reynolds' Office. Onyx Station, Paladin System.

Lance sat with a cigar in his mouth, puffing smoke into a special vent he'd had installed a while back. He stared at the view-screen on his desk, taking a long puff and exhaling.

The findings from the Ox King's database were far worse than he imagined. Not only was there someone higher up the chain than Ox, but it seemed the network was more extensive than the General initially believed.

Messages between Ox and a mysterious entity known only as T detailed plans to expand and attack dozens of Federation colonies, with one goal being to seize and occupy Onyx Station. The timetable for that action was currently unknown, but the letters suggested efforts were already underway.

Onyx Station was a major political point of interest in this region of Federation-controlled space, acting as the central transport hub between at least a dozen worlds. Its creation marked the beginning of a new balance between the neighboring species, providing a neutral ground to share political and social discourse, perform trade agreements and treaties, and provide a useful Federation footing in an otherwise fringe territory far outside the core planets.

Should anyone discover this station was under threat, many would return to their home systems, and Onyx Station would lose its political significance, ultimately disrupting the balance in this developing region.

For nearly a thousand years, war had raged between Kezzin, Trid, and the Londil, but such hostility had quickly diminished after the construction of the station and the formation of the Federation. Granted, the Kezzin remained independent, priding themselves on their isolationism, but they often agreed to meet on the station, as neutral territory to discuss important matters as they related to the region and its many inhabitants. The Kezzin were, after all, spread across four-star systems.

In short, Onyx Station was an essential Federation asset; for anyone to threaten its existence was unsettling.

Not long ago, back when the Federation was still the Etheric Empire, it had vowed to its members that once the old war was over, the military would be significantly downsized. It would only be used for peacekeeping missions, and then, only within Federation space. The non-human species agreed to these assurances, vowing to come together with humanity in order to officially form the Federation.

Lance remembered the ceremony and the joy

surrounding it. So many old friends and allies, brought together under a single, unified cause. He thought about those days often, and never with any regret. His daughter, the Empress herself, had given humanity a new beginning, bringing them together with the rest of the universe. It was an unparalleled feat—one that he still could hardly believe.

But that was Bethany Anne, always exceeding expectations. Always going above and beyond.

For the past couple hundred years, such tasks had been left to Lance Reynolds. His daughter had given him the tools to expand the Federation. The equipment to ensure a brighter tomorrow.

He *had not* let her down. He *would not* let her down.

Lance dabbed the end of his cigar on the ashtray, eying the screen and taking a deep breath. "T" or whatever his name was, must be the next rung on the ladder. Using his cigar, he pointed at the screen.

"I'm sending a little party your way, just to say 'hello,' give you a taste of how we deal with scum like you rising from the cesspool of the universe. You'll wish you stayed on your own playground, you ass-hugging piece of shit."

Nobody fucked with General Lance Reynolds or the Federation. That was for damn sure.

Docking Station 211, Laden City, Ronin, Behemoth System.

"You sure he can fit through the door?" asked Eddie, pointing at Hatch.

"I'll have you know, I'm very flexible," said Hatch, stepping onto the boarding platform. In only a few seconds, he deflated and compressed into a smaller shape, waddling through the doorway and into the spacecraft. "See?"

"That's great, but what about when you get inside and have to sit down? Those seats are built for humans."

"I had a special one installed while we were out," Julianna assured him.

"Smart thinking," said Eddie.

"The woman knows me," said Hatch, continuing inside.

Eddie followed, waiting for the alien to take his seat, which was larger than the others and seemed to have multiple armrests all along its sides for tentacles.

Julianna sat across the aisle, similar to the last trip, while Eddie sat a row in front of her. "No getting drunk this time, Captain," she told him.

"You aren't the boss of me," he shot back.

"You must not know Julie very well," said Hatch. "She's the boss of everyone."

Julianna grinned. "*He* gets me."

The ship ignited its thrusters a few moments later, since there weren't any other passengers to board. As the ship lifted off, Eddie noticed Hatch begin to bloat and squeeze, changing his size every few seconds. The seat seemed to conform to these fluctuations, like it was built to deal with this. "What's the problem?" asked Eddie.

Julianna looked unconcerned. "He can't talk right now. The Londil don't do well with altitude changes. They lose their ability to control their size."

"Will he be okay?"

"It'll stop in just a minute," she explained.

Eddie sat back in his seat. "That's so weird."

"He probably thinks it's weird when your ears pop," she said.

"Isn't he supposed to be a pilot?" asked Eddie.

"There's a special flight suit they wear," she started to say.

"We only wear it when we have to," interjected Hatch, who had finally regained his composure. "Londil don't like having tight fitting clothes against our skin."

Eddie sat up and looked at him. "Welcome back."

Hatch reduced his size and seemed to relax. "I hate traveling."

"Well," continued Eddie. "The good news is that you can eat or drink whatever you want on this trip. It's comped."

"Is that so?" asked Hatch. "How about some Ronin slugs?"

Eddie cringed at the words. "Seriously?"

"It's a delicacy," said Julianna.

"Not to me. That sounds disgusting."

Julianna looked at Hatch. "I made sure they stocked up on food for you. Pretty certain I saw slugs on the list."

Hatch's cheeks puffed up. "You're so good to me."

"If I didn't know any better, I'd say you two have a special kind of history," said Eddie, raising his brow at Julianna.

"Oh, man, you figured us out," Julianna said, unmoved by the accusation.

Eddie's mouth fell open. "What?"

She laughed. "Come on, Teach. I'm fucking with you. Hatch thinks humans are ugly as hell."

"It's true," agreed Hatch. "You all look like giant toadstools with fur on your heads."

"Hey," snapped Eddie. "You're not exactly a looker yourself, you know."

"I'll have you know I'm quite the female magnet, kid," remarked Hatch.

"He's telling you the truth. Hatch has about five wives, last I checked," said Julianna.

"Six, now," said the alien.

Eddie's eyes widened. "Seriously?"

"And fifteen kids," added Hatch.

"You've got fifteen children and you're leaving them to come with us?" asked Eddie, a look of shock on his face.

Hatch's cheeks puffed up. "All of them are grown and on their own now. They stay busy with school and work, but I still keep tabs on them."

Eddie sank down in his seat. "That sounds exhausting."

"You're telling me, kid."

General Lance Reynolds' Office. Onyx Station, Paladin System.

"Welcome back," said General Reynolds as he sat behind his desk.

Eddie and Julianna sat across from him, finally returned from their trip to Ronin. "Hope we didn't keep you waiting, sir," said Julianna.

"I stayed busy," said Lance. "Speaking of which, while you were out there getting drunk and spending all my money—" He paused, looking at Eddie. "—yes, I know all about the booze."

Eddie, rather than cringe or shy away from the accusation, simply smiled.

"Anyway, while you were doing your thing, I managed to decipher the data you retrieved from the Ox King's network database."

He shoved a pad across the table to Julianna.

"Interesting findings, to say the least," he added.

She took it and swiped the screen. Eddie watched her expression grow more and more intrigued as she read. Finally, her eyes widened and she seemed surprised. "Is this accurate, sir? Who is 'T'?"

"Your guess is as good as mine, Commander."

"'T'?" asked Eddie.

Lance motioned at the pad. "That's the initial used to sign certain emails pertaining to attack plans and other orders given to Ox during his campaign against our Federation outposts."

"So, that's our man, right?"

"I believe it is," confirmed Lance. "But the real issue is finding him. We'll need some help decoding the source of these emails."

"I can put Pip on that right away," said Julianna.

"As good as Pip is, he might not be up to the task," said Lance.

"Did you have someone else in mind, sir?" she asked.

"I did," he confirmed. "In fact, I'd say it's due time to introduce the two of you to an old friend of mine. I was saving this as a surprise, but maybe now is as good a time as any."

"Sir?" asked Julianna.

Lance leaned over to his screen and tapped it, holding his finger up to the two of them. "Status check," he said to whoever was on the other end of the line.

"Standing by as ordered, sir," said the unknown voice.

"Right. Thank you," said Lance. "I'll be arriving within the hour."

"Affirmative, sir," said the voice. "See you soon."

The transmission ended, and Lance turned to Eddie and Julianna. "Care to take a stroll with me?"

"To where, sir?" asked Julianna.

"I've got a present for you two that I think you'll want to see. It's parked near the asteroid belt."

"Parked?" asked Eddie. "What the hell did you—"

"Not what," interrupted Lance. "*Who.*"

Cargo Bay 06. Onyx Station, Paladin System.

Eddie stood next to Julianna as Lance shook hands with Hatch. Or tentacles, depending on your perspective.

"Good to see you again, Doctor," greeted the General.

"Likewise," said Hatch.

Eddie leaned over to Julianna. "They know each other?"

She nodded. "The General was the one who introduced me to Hatch. They go way back."

"I assume you'll want to see the Q-Ship, now that you're back," said Lance.

"You assume right," agreed Hatch. "Is she nearby?"

"I've had both ships transferred to a new location. The shuttle will take us there in a few minutes."

"Don't I need to receive a security clearance or go through in-processing first?" asked Hatch.

"Already taken care of. I knew my team would go after you and bring you onboard. I was the one who planted the file for Julianna to find."

"And you expected me to agree to help? What made you so sure I'd say yes?" asked Hatch.

"Are you saying you'd rather keep working in a garage than a starship?" asked Lance.

"Still, you shouldn't presume to know me, Lance. I don't care how long I've known you."

"Sixty years, last I checked," said the General.

"Holy shit," Eddie blurted out.

Everyone looked at him.

"What? That's a long ass time," said Eddie.

"Maybe for you," said Hatch. He returned his glance to Lance. "Speaking of living, I'm glad you're still in one piece."

"You too, Hatch," said the General, smiling.

The shuttle was parked near the back of the bay, with only a single crew member waiting—the pilot. Eddie found this odd, since it was standard procedure to have at least two people onboard at any given time.

The four passengers took their seats, and once again, the ship was outfitted specially for Hatch and his alien physiology. Julianna and the General were well ahead of Eddie in mission preparation.

The shuttle departed through the shield and into open space in the direction of the asteroid belt. From what Eddie could tell, which wasn't much, given how vast and dark the void of space actually was, there were no ships or other manmade vessels waiting for them.

Eddie leaned across his seat, motioning at Lance. "Hey, General, sir, if you don't mind me asking, what did you mean when you said 'who' earlier?"

Lance turned to look at him. "It's complicated, but let's

just say we're on our way to see someone who can help. A valuable asset to the fight, so to speak."

"Someone?" echoed Eddie.

"An A.I. with the capability to sort through the data we've collected. Someone I've known for a long time."

Eddie squinted, trying to see through the window up ahead. "But I don't see any ships."

"That's because the ship is cloaked," said Lance.

"Like the Q-Ships?" asked Eddie.

Lance nodded. "Exactly."

The pilot, who looked about as average and forgettable as anyone Eddie had ever seen, thumbed the console in front of him, activating the com. "Eagle One inbound for arrival."

Eddie's eyes perked up at the sound of the callsign. He recalled from his early training that wherever the head of the military was, if it was an aerial vehicle or spacecraft, received the new temporary designation of Eagle One, signifying its importance. He'd never seen or heard it in action, but it was a longstanding tradition going back centuries.

"Docking request acknowledged," said a voice over the com. It was very subdued, almost relaxed. "Please proceed, Eagle One."

The shuttle continued forward, maneuvering around one of the larger asteroids on the outer edge of the belt, heading above the ring. Eddie kept his eyes forward, trying to see what their destination could possibly be, but all he saw was darkness. No ship, no space station. Nothing at all.

He opened his mouth to ask where it was, but that was

when he saw it—a slit of light in the middle of the dark, a line breaking across the void.

It opened, growing larger by the second, revealing the innards of a docking bay—of a Federation ship.

"Ain't she a sight?" said Lance, smiling as the shuttle entered through the loading doors.

"Sir, what is this?" asked Julianna. "From what I can see, this is a battleship. I don't know of too many with cloaking technology."

"That's because we don't have any yet," said the General.

"Then, what is this? A secret one? Did you build this in private?"

He chuckled. "That's not far from the truth."

The shuttle landed and the door opened. Lance walked out onto the platform and stretched his arms. Eddie, Julianna, and Hatch quickly followed, waiting for the General to explain just what the hell was going on.

Lance held out his hands, almost in an inviting way. "Ladies and gentlemen, boys and girls, you are standing on the ruins of a once-dead ship, the *QBS ArchAngel*, the original flagship of the Queen's Fleet." He grinned again. "And, I might add, your new home."

Loading Dock 01, *QBS ArchAngel*, Paladin System.

Julianna wasn't sure if this was an elaborate joke or the blatant truth. Based on what she'd seen with her own eyes, back when the *QBS ArchAngel* had been destroyed, there was no way she could be standing on it now.

But here it was...or at least, that's what the General had claimed. How *could* it, though? She'd been a member of the Black Eagles during the war. Back then, the *QBS ArchAngel* had been destroyed, following mankind's move through the Gate. Much of its database had been salvaged and transferred to another ship. That vessel was consequently dubbed *QBS ArchAngel II* in honor of the first. Even the A.I., also known as ArchAngel, had been transferred.

The whole thing was beginning to give Julianna a headache.

"Sir, can you please explain what exactly is going on? I saw *the ArchAngel* blow up firsthand. Are you telling me this is the same ship? Did you just rebuild it from scratch?" she asked.

"It's the same ship," Lance confirmed. "In fact, you'll never guess who else is here."

"Who else...?"

A screen lit up on a nearby wall and a woman's face appeared on it. Her eyes were so large that they seemed intimidating. "Greetings, everyone," she told them. "I'm ArchAngel. It's good to meet you. The General has told me a great deal about each of you."

"ArchAngel?" asked Julianna. She stared at the face before her, the same face that also belonged to Empress Bethany Anne, a face that Julianna had not seen in years. "Sir, how can that be?"

"What's wrong, Commander?" asked Lance.

"I thought the A.I. was moved to the other ship, *QBS ArchAngel II*?"

"Ah, I see where you're confused," he said, nodding. "No, she was only copied, not transferred. The original A.I. had to be left behind."

"I was salvaged, though, after several decades, I'm told," said ArchAngel.

"Salvaged? So, this is the original copy?" asked Eddie.

"Can't be a copy if she's the original," said Hatch.

"Oh, right," Eddie replied. "Say, why does she look so familiar? I feel like I've seen her before."

"That's because she's modeled after the Empress," explained Julianna.

"Queen Bethany Anne?" asked Eddie, staring at the screen in awe, his mouth fully agape. "Holy shit."

Lance chuckled. "Imagine being the Empress' father

and seeing ArchAngel's face. It's definitely strange at times. We had to leave the ship behind for a while during the war, but a few decades ago, I had her rebuilt. We used the original as much as possible, but scrapped everything that wasn't up to code."

"That's amazing," said Julianna. "Sir, with all due respect, why didn't I know about this?"

"A few reasons," said the General. "To start with, this project has been on a need-to-know basis since it began. Until this moment, there was no reason for you to know. More importantly," he said, smiling. "I like surprises."

Hatch stepped forward. "This is all fine and impressive, but where are my birds?"

"Birds?" asked ArchAngel.

"The Q-Ships," explained Lance. "Those are in the second holding area. ArchAngel, can you show him the way?"

"Of course," said the A.I.

Impressive design. I must inquire with ArchAngel regarding her regulatory protocols.

Are you asking me to network you in so you can chat with her, Pip?

If you don't mind, Julianna.

"ArchAngel, my E.I. would like to talk to you about something technical. Do you mind if I upload him?" asked Julianna.

"Certainly not," said ArchAngel. "I would love to meet him. What is his name?"

"Pip, unless he beats me in the next bet, but that's not going to happen."

We shall see about that.

What did I tell you about that sass?

That you like it.

Julianna pretended to laugh. Honestly, the banter reminded her too much of Ricky Bobby, her previous A.I. Well, he'd been an E.I. and then evolved. That had been the problem. She didn't need something in her head that was real. It was too much for her, so she'd sent him away. That was what was best for Ricky Bobby, she told herself.

The General started to walk toward the stairwell. "Get your E.I. taken care of and meet me on the bridge in the next twenty minutes, Commander. Captain Teach, you're with me."

"Yes, sir," said Eddie.

You heard the man, Pip. Just let me know when you're done playing around.

Eddie hurried after the General as they made their way down one of the corridors, toward the ship's bridge. From what he could tell, there weren't a lot of people onboard. In fact, it seemed like a skeleton crew.

"Sir, where is everyone?" he asked, after a while.

"What do you mean?"

"I only see a few personnel walking around. Are we picking more people up at Onyx?"

They approached a set of doors, which opened automatically, bringing them to another corridor.

"I'm afraid this is it for now," he answered. "You'll have to make do with the staff on hand. If it were up to me, I'd fully outfit you with all the people you need, but I can only relocate so many Federation personnel without someone noticing."

"How many of them are there?"

"Including your team?" asked Lance. "About Forty."

Eddie was surprised. A standard battleship had about three hundred active personnel working at any given time. That accounted for three overlapping work shifts for every department. It was hard to believe that a ship of this size could sufficiently get the job done with such a miniscule crew.

"I'm sure you're wondering how this ship can even be operational with so few people manning it," said Lance. "Let me assure you, Edward, it is."

They came to another set of doors, which opened, and General Reynolds walked onto the bridge of the *QBS Arch-Angel*. There were three people sitting at a large workstation, with several open seats throughout. All of them stood when they saw Lance and Eddie enter.

"General on the bridge!" barked a young woman with blonde hair as she snapped to attention.

The two men in the room locked their bodies at the position of attention, all three of them completely still.

"As you were," said Lance. "Carry on."

"Yes, sir," said the woman, sitting back down.

Lance turned to Eddie. "This ship has been upgraded with a largely automated system, which means ArchAngel, the A.I., not the ship, can handle most of the smaller tasks. I expect this ship to avoid combat, unless it is absolutely necessary, so you'll be relying largely on the Q-Ships.

When you aren't using them, this will act as your home and a place to regroup."

"I understand," said Eddie.

"I know you do, Edward. I also know you'll take good care of what I'm giving you. This ship means more to humanity, more to the Federation, than anyone can possibly know...and now she's yours to command, soldier."

Eddie blinked. "Me? I don't think I understand. Isn't there a captain?"

"In this case, that's you. Think you can handle a ship like this?" asked Lance.

"Are you—Are you sure about this, sir? Giving me a team is one thing, but an entire battleship?"

"I'm comfortable with it, and for what it's worth, I trust you. You won't be alone, though. Commander Fregin will be at your side the entire time, backing you up. I hope this ship reflects the importance of your mission, Captain."

"Thank you, sir," said Eddie, standing at attention.

"Relax, son, but you're welcome. You proved you're up to the job when you took out Ox and his men, so now we're moving on to the real fight. I was going to wait until you'd had a few more missions under your belt before I gave you command, but it seems the timeline has been accelerated."

"How so?"

"ArchAngel is already combing through the data we retrieved from Ox. Early analysis suggests a threat, a damn big one, coming out of nowhere. We aren't sure of their exact goal, but tearing up the Federation seems to be a big part of it. If they're successful, they'll undo every inch of ground we've gained. They can stand the fuck aside, though, because we're not going to wait for them to come to us. Hell no! Prepare yourself and your team. Somebody's ass is going to be kicked, and it sure as hell isn't going to be ours, is it, Captain?"

"No, sir!"

The General nodded proudly. "I'll call when Archangel completes her analysis, and we can launch you like an arrow at the bullseye."

"Yes, sir! But how am I supposed to do prep for a mission with no parameters?"

"By training with your team and by learning exactly what your Q-Ship is capable of. It's a lot to take, I know, but right now this is all we've got."

Eddie nodded, looking out across the large view-screen, which currently had Onyx Station on it, several ships coming and going as they docked and undocked. The people on that station, as well as the rest of the Federation, believed they were safe. They believed, perhaps naively, that nothing would ever threaten their safety or security.

It was up to Eddie and his team to continue that belief...to keep the charade going. The boogeyman was out there, somewhere, getting ready to try and hurt them, but Eddie wouldn't let him. With every inch of his being, every piece of his heart, he would fight to keep the people safe.

Loading Dock 02, *QBS ArchAngel*, Paladin System.

The two Q-Ships sat together in the bay. One was older, its mangled design far less aesthetically pleasing than the other, but it was like that for a reason. Practicality over sleekness. This was a ship built by someone who cared more about efficiency and practicality than how pretty it should be.

Hatch stood a dozen meters from the ship, his cheeks puffy with excitement, amazed at the sight before him. He'd spent years building this by hand, so much time that he knew it backwards and forwards. He understood every facet of it, from the smallest bolt to the gate drive. Every subsystem was special, every tube and wire a treasure.

Next to it, another ship was waiting. Nothing but a copy, he knew, soulless and devoid of heart, built by hands who didn't understand, couldn't understand *his* vision. That was always the case with pretenders, with copiers and replicators. They always tried to recreate the master's work, but always came up short.

If Hatch had stayed away forever, perhaps a fleet of other insufficient copies would have been built, eternally damaging his legacy.

But no longer. Hatch was back, and that meant things were about to change.

"A.I., are you here?" asked Hatch.

"My name is ArchAngel," said the A.I. She suddenly appeared on a display screen against the nearby wall. "Welcome, Doctor Hatcherik."

"ArchAngel," repeated Hatch. "Right, well, tell me something. How many engineers have touched these ships since the start of this assignment?"

"The Q-Ships were only recently transferred here, but based on the records associated with them, at least several dozen."

"That many?" asked Hatch.

"Is something wrong?"

Hatch shuffled over to the side of his original ship. "It just means I've got my work cut out for me, undoing the stupidity that those other engineers did while I was gone."

"According to my readings, both ships are operating within normal parameters. Are you certain they need repairs?"

"Listen, A.I.," he began.

"ArchAngel," she corrected.

"Okay, fine. Listen, ArchAngel, because I'm only going to say this once," said Hatch. "Your standard for acceptable parameters and mine are vastly different. You understand? I expect perfection, not some bullshit acceptable percentage of flaws that inferior engineers use to gauge their work. If you tell me that this ship is operating at 94%, all that tells me is that there's a 6% drop in quality. I expect 100% at any given time. That means fuel efficiency, gate capacity, acceleration drive, cloaking tech, and even the goddamn air conditioning." He leaned in, spotting a smudge on the side of the ship, beneath the canopy, and wiped it with his tentacle. "Every piece must be perfect. Every function must perform at optimal standards. Do you understand what I'm saying, Archangel?"

"I believe I do, Doctor Hatcherik."

"We have a lot of work to do, you and I," he said, squatting and deflating himself as he slid beneath the ship. "You'd better start calling me Hatch."

Bridge, *QBS ArchAngel*, Paladin System.

The doors on the bridge slid open and Julianna stepped through, joining both Eddie and the General. "What did I miss?" she asked.

"Apparently, this is our ship now," said Eddie. He was trying his best to contain his excitement. It wasn't every day that someone gave him a battleship.

Julianna tilted her head at the General. "Sir?"

"It's yours, Commander Fregin. The two of you are in command now. I've already had your belongings transferred to your personal quarters," said Lance.

"You did?" she asked. "When was that?"

"While you were getting Hatcherik," he answered.

"Pretty wild, right?" asked Eddie. He motioned to the three personnel on the bridge. "I haven't met the crew yet, but we should do that soon."

"Of course, right," muttered Julianna.

Eddie turned back to Lance. "Hey, boss, if you don't mind me asking, what's next on our agenda? I appreciate the ship and everything, but I'm pretty eager to keep going."

"Always ready to fight," said Lance with a chuckle. "As I expected. Follow me."

He turned to leave the bridge, with Julianna and Eddie following close behind.

"As soon as I catch up to you two, you leave," said Julianna.

"We're busy and important people. Haven't you heard?" asked Eddie, smiling.

"You'd better not get a big head just because you have a battleship now," she said.

He pretended to be shocked. "Me? A big head? I have no idea where you'd get such a crazy notion."

"Uh huh. Anyway, I'll be exploring the rest of the ship later, if you're interested. It seems like we have far more room than necessary."

Lance brought them into a small conference room, not far from the bridge. When they were inside, the lights automatically turned on, and a screen lit up against the far wall. As soon as it did, ArchAngel appeared. "Welcome," she said.

"Archangel, have you had a chance to decode the data I sent you?" asked Lance.

"I have, sir, but I don't know if you'll like it."

"What I like doesn't matter," said Lance. "Show me."

Archangel nodded, and immediately vanished. In her stead, a large planet appeared, rotating around a yellow star. "This is Exa. It's a world located in the Seolus system, 20 light years from our present location. As you might expect, it is outside of Federation space."

The planet rotated, then zoomed in on a specific continent.

"According to the data you collected," continued Archangel, "there is a weapons cache located here. I believe it is a key asset of the enemy's. Presently, if the logs are accurate, I suspect there is a small force occupying it in preparation for an assault on an as-yet unspecified world."

Eddie walked over to one of the cushioned chairs around the long conference table. "Are you saying they're already mounting another attack?" He scoffed. "Holy shit, that didn't take them long."

"Correct, Captain Teach," responded ArchAngel. "In

fact, I believe their plan is to move forward within the week."

"What about the man we're calling 'T'?" interjected Lance.

"Still unknown," answered ArchAngel. "I believe we will need more information before I can come to a conclusion on his identity and whereabouts."

"Sounds like we only have one option," said Eddie.

"You mean, attack the weapons cache?" asked Julianna.

ArchAngel appeared on the screen again. "I believe the safest course of action would be to detonate tactical bombs at key locations around the facility."

"How are we supposed to do that?" asked Eddie.

"Do we know anything about their security?" asked Julianna.

"Not much," admitted ArchAngel. "Presently, the data I have suggests a force of approximately six hundred personnel, but the number could be higher or lower."

"General, any suggestions?" asked Julianna.

He nodded. "Cloak yourselves in with the Q-Ship, drop the bombs, get out. That's really the only way."

"Can't we just nuke them from orbit?" asked Eddie.

Julianna and Lance looked at him.

"What?" he asked.

"We're just surprised at how fast you went to that extreme," said Julianna.

"Is there a reason we're holding back?" he asked.

"First off, we don't use nukes," said Lance. "ArchAngel has about five kinetic devices, which have the same power as a nuke without any of the fallout."

"Right, and still we don't want to use those," said Julianna. "They're a last resort weapon only."

"Okay, so no nukes," said Eddie, nodding. "Just thinking out loud here, but it's not like the smash and grab we did on the Ox King. This time, we'll be carrying bombs that we can't just drop. We need to put them into place. Is that about right?"

"Optimally, you will need to insert them manually, exactly where I've directed," ArchAngel replied.

"Ain't that some shit," muttered Eddie. "We might need some help on this one."

Eddie started to ask if anyone else had anymore ideas when the screen suddenly changed. The right side switched to a cargo bay, while the other half kept showing ArchAngel. "I might have a solution, if you're all interested," said a voice.

"Hatch?" said Julianna. "Have you been listening?"

Hatch's head popped out from the side of the screen. "ArchAngel asked if I wanted to listen in on this, since I'm a member of the team and everything...or did you already forget?"

"Of course not," said Lance. "I was the one who asked her to show it to you."

"You did?" asked Eddie.

Lance tapped his head. "Internal implant."

Hatch's tentacle held a socket wrench, which he began to wipe with a brown cloth. "Anyway, as I was saying, I might have an idea for you."

"We're all ears," said Julianna.

"You're familiar with the cloaks I developed for the Q-Ships?"

"Yeah, they're brilliant," she said.

"You're right about that," he answered. "But more to the point, I might be able to develop a personal version of that for each of you. A way to keep you hidden and out of sight while you run around and set your bombs."

"A personal cloak?" asked Eddie.

"It won't be perfect, obviously, because this technology isn't built for that kind of thing, but I might be able to put something together that can give you an edge."

"Your efforts are always greatly appreciated," said Julianna.

"By you, maybe. If I'm right about the tech, it should only take me two or three days, but check in with me in twelve hours. I should know whether it's possible by then."

Julianna and Eddie both nodded, then turned to Lance. "What do you think, sir?" asked Julianna.

"This one's up to you two," said the General. "You're the ones risking your lives down there."

"You can count on us," said Eddie.

"If Hatch can give us an advantage, all the better," added Julianna.

"In the meantime," said ArchAngel. "I believe Pip can assist me with hacking the system from orbit. The last data cache included several authorization passcodes that should be enough to let us into their network."

"Good," said Eddie. "With any luck, that'll mean another target."

"We haven't even taken this one down and you're already thinking about the next one?" asked Julianna.

"Maybe I'm in a hurry to kick some alien ass," said Eddie, giving her a half-smile.

"I heard that, you little punk," said Hatch.

Julianna laughed. "You better watch out, Teach. Hatch doesn't mess around."

"I'm sorry, I'm sorry," said Eddie, raising his hands, but still grinning.

Hatch puffed his cheeks. "You get this one, kid, but I've got my eye on you."

11

Captain Teach's Personal Quarters, Deck 06. *QBS Arch-Angel*, **Paladin System.**

Eddie stared around his new room with a slight bit of awe. It was larger than he expected, with a queen size bed, a pullout sofa, and a personal kitchen area with a dining nook. He'd never been in a position that warranted so much space, especially during his time in the service, but he quickly decided that it was definitely something he could get used to.

He wasn't sure he deserved the luxury, but since they offered, who was he to complain?

He opened the refrigerator, and to his surprise, found a dozen Blue Ales sitting on the bottom shelf. Beside them, a stack of Coca Colas, his favorite soda. "General Reynolds, you sneaky bastard," he said with a grin.

Eddie open one of the sodas and took a deliciously long drink from the can.

Ah. Perfection.

Eddie shut the fridge, leaving the beers for later. He certainly loved his Blue Ales, but nothing in the galaxy matched a good Coke. Empress Bethany Anne had known that. Eddie used to listen to stories about her conquests, about how she saved humanity and protected Earth, about all her many travels from this side of the galaxy to the next, and he idolized her. When he found out she was obsessed with Coke, he took it upon himself, at the tender age of ten, to give it a try.

He was instantly hooked, and to this day it remained his all-time favorite beverage, even more than beer...and that was saying something.

Eddie sat on the sofa, sinking into the cushion. There was a screen mounted on the opposite wall from him, which had to be a television. He didn't see a remote control, though, so it had to be voice-activated. "TV," he said, and the screen lit up instantly.

After directing the screen to show him the latest Federation news, he turned it off, slightly bored, and just sat there, quietly drinking the rest of his Coke.

It was hard to believe where he was right now, here in this mythic ship, this relic of a time before he was born, like sitting inside of a museum.

Three knocks at his door.

The screen lit back up, showing Julianna in the corridor outside his room. "Teach, you in there?"

"Come in," he said, standing to his feet.

The door reacted to his command, opening automatically. He should have been surprised, but he wasn't. *The ArchAngel* was a marvel and General Reynolds seemed to have a personal window into Eddie's future.

"Thanks," said Julianna, stepping inside. She had her pad in her hand. "I was thinking we'd check out the ship, if you're ready. Maybe meet some of—" She stopped, glancing around the room. "Nice quarters."

"Right?" asked Eddie. He raised his hand, showing her the Coke. "And it comes with all of my favorite things!"

"Your favorite thing is soda?" she asked, then paused. "Actually, I remember you had some cans of that in your bag when we met. Didn't that alien bust them open?"

Eddie furrowed his brow. "Don't remind me. Stupid bastard has no idea how hard Coke is to find way out in the fringe systems. All they have is Pepsi."

"I had no idea it meant so much to you," she said, sincerely.

Eddie took a final sip from the can, emptying it completely, and tossed it in the nearby trash recycler. "Speaking of awesome rooms, how's yours?"

"I wouldn't know. I haven't been there yet," she admitted.

"What? Seriously? Why the hell not?" asked Eddie. "Maybe the General got you something cool, like—" He stopped. "Wait a second, what kind of shit do you even like?"

"Wouldn't you like to know," said Julianna.

"I would, yeah," he agreed. "Let's go check it out!"

"No, I don't think so. We're too busy for that right now."

He frowned. "Aw, come on, Jules. Let's have some fun!"

"No fun for you," she said, turning towards the door. "It's time to work."

"Dammit, I'll find out what your deal is eventually," he said.

"You can try," she told him. "But you'll only come up short."

Bridge, QBS ArchAngel, Paladin System.

Lance Reynolds stood on the bridge, overlooking the barebones crew. At some point, he'd have to find a way to fill out the rest of this ship, but not yet. For now, Edward and Julianna would have to handle themselves with the resources they had.

And handle themselves they would, he knew. Lance wasn't the type to take a chance on just anyone, not when it came to the mission at hand. He believed in people, certainly, but he always made sure to pick the right ones. In this case, he believed he'd chosen well. If that turned out to not be the case, time would certainly tell.

"General, as you requested, I have a complete status update on the ArchAngel's system," said a woman by the name of Susan Deckard. She was standing at her station, waiting for his response.

"Let's hear them," said Lance.

"The ship is in optimal condition, operating at an astonishing 97%."

"That's great news, Deckard. Thank you."

"Yes, sir," said the woman.

"As you were," he told her, and she returned to her chair.

The crew of this vessel, few as they were, had been chosen by hand, specifically by General Reynolds himself.

He knew each of their records, each of their histories. It was a mountain of paperwork, but he wouldn't have it any other way.

The truth was, neither Edward nor Julianna fully understood the significance of what they were doing. The outer rim of the galaxy was rife with chaos, death, and terror, and if they didn't stop it here, the future of the Federation would be in jeopardy.

Lance knew this because the intel told him it was true. Names and dates of terrorist activities had been secured at various stages over the last five years, each indicating a rising movement outside of Federation space. Someone was making waves, attempting to undermine what Lance, Bethany Anne, and so many others had tried to do. While they had wanted peace and security, this unseen hand seemed to only want destruction and chaos.

The General was having none of that. He would be damned if he'd let all the hard work they had done turn to shit, just because of a bunch of terrorist thugs.

The treaties might prohibit certain things, but there were always loopholes—loopholes that Lance had exploited to get the resources he needed. If anyone came asking questions, he could always fall back on the fine print, but he hoped it wouldn't come to that. With any luck, his faith in Edward Teach and Julianna Fregin would pay off a thousand-fold, and the future would finally be secured.

A pay off that no one would know about. The Federation could not be formally tied to these operations. The member systems would balk at what many would call military adventurism. It wasn't. It was a proactive approach to securing the borders. The general wasn't about to let termites eat away at the foundation.

For now, however, all he could do was give his team room to move, to act, and to grow. He couldn't micromanage everything they did, not if he wanted them to stretch themselves and find their footing. No, he'd have to keep his faith. He'd have to believe in them.

And Lance *did* believe. More than anyone, he had faith in his people.

That was how this hidden war would be won. Not with giant guns, Q-Ships, or armadas, but with loyalty and trust, with the same sort of people who built the Federation. People like Bethany Anne and her friends. People like Edward and Julianna. Hell, maybe even people like Lance.

He smiled, standing there on the bridge of this ancient ship, and he pulled out a fresh cigar, running it along the base of his nose, and took a whiff. "Ah," he sighed, lighting the old stogie.

Looking around the bridge, he took a few puffs of the cigar, sending tiny clouds of smoke into the air.

"Smoking on the bridge isn't advised," ArchAngel said overhead.

"Telling me what to do isn't advised." Lance tapped his cigar, making ashes fall to the floor.

"Actually, smoking in general is a nasty habit," retorted Archangel.

Lance blew out a plume of smoke, doing his best to ignore the intrusive A.I.

Dining Hall 03, Deck 12. *QBS ArchAngel*, Paladin System.

"This is one hellavah ship," remarked Eddie as he and Julianna walked through the dining area. It was lined with long tables, but only a few people were currently eating.

Eddie could smell warm food coming from somewhere, but there didn't seem to be any tray lines or lunch ladies like your typical mess hall. Instead, there were only cabinets, fully automated to deliver warm lunches from an assembly line behind the wall. He'd seen this type of system before, but only in smaller ships with fewer crewmembers.

"Is there a mess hall with a kitchen on this ship?" he asked.

"They all have them," said Julianna, motioning to the far side of the room. "There are just no chefs."

"I guess we don't have the manpower," he reasoned.

"Yet," added Julianna. "But give it time. One day this ship will be bustling with activity, the same way it used to."

He examined her expression, and for a moment she almost looked happy. "You act like you know that firsthand."

"I do," she answered.

"What do you mean, you do?"

She stopped at the door, turning to look at the room again, and crossed her arms. "I used to eat my dinner right there, near that corner," she said, motioning.

"Huh? Wasn't this ship decommissioned until recently?"

"It was," she said, nodding. "I'm talking about before that."

"You mean you were onboard *the ArchAngel* before it was…"

"Blown up," she said, turning to him.

His eyes widened. "But that was centuries ago!"

"So?"

"That means you're as old as this ship, doesn't it?" He dropped his mouth, looking her over, almost like it was the first time. He'd guessed that there was something incredible about her, but not to this extent. "Holy shit."

"Don't act so surprised. You'd know all this if you paid more attention."

"Hey," said Eddie. "I pay attention when it matters."

She gave him a look that said she didn't believe him. "If you say so."

"Anyway, if you were on this ship before it blew up, then that means you were also in the war, right?"

"That's correct."

"So, did you ever get to meet the Empress?"

"Bethany Anne?" she asked, smiling. "Who do you think authorized my enhancement?"

Eddie had watched countless archived speeches, interviews, and footage of the Empress when he was a child, growing up, but he'd never had the opportunity to meet Bethany Anne in person. She'd left this region of space long before he'd had the chance. Even now, he could hear the Empress's words in his head.

"I left Earth to save it," Bethany Anne had said in a televised speech, many years before Eddie was born. "I took to the stars to save us all, and in doing so, I discovered a galaxy of life, a universe of people not unlike my own. I saw with my own eyes that ours was but one of many in this universe...a voice in a chorus, bringing unity to the song of existence. And it must be protected, my friends. It must be shielded from all who would disrupt the music."

Eddie believed in her immediately and without hesitation. Something about her words, about her eyes, told him she was telling the truth, that she wanted to save people.

"Do you think she's alive?" asked Eddie, looking at Julianna.

"Bethany Anne?" she asked.

He nodded. "No one has seen her in years."

She gave him a sly grin. "Oh, I expect she's doing just fine."

"What makes you so sure?"

"Because I know her," she Julianna, continuing down the hall. "And trust me, nothing can stop the Empress."

"You really believe that, don't you?" asked Eddie, smiling. "Good. I'm happy to hear you say that."

"Are you?"

He nodded. "I'd like to meet that woman someday."

Julianna laughed. "Maybe you will, Teach, if you can stay alive long enough."

"I plan on it," he said, clasping his hands.

"Good," said Julianna. "Because the Queen Bitch is worth the wait."

12

Loading Dock 02, *QBS Archangel*, Paladin System.

Hatch fiddled with the MX screwdriver in his tentacle, opening the CLK-01 box. It was a tricky procedure, given the contents, but not in a dangerous sort of way.

The casing was created using an experimental magnesium-based alloy known as MX-99. It made the box nearly indestructible, which was especially useful given the ship's active combat status.

The actual genius lay within, however, as the CLK-01 box housed the central core of the technology, a powerful energy crystal from Berosia known as Aether. These crystals were some of the rarest in the known universe, consisting of condensed Etheric energy that could not be reproduced. Rather, they had to be mined from a single location, deep within the mountains of the upper Berosian continent. They were so rare that only a handful were found every decade, which made each of the Q-Ships all the more valuable. The same was true of *the ArchAngel*, since it used not one, but six Aetherian crystals in order to cloak the ship in its entirety.

Hatch was far more concerned with what he could *do* with them, however, than where they came from. Specifically, creating a personal cloaking device that could be used to hide a couple of his teammates as they planted explosives around the walls of an enemy outpost.

He set the casing on the floor beside him and examined the Aether—a glowing blue crystal, cold to the touch. It illuminated the space around it, creating a soft glow inside the box and along Hatch's tentacles.

He took another device from his other side—something he'd crafted himself over the past several hours—and brought it closer, preparing to transfer the crystal. The device was hooked onto the side of a brown belt, which Hatch had borrowed from one of the supply lockers. He popped the Aether out of the CLK-01 box and inserted it into the new device, strapping the crystal in tightly and closing the latch.

The device powered on immediately, but gave no indication other than a small green light.

Hatch looked around the cargo bay, but saw no changes. "AI," he said.

ArchAngel's face appeared on the display. "I believe I told you my name is—" She paused. "Hatcherik?"

"No," said Hatch, staring at the A.I. "That's my name."

ArchAngel blinked. "Scanning area…"

"You won't find anything," said Hatch. He turned off the device. "See me now?"

"Fascinating," she said. "I ran over one hundred scans and found no results. What happened?"

Hatch grasped the belt in his tentacle and brought it up to eye-level, and he grinned. "Just another day at the office, my wall-sized friend. Now, do me a favor and call the others. They're going to want to see this."

Loading Dock 02, *QBS ArchAngel*, Paladin System.

Eddie, Julianna, and General Reynolds stood side-by-side as they waited for Hatch to show them what they'd all be waiting for.

"You sure this is going to work?" asked Eddie, watching the alien fiddle with a small box.

"Have your doubts, do you?" asked Hatch.

"In his defense, you did suggest you could alter highly advanced technology that only a few people in the Federation have experience handling," said Julianna. "In a matter of hours, I might add."

Hatch motioned with one of his tentacles. "So? Did Q'Thur Ock Mo'Shall stop to consider whether or not anyone else was capable of creating the first matter displacement chamber? Did Otto Seraph K'Kurn ever stop to ask if he was worthy of developing the second warp theorem? I don't think so."

"Whoever they are," said Eddie.

Hatch paused, blinking at him. "I swear, I'm surrounded by children. What do they teach you people in school these days?"

Eddie pretended to gasp. "You people?" He looked at Julianna. "Are you hearing this?"

"Let's see what you've got here, Hatcherik," said Lance, who had remained composed throughout the exchange.

"At least someone appreciates what I'm doing," said Hatch as he lifted the box with one of his eight tentacles, simultaneously using three others to hold various tools and make adjustments. "Prepare yourselves, everyone."

He turned a small dial on the side of the box and a green light appeared. Eddie waited for something else to happen, but there was nothing. No sign of a cloak or anything else.

"Is that it?" asked Julianna.

"Were we supposed to see a change?" asked Eddie, looking around. "I don't get it."

Hatch puffed his cheeks, amused. "Of course, you don't. You're still in the safe zone."

"The what?" asked Eddie.

Hatch waved his tentacle. "Take a few steps back, would you?"

"Uh, sure," said Eddie, doing as the mechanic suggested. "There. Two steps back."

"A few more," said Hatch. "Keep your eye on me as you do."

Eddie took another two, watching the alien as he did. On the second step, he noticed a change. Hatch, along with both Lance and Julianna, faded. It was like they'd suddenly ceased to exist, like they had teleported or phased out of existence. "Holy shit! Would you look at that?" he asked, dropping his mouth. "You guys just disappeared!"

"Quite the opposite, don't you think?" asked Hatch's voice. A laugh bellowed from the emptiness. "You see? He can't see us anymore."

"But we can see him," said Julianna, who was nowhere to be found.

"Come back," suggested Hatch. "Step forward, Captain Teach."

Eddie did as the mechanic instructed, taking a single step. As he did, everyone phased back into view. "Hot damn."

"That's right, kid," said Hatch.

Julianna looked back at Eddie. "That cloak covers a lot of area, doesn't it? Can you lower the field so it's only around the individual?"

"I'm afraid not," said Hatch, turning the dial and changing the green light to a red one. "This came from the Q-Ship, so the range is built in. I'd have to create an entirely separate device, which would take longer than we have."

"So," said Lance, who had been carefully observing all of this in silence. "It seems you two will have to keep some distance."

"Three meters," said Hatch. "You go outside of that and they'll see you."

"It's not ideal, but it's better than the alternative," said Julianna.

Lance looked at Eddie. "Can you work with this, Captain?"

"Of course," said Eddie. He walked over to Hatch, letting out his palm. The mechanic handed him the box, and Eddie stared down and studied it for a moment before finally turning the dial. "We'll be in and out with the bombs charged and set before anyone down there is the wiser."

"Just don't get close to anyone," cautioned Hatch.

"Not to worry," assured Eddie. "They won't even know we were there."

Lance nodded. "We'll form a gate and be there in a few hours, so long as you two are ready."

"We're good to go," said Julianna. "Right, Teach?"

Eddie gave the device back to Hatch. "Hell, I'm ready to go right now. You kidding?"

"I love the enthusiasm," said Lance, smiling. "Motivation is key to a successful operation."

"That and kicking ass," said Eddie. "Which, I assure you, I'm ready and willing to do."

Loading Dock 01, *QBS ArchAngel*, en route to Seolus system.

"How long before we arrive?" asked Eddie, his flight helmet under his arm, fully geared.

"Fifteen minutes, last I checked," said Julianna. She was already dressed, her helmet sealed.

They both wore their black combat suits, ready for the job. The difference now was that Eddie's belt had a small box on it with one of the most powerful pieces of technology known to man: an Aetherian crystal. He couldn't help but glance down at it every few minutes. Hatch had given him a lengthy speech about how expensive and rare the crystal inside of the box was, which made Eddie more nervous than he expected. Despite the oncoming mission he was about to undertake, he was actually more concerned with misplacing the cloak than getting shot.

The screen on the wall near the Q-Ship lit up, revealing the face of ArchAngel. "Greetings. Is there anything I can do for you two before we arrive?"

"Just keep the engines running for us," said Julianna. "We'll try to hurry back."

"Understood," said the A.I.

"ArchAngel, where are you parking this rig?" asked Eddie.

"On the opposite side of the star from the planet Exa. Between the cloak and the solar radiation, we should be shielded from any known sensors the outpost has in their possession."

"Good to know," he responded, lifting his helmet and placing it over his head. With a quick turn, it locked into place. "All set."

Julianna nodded. "We'll be landing there under the cover of night. It won't do much, but the patrols should be lower than normal."

"Even better," grinned Eddie. He grabbed hold of the Q-Ship's handhold and boosted himself up, into the opening, and slid inside.

Julianna followed, and took her position in the co-pilot seat. "Performing pre-flight check."

Eddie reached beside him and took the rifle in his hand, then proceeded to check it over. After some quick consideration, he returned it.

"What's wrong?" asked Julianna. "Your rifle okay?"

Eddie took his pistol next to the rifle and holstered it on his side. "I'm going with the handgun on this one. Better for the job. You bring yours and back me up if things go south, but I'll need my hands free to handle the explosives and the cloak."

"Understood," she said, tapping the butt of her rifle, which was sitting next to her.

The *ArchAngel* came out of the gate a few seconds later, cloaking immediately. "All clear," announced Pip over the comm inside the helmet. "You're both good to go."

"We'll see you when we return, Pip," said Julianna.

"Didn't Hatch tell you?" asked the E.I. "He upgraded the system on this ship so I could interface during your missions."

Eddie blinked. "When the hell did he have time to do that?"

"As I understand it, he simply replaced the data-drive with the one from the other Q-Ship," said Pip.

"So does that mean the second ship doesn't have one anymore?"

"Affirmative," said Pip. "But I believe he's working on a workaround."

"Regardless, that's great news," said Julianna, smiling a little.

"Most certainly," agreed Pip.

"Okay, you two, enough bonding. Let's kick some alien ass," said Eddie, gripping the controls.

The Q-Ship lifted off the deck, hovering into position. Eddie ignited the thrusters and took them through the shield, entering open space. Behind them, the cargo bay sat floating in darkness, the rest of the ship shrouded in cloak.

The thrusters hit their second burst, pushing the ship into full speed. Eddie brought the Q-Ship around the star, a dying white dwarf. He was finally used to the controls, letting himself relax as he cruised towards the first planet, a largely empty rock no bigger than a fat class-3 moon.

The Q-Ship was already cloaked and ready to enter Exa's orbit. Exa was the second planet in a string of three.

This system, aside from its galactic position as it related to Federation space, would typically be of little interest. Exa itself was barely habitable. The atmosphere around the bulk of the planet was too thin for habitation, excluding a handful of adaptable species. The only exception to this was around the equator, which had a balanced temperature as well as clean air. This was also their current destination.

The Q-Ship approached Exa, fully cloaked, and dropped to a slow cruising speed as it entered the atmosphere. It wouldn't be long now.

Kezzin Battlebase 44, Planet Exa, Seolus system.

The Kezzin base on Exa was silent and still. A soft breeze from the nearby valley blew through the window of the quiet room as the Kezzin called Lars Malseen lay in his bunk, counting the stars.

He couldn't sleep, but what else was new? Ever since he arrived on this gods-forsaken planet, he'd wanted to leave. He'd wanted to go home.

Lars released a long sigh. Oh, how he missed Kezza. His homeworld felt so far away. He was stuck here on this rock, separated from his Kezzin friends and family, forced to work with these pirates and criminals.

All because of a debt.

Lars could still remember it, the day they had come for his brother. The pirates owned the colony his family lived on and they expected their payment for "protection." When his brother couldn't meet the demand, the soldiers had come to conscript him. The poor farmer couldn't leave his family behind, though. He was a father and a husband, and he was needed, but if he didn't leave, the farm would be destroyed.

Lars couldn't let that happen, not to the only family he had left. Not to his brother, his nieces, his nephews.

He offered himself and the pirates accepted. Blood-for-blood had always been the Kezzin way, to exchange one life for another. It was a fair trade.

Now, he was here, stuck in this place, watching foreign stars through stone-rimmed windows, longing to be elsewhere.

Lars had no love for these people. He only wanted to see his family again, to keep them safe. If only the Brotherhood wasn't so powerful, so corrupt, perhaps he could find another way. Perhaps he could save them.

But such a life was far beyond his means. He was a cog in the machine, an insect beneath the boot.

Lars took a long breath, closing his eyes.

As he did, a cough forced him awake. He looked to the side of the room to see a soldier entering. It was Chan, returned from his rounds. "What a boring night," muttered the large pirate, his metal armor clanking as he shuffled to his own bunk.

Lars watched as he plopped down on the side of his bed, opposite Lars, and began taking off his boots and leg-guards. "Welcome back."

Chan raised his head, apparently not realizing he'd woken Lars. "Hm? What are you awake for, Malseen?"

"Nothing," said Lars, turning on his back.

"You'd better sleep if you know what's good for you. Your shift is in an hour, ain't it?"

"Sure," said Lars.

"They catch you sleeping on the job and you'll lose a hand, you know." Chan removed his chest-piece. "Lazy asshole."

Lars took a deep breath, trying to shut Chan out as best he could. The moonlight beamed in through the open window, shining against the nearby wall adjacent to his bunk. He stared at it, wide awake. The soft glow of silver light reminded him of something familiar, a night he once spent in the forest when he was young with his brother.

He tried to imagine his brother's face right now. He hoped with all his will that the man whose place he'd taken was, perhaps, out in those same woods, spending time with his own children. If fate was merciful, if the gods themselves were kind, then such a scene would become reality.

Chan began to snore, his throat flapping so loud it was almost too hard to believe. After months of being stationed here, Lars was used to such things, but he still loathed them.

No matter.

Lars stared at the light on the wall as his eyes began to close, and he felt his whole body grow more relaxed. Rest now, he felt it say. Time to sleep.

But as his focus dipped from the wall, the light stirred a bit, flickering in a way that gave him pause. Lars felt himself tense up, surprised at the distortion. Was he so tired that his senses were playing tricks? Did he need to rest so badly?

Another break in the light, like something was interrupting it. Lars leaned up on his shoulder, then turned around to face the window. Could it be a bird? Perhaps a cloud passing overhead. Or maybe...

The light of the moon shined with such brightness that it made him squint, but he kept his eyes fixed.

That was when he saw it. A distorted shadow against the celestial light. A faded blur that wasn't there. Lars had spent many years as a tracker, living in the wilds of Kezza. His eyes were stronger, more refined than most, and so he knew better than to ignore what he was seeing. He knew there was more to the moon tonight.

Lars twisted around on his bed, all the while keeping his eyes on the shadow in the night, the distant, foreign thing that shouldn't be...

And then, without a word to his roommate, he got to his feet and went outside.

An Empty Field Near Kezzin Battlebase 44, Planet Exa, Seolus system.

The Q-Ship entered a darkened sky, countless stars behind it. The planet was currently experiencing the middle of the night, the eighteenth hour in Exa's twenty-hour cycle. There would be plenty of time before dawn to get the job done.

Eddie brought the ship down, hovering momentarily before releasing the landing gear, and setting the Q-Ship gently on the ground. They were in a small field just north of the base, half a klick out, or a slow ten-minute walk. He decided to bring them in close since they had to carry the explosives.

Eddie wasn't a fan of moving slowly, preferring the faster route when it came to it, but he also understood that certain situations often called for some restraint. In this case, a hundred pounds of explosive death hoisted on his back as he and Julianna stayed quiet and invisible, avoiding several hundred-armed soldiers in the process. It wasn't the easiest task in the universe, but he could do it.

"Ready?" asked Julianna as the two prepared to leave the cloaked ship.

Eddie slid his thumbs behind each of the straps around his chest, feeling the weight of the bombs he was carrying. He was pretty sure he had enough explosives to blow up the whole goddamn world if he wanted to. "I'm ready to kick some ass. You?"

She already had her own pack on, having a far easier time with the weight. She grinned, raising her rifle. "In and out before they know what hit them."

"Right, then." Eddie turned the knob on his belt. "Time to kill us some bad guys."

The enemy outpost wasn't far. Eddie could already see several lights in the distance. As they drew closer, it became apparent that these were from the base's many rooms. As expected, the residents were not entirely asleep, despite the late hour, nor should they be. Any reasonable military stronghold would be operating at all hours, with around-the-clock shifts. But as everyone knew, the late-night crew was always the thinnest. Eddie was happy to see that applied to Kezzin every bit as much as it did to humans.

Eddie and Julianna moved silently in the night, invisible to any guards who might be watching. They crept through a small forest and approached the side of the base's western wall, crossing another field to reach it. Near them, five sentry towers stood, sporting guns and lights to scan for intruders. No doubt, this place was hardwired with scanners of all kinds, old and new. Lucky for Eddie, the cloaking device he was carrying on his belt worked against all of them.

Julianna stayed less than a meter away from him at all times, never moving too fast or too slow. When they were finally close enough to the wall, but still walking, she withdrew the first of the explosives and began prepping it.

Eddie said nothing during this, nor did he need to. The woman knew what she was doing. She was a pro, after all, and the cloak didn't stop sound from escaping. If they talked or made noise, they could be discovered, despite Hatch's technological marvel.

The base was large, but not as intimidating as he had expected. It looked as though it had been thrown together overnight, like there was no history to it, no soul. Structures like this were often the result of ARCs (Automated Redistribution Construction), where a series of robotic drones would build something overnight, depending on the specifications. ARCs were expensive and hard to come by outside of Federation space, so it was curious to see one here in the hands of a group of pirates. Eddie would have to ask ArchAngel about this later.

Eddie motioned silently with his hand as the two reached the large wall. Julianna had, by this point, already assembled the first explosive. All she needed to do was flip a small switch to prime the device. Once they had about a dozen of these in place, they'd leave and detonate them all at once.

Julianna set the bomb on the soft ground, right up against the wall. She covered it with some nearby dirt and leaves, hiding the bulk of it. Once she was ready, they proceeded farther down the wall to the next location.

After the second drop, as they were walking to the third, Julianna paused, touching Eddie's shoulder. He looked at her, curiously, and she put her finger to her lips and then pointed up. Her enhanced eyes were far more acute than his own, but he could still make out a shadow moving along the wall. A guard, no doubt, making his patrol.

When the figure was gone, moved on to some other post, the two continued to their next point of interest, followed by the next. Before the hour was through, they managed to plant six bombs along the western and northern walls, all without saying a word or getting spotted.

So far so good.

13

Kezzin Battlebase 44, Planet Exa, Seolus system.

Lars felt the wind against his thick scales, cold as it was, and observed the field beyond the walls. The tall grass danced as the gust blew through, giving movement to the greenery. He longed for this, more than metal or stone, more than anything in all the galaxy. A soft and natural splendor that only existed in the wilds.

The wind settled soon, and Lars leaned against the artificial stone at the top of the wall, accepting that tonight he would not sleep. His mind was far too busy… overflowing with memories and nostalgia.

That was fine, he decided. Sometimes it was better to be alive than asleep. Maybe the soul needed moments like this, filled with quiet reflection.

Lars took a breath, watching the moonlight sweep across the field. He'd come out here to investigate the strange shadow he saw from his window, but now decided it was nothing. Perhaps his mind had played a trick on him. A way to get him out of bed.

The other soldiers were still patrolling, but nowhere near him. Two were stationed at each at corner of the facility, but the bulk of the base had video feed for surveillance. If anything actually had been out here, surely the cameras would have caught it and the entire base would've been alerted.

He licked his hard lips, debating, as he often did on nights like this, how he could possibly rid himself of this accursed life and return to his old one.

Lars pushed the thought out of his mind, focusing on the field and trying to forget. As he did, the grass moved again, no doubt from yet another gust of wind. He ignored it, turning back towards the base, wondering how long he had before his shift.

He heard a snap behind him, like a twig breaking, and he instinctively turned and found nothing. This planet was largely devoid of animals, but it had its share of insects and foliage. Had his mind played another trick on him?

Was he so sleep-deprived that he was hearing and seeing things? If so, it would have been a first. Lars had always been able to rely on his senses. Perhaps it was due to all his time spent tracking and camping in the wilds of Kezza, or maybe it was a natural gift. He couldn't say, but he could only hope that—

A light snap echoed near the base of the wall. Lars glanced over the side of the stone, but saw nothing. Another phantom sound? No... his instinct told him there was more to this. He stared at the dirt and mud beneath the wall, watching with focused eyes.

That was when he saw it.

The dirt compressed, forming an outline. A footprint, he realized, fresh and newly defined. Lars dropped his mouth and, without realizing it, leaned closer to the edge of the wall. What in the gods' names could this be?

Another boot print formed in the mud, followed by a third. As Lars observed them, more appeared in the same direction. It was as though a ghost was moving before him, traveling the border of the wall.

But Lars did not believe in such things. He'd spent enough time in the darkness to know that such specters were nothing more than superstition. This was a person, he knew it. A living, breathing thing that had, somehow, found a way to hide itself.

Lars watched as the footsteps continued, and he moved quietly along the top of the wall, observing, staying in the darkness. He'd spent his whole life tracking game, keeping silent and remaining hidden. He would watch this entity, this intruder, and see where it went. Whatever this was, like Lars himself, did not belong there.

Eddie stopped while Julianna set another bomb against the wall. They'd finally placed all but one of the explosives. In only a few moments, they'd return to the Q-Ship and blow this place to hell and back.

Julianna covered the bomb with some dirt, the same as before, and looked at Eddie, giving him a nod. *Just one more to go,* he thought. *Another two dozen yards and we can high tail it out of—*

A shadow formed in front of him, there on the ground, and grew rapidly. Eddie turned towards the top of the wall, only to see a looming mass as it came towards him.

The object slammed into both him and Julianna, pinning them to the earth. It didn't take Eddie long to realize that this was a body—a massive, hulking alien who was strong enough to bend metal.

Eddie wheezed, having had the air knocked out of him. The two arms wrapped around him, pinning him tight. "What the actual fuck?!"

"Hold yourselves!" ordered the Kezzin soldier.

"Fuck off!" returned Eddie, digging his knuckles into the alien's waist.

But the Kezzin didn't flinch. His armor was thick and he was strong. He clung to both of them with all his strength. "Intruders! Intruders!"

Julianna pulled her forehead back and attempted to head-butt the guard, but he buried his head between the both of them, holding their bodies close. A second later, three other guards ran up, armor clanking as they arrived. The first two took Eddie by the shoulders while the third kept a rifle pointed at him. He gritted his teeth and flinched at them, about to fight back. He'd rather die than be taken prisoner.

"Go with them," said Julianna, jarring Eddie. Her words pulled him out of his rage.

He looked at her. "But we can't just—"

"Trust me, Eddie!" she snapped.

He snarled, looking at the guards. "Bastards."

Once they had him handcuffed, the group turned to Julianna. The one who had tackled them put another set on her wrists. She said nothing, and instead got to her feet.

The guards escorted them to the front of the base and into the facility. *Shit*, thought Eddie as they entered the gate. *Shit shit shit shit.*

———

Lars watched as the other guards locked the prisoners inside their cells. When it was done, they called for Commander Orsa, who took reports from each of them, one at a time.

"Excellent work, Lars Malseen," said Orsa, once he was done. "You have performed well, and before your patrol was even scheduled."

"Thank you, sir," said Lars.

"I have to wonder, though, what were you doing out before your shift? And how did you know of the intruders? It seems no one else was aware of them."

"I was restless," replied Lars. "And I saw them moving beneath the wall. They had some kind of invisibility."

Orsa gave him a skeptical look, but left it alone. "Very well. Return to your quarters for now."

Lars looked at the two humans in the cells. One was calm and motionless. She sat with her hands on her knees, taking steady breaths. The other, a male, seemed to be fuming. "Sir, if you would allow it, I would like to question the prisoners."

Orsa raised his brow. "Would you?"

"I have some experience extracting information," explained Lars.

"We have no official interrogator here," said Orsa, apparently considering the notion. "Very well. Do what you want, but don't kill them. Find out if there are any others out there. Ask them why they're here. Do whatever you have to in order to protect this base. Do you understand?"

"Of course, sir," said Lars.

Orsa looked at the three guards, requesting they join him. "Let's go."

As the group left, Lars turned to the cells. The cages were both made of hard light, making them impossible to penetrate, which meant that no matter what these prisoners did, they couldn't leave.

Lars went to the side of the first cell where the male was sitting. The human glanced up at him. "You there."

"What?" the man retorted.

Lars stared at him. "What are you doing here?"

"None of your business, asshole."

Lars ignored the insult. "Are there more of you outside the walls?"

"Hundreds," said the intruder, giving him a slight smile.

"Is that so?"

"Maybe. Who knows? I'm not telling you shit."

"If you don't, the Captain will have you killed."

The human laughed. "We'll see."

"You seem overly confident for someone in a cell," said Lars. "What is your name?"

"You can call me Ed."

"Ed?" repeated Lars. The name was simple, yet strange, like something a child had thought up.

"Got a problem with it?" asked Ed as Lars understood the human's name.

"No," Lars said, simply. "Where did you come from?"

"My mom," said Ed. "You know how babies work, right?"

"I mean, why did you come to the base? What faction are you with? What organization?"

"I'm an independent contractor," said Ed.

"You operate on your own?" asked Lars.

Ed tapped his nose. "Right you are."

"I find that difficult to believe."

"Believe what you want," said Ed. "But I'll tell you one thing. If you don't let me out of here, I'm going to break out, and then I'm going to kill every last asshole terrorist in this place."

"Terrorist?" asked Lars. "You're the one planting bombs."

"To stop you from killing innocent people, you jackass."

Lars paused, trying to understand. "What are you talking about?"

"Your people have been attacking colonies! You keep killing all those—"

"That's enough!" barked the female. "Contain yourself, Eddy. You're speaking with the enemy."

Lars had heard of the colony attacks. It was difficult not to notice or overhear the way the higher ranks celebrated their slaughters. They made a habit of pillaging, it seemed, but such was the way of these people. The Kezzin Brotherhood owned a third of the Kezzin-occupied systems, which made them one of the most influential independent military factions in this region. The way Lars had heard it, the

Federation had invaded their territory, killing Kezzin soldiers and stealing their worlds. "You must face the consequences of your actions. I'm sorry."

"By consequences, you mean death," said the female.

"That is none of my concern," Lars said.

"Concern?" asked Ed. "Wait until I get out of here. I'll make it your concern."

Lars didn't answer, but turned and walked to the door, leaving the angry man to himself. He stepped out into the hall and proceeded towards Orsa's office. He'd have to tell the Captain all about this, about what the human had told him regarding the colonies. If it was true, there could be more of them out there, waiting to strike. The entire base might very well be under siege before long.

Lars knocked, entered the office, and stood before Commander Orsa as the elder soldier ordered three squads to patrol the walls in search of hidden bombs. "There must be more of them. Go and search!" ordered the Captain.

"Yes, sir," said several of the men.

As the soldiers began to leave, Orsa turned to him. "Lars, what did you discover from the prisoners? Anything important?"

"They claim to be avenging the Federation colonies," said Lars.

"The colonies?" asked Orsa, though he didn't seem very surprised. "I see. What else did they say?"

"Nothing else. The female stopped the male from speaking further on the subject, but I learned his name is Edward."

"Edward, you say? Interesting. I'll have to include that in the report. Good job, Lars."

"Thank you, but there was something else."

"What is it?"

"The male mentioned that the Brotherhood was responsible for terrorist attacks on the colonies. He made it sound like we were the aggressors."

Orsa chuckled. "Is that what he said?"

Lars nodded. "It's a lie, isn't it?"

"A lie?" asked Orsa. "What do you mean?"

"I've heard the Federation colonies once belonged to the Kezzin. Isn't that true?"

"Something like that," said Orsa. "That area was lost in the War of Division. The Federation moved in when it was unoccupied."

"You mean to say they didn't steal it?" asked Lars.

"Of course they stole it," insisted Orsa. "Those worlds are ours by right. Just because we left them vacant for three hundred years does not mean the claim is rendered null."

Lars considered this for a moment. "Who attacked first?"

"They attacked when they established those colonies," explained Orsa. "Colonizing those worlds was an attack on our dignity. Our very pride."

"But they didn't fire weapons," said Lars.

"No, they didn't, but they might as well have."

"But that means—"

"Lars, let it go. Remember why you are here. The Brotherhood exists to ensure Kezzin prosperity. To hell with those aliens. They are all garbage, especially humans. You know that."

Lars stared at his superior, blinking. "Yes, sir."

"Now, if that's everything, then leave the rest to me. I'll see these humans punished for their attempted attack."

"Of course," said Lars. "My shift is about to begin, so I should prepare."

"No, just go to your room and await instructions. Get some rest until I need you."

"But what about—"

Orsa raised his brow. "Don't make me repeat myself, Lars. I'm giving you a reward. Do you understand?"

"Yes, sir. Of course." Lars backed away, towards the door. "Thank you."

He turned and left, leaving the office and proceeding down the hall. It had only been a short time since he'd gone outside, but already so much had happened. He couldn't believe it, everything Orsa and the two humans had said.

Did those colonies really deserve the fate they received? Had the Brotherhood attacked them simply for existing?

Galactic politics were cruel, and Lars knew better than most about how an innocent person could get caught up in them, unable to do anything. Unable to fight back.

What an awful life it is, thought Lars, *to be the pawn of an unjust empire.*

14

Inside a cell. Kezzin Battlebase 44, Planet Exa, Seolus system.

Julianna sat on the bench, quietly staring at the translucent hard-light cell wall.

She was breathing steadily, totally calm and without concern. There was no need for it. Not yet, anyway.

The Kezzin guards had taken her rifle, but she was still armed. They had separated her from Captain Teach, yet she was not alone.

Pip, thought Julianna, mentally calling out to her E.I. companion.

I am here, Julianna.

Have you had time to crack the security network yet?

It is nearly finished. Please be patient.

Go as fast as you can. I'm not sure how long I can let this façade go on.

Getting captured was unfortunate, but this could prove to be even more fortuitous.

If you manage to crack that digital safe and get us the data, then you could be right.

Shouldn't you let Captain Teach know what we're doing?

Not without alerting the other guards, but he'll find out in a few minutes.

You're right, of course.

Julianna glanced over to the other cell where Teach was standing, leaning with his fist against the hard-light wall. He looked absolutely furious, so much that it made her want to smile. If only he knew what she and Pip were planning.

The door to the room opened and in walked a Kezzin guard. He looked at each of them for a long moment before Teach smacked the wall. "What's the deal, buddy?" asked the Captain. "Got something you wanna tell us?"

The guard looked him over. "Which of you is in charge?"

Teach chewed on the inside of his lip before he answered. "That would be—"

"Neither of us," interjected Julianna.

Teach looked at her, curiously.

She winked at him. "We're just grunts like you, doing our jobs. Our boss is outside in the ship, along with the others."

The Kezzin laughed. "I am no grunt, human. My name is Commander Trill Orsa, the head of this instillation."

"So, you're the boss here. Is that right?" asked Teach.

"It is," answered Orsa. "And if you think I'm stupid enough to believe there are more of you outside, then you must be a poor judge of character."

"It's true, we are," said Teach, nodding and tapping his chin.

"Very poor," agreed Julianna. *How's it coming, Pip?*

Infiltration process complete. I'm inside the network.

Upload their files and logs to the Q-Ship as soon as you can.

I've already started. Estimated time to completion is ninety seconds.

Which still leaves us with enough time to hightail it out of here, thought Julianna.

I would suggest waiting a few minutes. An escape could trigger an alert to their system, which may slow me down.

Julianna sighed inwardly. *Fine.*

Commander Orsa crossed his arms and glared at Teach. "I've decided you will both be executed for your crimes against the Kezzin people. What do you say to that?"

"Shove it up your ass," said Teach.

Orsa ignored the crude comment. "I'll give you one last opportunity to get out of this. Tell me everything you know about the organization you work for, including any intelligence relating to our operation. Do this, and you might make it out of this alive."

"You want us to flip?" asked Julianna.

"Flip?" repeated Orsa, apparently not understanding the expression.

"Betray our side," explained Teach.

"Ah," said Orsa. "Yes, that. If you do, I'll see to it that you're treated with respect. In time, perhaps in a few years, you may even be allowed to leave."

Teach leaned forward, raising his fist to Orsa. "I'll say it one more time so you understand exactly what I mean. Take your offer, ball it up, and—" He slammed his fist into his other palm. "—shove it so far up your own ass that it clogs your goddamn throat and chokes the blood to that tiny, little Kezzin brain of yours. You got me, fuckwit?"

Orsa gave an odd expression. Julianna took a guess that it probably wasn't good. "I'll come back when you two are feeling more talkative," he said, stepping towards the door. "Just remember, if you don't talk soon, I can't ensure your protection."

Julianna watched as Orsa left, closing the door behind him.

"Asshole," muttered Edward, loud enough that the Kezzin captain was bound to hear.

Lars watched as his captain walked across the hall from the brig and re-entered his office. Judging by the look on his face, Lars guessed the discussion with the prisoners had not gone well.

He followed after Orsa, curious to find out what he planned to do. The Captain had ordered him to return to his room, which he had done, but with so much going on, Lars could hardly sit still. It bothered him to believe what the humans had said was true, that the Brotherhood really was attacking defenseless colonies.

When Lars finally entered the office, he was met by two guards. "The Captain is not to be disturbed," said one, whom Lars recognized as a Kezzin named Kal Drog.

"I need to ask him something," said Lars.

"The Captain gave specific orders," said Kal. "Sorry."

"Can you tell him it's me?" asked Lars.

"I will," agreed Kal. "But you should leave now. He's very upset. If you think your capture of the invaders will garner you any special privileges, you're mistaken."

The second guard nodded. "You should return to your room, like the Captain instructed."

"I have questions," said Lars.

"Not for the Captain, you don't," said Kal. "Why not ask us your questions? Maybe we can save you the trouble of getting killed."

Lars considered the proposition, but decided against it. "No, I think I'll do as you suggested and return to my room. I don't know what I was thinking, bothering him."

"Good idea," said Kal. "It's good to see you aren't a complete idiot sometimes."

"Right," said Lars, leaving it at that. He marched away from them and into a separate hallway. It was empty, giving him a moment to think. He wanted to find out more about these prisoners and their accusations.

Lars shot a glance in the direction of the brig. If those humans were right, then the Brotherhood had killed hundreds, maybe even thousands of civilians. There was a good chance that they might even incite a war with the Federation. If that happened, Lars' family would be in serious danger.

He felt panic rising in his chest. He'd gone and volunteered for this job with the hopes of protecting his brother, but what if it was all for nothing? What if a fleet of ships showed up next month and destroyed Kezza and all its colonies? All of Lars' sacrifices would have been for nothing.

Did Orsa understand any of this? Did the rest of the Brotherhood? Or were they more concerned with vengeance and land than the lives of innocent Kezzin families? Knowing the people in this base, Lars was certain he knew the answer to that question.

Eddie kicked the hard-light cell door with his foot. He hated small spaces. Specifically, cages like this one. *Just wait until I get out of here,* thought Eddie, staring at the door to the outer hall, like he was trying to burn a hole in it. *I'll kick that Orsa guy's ass.* He shook his head. *No, I need to focus on getting the hell out of here first. Think, Eddie.*

Just then, the door opened and in walked the same Kezzin guard that who originally captured them. The same one who had also questioned them about their mission.

"What the hell do you want now?" asked Eddie. "We already told you, we're not talking."

"I just want to know something," said the alien.

Eddie crossed his arms and leaned against the wall.

"Were you telling the truth about those colonies?"

"What do you mean?" asked Eddie.

"About how they've been attacked by Kezzin soldiers?"

"Of course," said Eddie. "What kind of question is that?"

"You have to understand," said the alien. "I've never heard of such attacks. I had to confirm with my superior."

"You mean the guy we just talked to?" asked Eddie.

"Correct. That would be Commander Orsa. He runs this outpost."

"Friendly guy," said Julianna.

"Not really," said the alien, apparently oblivious to the sarcasm. "So, will you tell me who sent you here?"

"You know we can't tell you that," said Eddie, conversationally.

"Then, at least answer this, please. If our attacks continue, what will happen? What will your people do?"

"You mean, if you continue to slaughter innocent people across dozens of worlds?" asked Eddie.

"Yes," said the alien.

"We'll respond with due force," said Julianna.

"Due force?" asked the Kezzin.

"That's the polite way of saying we'll destroy every last one of you," answered Eddie. "You got that?"

The alien stood there, quietly, contemplating the message. He didn't respond right away. After several seconds, just before Eddie was about to make another joke, the alien stepped toward him. *Here we go,* thought Eddie, expecting the worst. *I finally went too far, didn't I?*

The Kezzin touched the side of the hard-light cell wall, spoke a word in his native tongue, and suddenly the door dissolved.

Eddie blinked, staring at the empty space where the wall had been. He reached through with his arm, surprised to find it gone. He looked at the alien, raising his brow. "What's this about?"

"You're free to go," said the Kezzin. "Please, leave as fast as you can, before the guards notice you."

"What are you doing this for?" asked Julianna.

"I have no loyalty to the Brotherhood," said the guard.

"Is that what you call yourselves?" asked Eddie.

The alien nodded. "The Brotherhood of Kezza. It is a collection of militia, many of which were conscripted and forced to join. I am here because I chose to take my brother's place. It is for his sake, and his children's sake, that I release you now. Please, return to your people and tell them that the attacks are not of Kezza. They are only the Brotherhood."

"I understand," said Eddie. He took a step out of the cell. "Thanks for your help, uh...what's your name again?"

"Lars Malseen," he answered.

"Nice to meet you," said Eddie. "And thanks for the rescue, even though you were the one who brought us in."

Lars started to walk to Julianna's cell when the hard-light wall dropped, a little before he could reach it. Lars stared at it, tilting his head. "That's odd."

"Is it?" asked Julianna, stepping out. "Sorry to tell you, but we were already planning on busting out."

"How did you do that?" asked Lars.

"Yeah," agreed Eddie. "What the fuck did you do?"

"It wasn't me," said Julianna. "It was Pip."

"Pip got you out? How? Didn't they take your gear? How did you even communicate with him?" asked Eddie.

"I don't use the pad to talk to him," she explained, tapping her head. "He's tied directly into me."

"Then what the hell is your pad for?"

"Online poker, obviously. I'm addicted to the stuff."

Eddie's mouth dropped slightly. "Are you kidding me?"

Julianna grinned. "Maybe next time you'll ask before you make assumptions. Oh, and Lars, was it? You may want to run the fuck out of here, because we still have orders to blow this facility to hell. I hope you understand."

"Is that necessary?" asked Lars. "Not every soldier here is the same."

"That might be true, but this is war. Sometimes that means making the hard choices. In this case, this facility has a stockpile of weapons large enough to take out a dozen colonies. We blow it up, maybe we delay that."

"Sorry, Lars," said Eddie. "She's right, but you still have time to leave."

"If you're after the weapons cache, setting charges around the outer walls won't do much. The storage rooms are underground. You can bring down those walls, but it would not eliminate the weapons or their holding areas."

"Do you have a better suggestion?" asked Eddie.

Lars thought for a moment before he answered. "Flood it," he finally said.

"What?" asked Eddie.

"Activate the emergency system and flood the compartment," said Lars. "Can your Pip do that?"

Julianna was quiet for a second, her eyes distant, and then she blinked. "He says he can, but we'd have to get to the control center. That area of the base has its own network."

"How do we do that?" asked Eddie.

"I can take you," said Lars. "It's not far."

"You?" asked Julianna. "I'm not sure we can trust you. No offense."

"Your response is understandable, but I'm already committed," said Lars, motioning at the cell. "I just freed you, after all."

"You freed Captain Teach," Julianna corrected.

"Funny," said Eddie. "Okay, Lars, if you can get us to this control room and help us flood the weapons cache, we'll promise not to kill everyone in this outpost. How's that?"

"A fair compromise," said the Kezzin.

"Before we go running off into the belly of this beast, I suggest we grab our gear," said Julianna.

"They have your things in another section. I tried to get all your gear, but they would have noticed. I was able to retrieve this without them spying me. It looked important." Lars unfastened the cloaking belt from his waist and tossed it through the air. Eddie had been too overwhelmed and hadn't even noticed it.

He grabbed the belt in the air and fastened it around his waist. "Oh for fucksake. You just saved my ass." Hatch would have killed him if he left this behind. Slowly. Painfully.

"We still need weapons. How do we get to our gear?" asked Julianna.

"You don't. It's too heavyily guarded. But there's another option." Lars walked over to the side wall and opened a storage locker. He took out a rifle with a strap and held it out. "How is this?"

Eddie took a few steps towards him and took the weapon, examining the rifle. He'd handled his share of Kezzin weaponry over the last few years, so this wouldn't be too difficult to adjust to. "This'll work, but aren't you worried about killing your own kind?"

"These rifles have a stun option." Lars flipped a switch

near the trigger. "It will knock the target out for over two hours."

Eddie scratched his head. "I gotta say, I'm not used to using a soft touch, but if that's what we have to do, I'm game."

"Thank you," said Lars.

Julianna took a rifle and cocked it, squeezing the grip with her fingers. It had a different feel to it than her typical rifle, but she'd manage well enough. "If the two of you are ready, I'd like to get this over with."

"Of course," said Lars with a quick nod. "Please, follow me."

15

Kezzin Battlebase 44, Planet Exa, Seolus system.

Eddie and Julianna followed Lars as the alien led them through the inner halls of the facility. Eddie knew he should be wary of Lars, but something about him felt genuine, like he'd known him for years. Maybe it was only because the alien had opened the cage or perhaps it was the story about Lars' brother, but Eddie trusted him.

He hoped his trust wasn't misplaced, but he was ready to kill the Kezzin, just in case. Trust but verify, he'd heard someone once say.

With their weapons at the ready, the group moved quickly through the corridors. Julianna spotted a few guards as they approached, and she sprinted to meet them, blasting each in the chest with a stun shot. The two aliens flopped to the floor like ragdolls, still alive but unconscious.

Lars motioned for Eddie and Julianna to keep going, and he led them to a small stairwell. They descended into a lower deck that smelled older than the rest of the building. It probably was, Eddie decided, given how the walls were made of another kind of stone.

Not far from the stairs, another set of guards appeared, mumbling to each other about dinner. One of them looked in the group's direction, a surprised expression overcoming him. He started to open his mouth, probably to call for help, when Lars charged at him, firing his weapon at the soldier and slamming his fist into the second one's face. The first guard fell instantly, but the other only stumbled, surprised by the sudden attack. Lars went to hit him again, but Eddie raised his own gun and shot the soldier instead, knocking him out.

Lars turned to see Eddie, giving him a nod of gratitude, to which he returned.

They pressed forward. "Not far now," whispered Lars, motioning to the end of the hall.

But before they could reach it, a scream rang out, coming from nearby. Eddie looked to see a female Kezzin there, pointing at the three of them. "Help!" she cried with an ear-piercing voice. Julianna responded with a shot to the woman's neck, instantly knocking her out.

Eddie blinked, surprised by his partner's lack of hesitation. *Glad she's on our side,* he thought, not for the first time.

A door opened nearby, and a Kezzin male appeared, surprised and confused by the arrival of a couple of humans. Before he could act, Eddie dashed towards him, almost instinctively, bashing him with the butt of his rifle, square in the face. The Kezzin stumbled back, completely taken by surprise. Eddie flipped his rifle back around and fired, disabling him.

"Let's go!" snapped Eddie, looking at Lars. "Quick, there'll be more soon."

"Follow me," responded Lars as he began to move.

Eddie did as his new friend suggested and, with Julianna beside him, started running. The three of them moved through the corridor as fast as their feet could carry them, bringing them close to several open rooms.

As they went, several more guards appeared, but the moment they did, the two soldiers had their rifles ready. Body after body hit the floor, limp and unconscious. Before long, there was a trail of Kezzin dispersed throughout the halls, each of them left in the wake of the intruders' charge. By the time they reached the control room, Eddie and Julianna had stunned at least two dozen Kezzin.

Lars swung open the door and motioned for the two of them to enter. Three guards were inside, waiting with their weapons at the ready, apparently anticipating this encounter.

Julianna slid inside, blasting one of them in the forehead. The blast threw the alien into the air and down on a nearby workstation.

Eddie took another, shooting him in the stomach as he entered.

The last remaining guard went for Lars, and the two Kezzin clashed like bulls. Lars headbutted the guard, who seemed unphased. "Traitor!" yelled the soldier, but Lars gave no response.

Instead, Lars reached for the Kezzin's neck, gripping him tightly and pushing him back. The alien attempted to punch Lars in the side of his head, but Lars blocked the blow with his other hand. The guard struggled to try again, but he was losing strength as Lars' fingers tightened around his throat. He could barely breathe now, so instead he tried to pry the hand from his throat, but Lars wouldn't release him.

A few seconds later and the alien dropped to the floor, completely unconscious.

"Holy shit," said Eddie. "Is he dead?"

"A Kezzin is not so easily killed," remarked Lars. "His lungs closed to preserve his oxygen. He'll wake up soon."

Julianna stood beside the unconscious alien, aimed her weapon, and shot him. "That'll keep him down."

"Ruthless," said Eddie.

Julianna raised her brow at him. "Would you rather I be soft?"

Eddie grinned. "You know I wouldn't."

"The controls are here," said Lars, motioning to the centermost console.

"Pip says he can access them now," said Julianna. "It should only take a few—"

Before she could get the sentence out, an alarm sounded overhead. "Intruders detected in section sixteen, sub-basement three!"

Eddie twisted his lips. "You were saying?"

The soldiers came running through the far opening, weapons in hand, searching for the intruders and shouting.

Eddie and Julianna took spots against the doorway to the control room, preparing to fire. As the wave of guards barreled down the hall, the two humans unleashed a barrage of firepower, stunning them en masse.

"This isn't good!" snapped Eddie, taking aim with his rifle and firing. He hit three men within four seconds, downing them.

"Keep firing," said Lars, behind them. "I believe I have a solution."

"What's that, exactly?" asked Julianna. She ducked behind the wall as two shots flew beside her.

Lars fiddled with the console, tapping the screen to bring up another set of controls. "Here!"

Just then, the door behind the invading soldiers slammed shut, blocking out the rest. Only a few remained inside the hall. "That's a start, but what's next?" asked Eddie, shooting one of the still-standing soldiers.

Lars typed in a command on the screen. "There's another way out of this level. A sewage drain."

"A what?" asked Eddie, hoping he'd misheard him.

"A sewage drain," repeated Lars. "It's behind this control room, down one of the other corridors. It should take us outside, some distance away."

"Sewage?" balked Julianna. "If you think I'm crawling through a bunch of alien shit, you've got another thing coming."

"It's not like that," Lars assured them. "There's a walkway along the side, adjacent to the pipes. The smell won't be the best, but you won't get anything on you."

"Is this our only move?" asked Eddie.

"Unless you would rather fight your way out," said Lars.

"I'm not opposed to that," said Eddie.

"Then you should know, there are roughly six hundred

soldiers here, and I would wager each of them is on their way to kill us."

Eddie hesitated, thumbing his chin.

"Well?" asked Lars.

"Fine!" snapped Eddie, firing one last blast and hitting the final soldier square in the chest. "Let's take the shit path."

They raced through the corridor, leaving three dozen unconscious bodies in the hall behind them.

Eddie never thought he'd have to wade through a river of shit, no matter the mission or circumstance. In fact, if General Reynolds had told him this was going to happen, Eddie wasn't quite sure whether he would have still taken the assignment.

He wrinkled his nose at the overwhelming smell, which seemed to come in waves. Sometimes overpowering, sometimes light enough to breathe. But who would *want* to breathe right now?

"We're nearly there," said Lars, who didn't seem to be affected by any of it.

Eddie crawled behind Julianna and Lars, trying not to touch the grime on the walls inside this tunnel. "How can you—" Edward paused, nearly gagging. "—talk right now."

"I have the ability to stop my breathing for extended periods of time, which keeps the smells out," explained the alien. "Were you unaware?"

"Must be...nice," muttered Eddie.

"It's common to several species on my homeworld," said

Lars. "It's convenient at times, but my nose isn't as acute as yours, from what I understand. I find it difficult to differentiate between certain scents."

Eddie didn't answer. He'd rather avoid opening his mouth if he could help it right now.

Julianna seemed unaffected by everything, although she might simply have been too focused to say anything.

In either case, Eddie could already see an opening ahead of them—a larger room that was tall enough to stand in, with what appeared to be natural light coming in, perhaps through a window.

As they entered, one-at-a-time, Eddie stood and stepped a few meters away from the hatch. "God, let's never do that again," he finally said.

"Agreed," said Julianna.

"Oh, it bothered you?" asked Eddie. "I thought maybe you liked it."

"I was holding my breath," she said.

"For ten minutes?"

She nodded. "One of the perks of having this body. You should look into getting the treatment done sometime."

"I like my body just the way it is, thank you," said Eddie. "Shitty lungs and all."

"Suit yourself," she said. "Lars, where to?"

"We head straight out from here. The path will take us directly through the western wall, which is close to where we found you."

"Let's get the hell out of this place. I've had my fill for the week," said Eddie.

The alarm was still blaring overhead as the three of them made their way through one of the corridors. As Lars had suggested, the path took them to an emergency exit, which opened into a grassy field. The same one as before.

They were almost free.

That was when Eddie heard it, a thunderous voice ringing from nearby. "Sensors show movement near the wall! They're trying to escape!"

Lars looked at the two humans. "There's no avoiding it. They'll find you if we run now."

"Right," said Eddie, cocking his weapon. "Guess we'll have to do this the old-fashioned way."

The three of them ran out into the field outside the wall, and the same voice from before called out to them from high above. "There! There they are!"

Eddie turned, his rifle primed and ready, and in a single, fluid motion, let loose a barrage of firepower, sweeping from one side to the other.

In seconds, a hundred shots hit the wall, breaking it apart and sending debris in all directions.

"Those don't look like stun rounds," observed Julianna.

"That's because I switched them to armor piercing!" yelled Eddie, his voice only slightly louder than the weapon.

Chunks of the wall broke off and fell to the grassy field below as the aliens ducked for cover, screaming in a panic as the unexpected fireworks unloaded on them.

Julianna stepped up beside Eddie and, with the flick of her wrist, primed her rifle as well. "Save some for me."

The Q-Ship stood in the middle of the field, its cloak

hiding it from any eyes or sensors that might be watching. In the distance, shots erupted near the alien outpost.

Inside, the ship was dark and silent. Without anyone around to use it, the vessel could only sit and wait, doing nothing until its pilots returned.

Or so it seemed.

There, in the darkness, a light appeared. The activation icon for the ship's engines.

A second later, several more lit up, indicating weapons and thrusters. Soon, the Q-Ship was fully online, preparing for departure. In almost no time, it began to lift off from the grass.

No human or alien had told it to do this. No orders from space had been sent.

The command had come from another program. The one known only as Pip, who had, during his short integration with the Q-Ship, written an emergency command package, which would respond only in case of emergency.

And that emergency had come.

The ship, still invisible, hovered off the ground and began to move towards the alien facility, its cannons aimed and ready.

―――――――

The aliens were beginning to reform, despite Eddie and Julianna's assault on the wall. It wouldn't be long before they managed to reorganize or call for reinforcements.

Despite his bravado, Eddie was pretty sure his team was running out of time. They'd have to make a run for it soon, exposing their backs to the enemy while they made their escape. Things could go very wrong, no matter what they did next.

He stopped firing, but not on purpose. "Shit," he muttered, glancing down at the rifle.

"What is it?" asked Julianna as she continued firing at the wall.

"I'm out!" he replied.

Julianna gave him a look that said, *Well, isn't this just fucked?*

But before he could answer, Eddie felt a vibration in his chest, growing stronger by the second. It felt like thunder, roaring in the sky, shaking the very ground beneath his feet, but it wasn't. No. This was something else. Something familiar.

He looked up and saw a strange blur in the sky, bending starlight, but only slightly. It was like looking through a glass window.

He opened his mouth, pointing. "Is that...?"

The stars disappeared, turning black as the darkest night, and something else replaced them.

The Q-Ship.

Eddie watched as the unmanned spacecraft released a missile directly at the wall. It flew, trailing smoke, and blasted into the facility without mercy. Half the western wall came crashing down, sending a dozen men flying in several directions, mostly in pieces.

"Hot damn," muttered Eddie, watching as the scene unfolded.

"Is this your ship?" asked Lars.

"It sure is," answered Eddie. "But I don't know who's flying it."

"That would be me," said Pip, his voice booming from the Q-Ship above their heads.

Eddie looked at Julianna. "Did you know about this?"

"This is news to me," she answered.

A blast fired from the base, nearly hitting the Q-Ship. Pip responded with a counter-shot, sending another missile and evaporating four aliens as they attempted to load an anti-aircraft gun.

"May we discuss this at a later time?" asked Pip, bringing the ship right above them and opening the lower hatch.

"Fine with me," Eddie agreed, signaling the others to get inside. "Let's get out of here."

Julianna leapt up and onto the side of the ship. She let out her hand to Lars. "You heard him!"

Lars looked reluctant. "I can't go with you. I…"

"Get your ass on the ship!" ordered Julianna. "If you stay, those bastards will kill you."

Eddie grabbed his shoulder. "She's right, Lars. You're one of us now. You understand?"

"One of you?"

Eddie nodded. "You said you had a family waiting for you. A brother, right? Come with us and I promise we'll do whatever it takes to help you find them."

"You would do that for someone you don't even know?"

"I know enough," said Eddie with finality. "Now, get your ass on this ship so we can get the hell off of this rock!"

16

Loading Dock 02, *QBS ArchAngel*, Seolus system.

The screen on the wall came on, revealing the A.I. ArchAngel. She stared down at Hatch as he finished the final install on the Q-Ship. "Come to see how the work was going?" he asked, fanning a tentacle at her. "No need. I'm all done."

"On the contrary," she remarked. "Captain Teach has requested your presence in Loading Dock 01. His ship is about to arrive."

"Teach wants to see me?" asked Hatch. "He better not have broken my ship."

"I don't believe that's it," said the A.I.

There was a loud clank as Hatch tossed his screwdriver into a nearby case. "Tell him I'm on my way," he said, lifting off the floor with his lower tentacles.

This wasn't the largest ship Hatch had ever been on during his time with the Federation, but it certainly felt like the most personal. Projects that he had worked on previously, or at the very least contributed to, had since been implemented on this ship. The cloak was only the biggest, along with the Q-Ships themselves, but there were also other, smaller features. The material in the bulkheads that doubled as computer screens, for example, had originally been one of his pet projects. He wanted to create a thin material that could be plastered on any surface, whether it was inside a ship or in the middle of a wet cave. There weren't any caves here, of course, but it seemed the basic idea had been used. That was why ArchAngel could pop up on just about any wall inside the ship.

Hatch had always wondered what became of his work, but now he knew. This refurbished ship, the one taken from the wreckage in an ancient battle, had become something of a personal showcase for him—the manifestation of his legacy.

Maybe that was why he felt so comfortable here, like he was home again. Except it was better than that, he knew, because Yondil was never where he truly belonged. It was damp and dirty, filled with too many people and not enough quiet. Not enough stars.

Because A'Din Hatcherik was made for all of this. He was back where he belonged.

"Whoop whoop!" called Eddie as the Q-Ship door opened. He leapt down the steps and onto the floor, landing in a loud smack.

"You're late," grunted General Reynolds, whose face was displayed on one of the walls.

Hatch stood just to the left of the screen, observing the ship, puffing his cheeks.

"Sorry, we were tied up," apologized Eddie.

Julianna stepped down from the Q-Ship, following him. "Almost literally."

"You were captured?" asked Hatch.

"Yep, but not to worry," said Eddie, raising his finger. "We had a man on the inside helping us out."

Lance cocked his brow. "What are you talking about, Captain?"

Julianna turned and motioned at the ship. "Come out and say hello."

Four red fingers reached from inside the ship and grabbed the side of the open doorway. The large Kezzin soldier known as Lars Malseen stepped forward, presenting himself for all who could see.

"This is Lars," said Eddie, grinning at his new friend. "He helped us escape."

"He was also the one who captured us in the first place," added Pip, his voice coming from *the ArchAngel*'s speaker system. Apparently, the E.I. had already transferred back into the main system.

"Sure, sure," said Eddie, waving his hand dismissively. "We all make mistakes. The point is, he helped us get out of there and successfully complete the mission."

"I gotta say," said Lance, eying the alien with some reservation. "This is a surprise, Captain. We'll have to discuss this further during your debriefing."

"A Kezzin, eh?" muttered Hatch, tapping one of his tentacles to his cheek. "Interesting."

"Why's that?" asked Eddie.

"Oh, I've just heard they aren't very keen on humans. It's strange."

Lars frowned. "The Brotherhood hasn't represented my people in the best light, but they're largely the only Kezzin who leave our territory. The rest stay mostly to themselves, aside from traders."

"Sounds like the Kezzin government needs to take action," suggested Hatch.

"You're not wrong," admitted Lars. "There's a political movement to do just that, but the Brotherhood's grip on Kezzin space is so strong that most are afraid."

"Let's save the politics for later. I'm starving!" said Eddie, who was ready to eat his way through a pound of beef and down a few beers. "General, are you coming to the ship to do the debrief?"

Lance shook his head. "No, you're coming to me. Strap in and get ready to jump to *Onyx Station*. I'll be in my office when you get here."

ArchAngel's face appeared next to Lance's. "Shall I set a course, sir?"

"Do it," said Lance. "And Captain, I'd like your Kezzin friend to wait in his new quarters until you arrive. I'm sure he understands."

"I do," answered Lars. "I'm essentially the enemy, after all."

Julianna looked back at him. "Don't say that."

"Yeah," agreed Eddie. "We're not at war with the Kezzin species. Just the Brotherhood, it seems."

"Nonetheless, your general is right. You met me while I was an enemy soldier, and you haven't known me for long. I'll do as you ask until I have proven myself."

"A sensible answer," said Lance.

Eddie didn't press the issue. He already felt a trust with Lars, foolish as it might be, but he understood it would take time. General Reynolds would see the value in Lars eventually. "Come on," said Eddie, tapping Lars on the arm. "Let's get you settled. ArchAngel, can you pick out a new room for our friend?"

"I have two hundred and thirty-seven rooms currently available," said the A.I.

"Oh, yeah. I forgot we had a skeleton crew."

"Try to get some rest before you arrive at the station," suggested Lance. "I'll see the four of you soon."

The screen clicked off and the wall returned to its former state.

Hatch came closer to Eddie, puffing his cheeks. "Now that you're back, you should know the second Q-Ship is updated and complete. I finished it less than an hour ago."

"That's great! I like that one better."

"Of course you do. I designed it from the ground-up, not like the one you just rode in on. If you want, I can tell you about the additions I made in more detail."

Eddie felt his stomach growl. "I'd love to hear it, Hatch, but maybe after dinner. I need food and a beer before I can do anything else."

Eddie bit into a half-pound cheeseburger, ripped a piece of turkey leg off, and then followed it down with a swig of cold Blue Ale. "Ah," he gasped, swallowing the crisp beer. "That's damn good."

"Easy or you'll choke," suggested Julianna.

"Who are you to talk?" asked Eddie, motioning to her plate, which was twice the size of his. "You eat more than any woman I've ever met!"

"That's because I'm not like any other woman you've met," she explained. "My body needs fuel."

"So does mine," he said, biting into the turkey leg. The meat was sweet and tender. It was so much better than the kind they had out on the fringe. Aliens weren't partial to human foods, so the only spots to find good quality beef and fowl was on a Federation ship, but those were rare. Eddie never realized how much he missed the taste of quality Federation food until he was out on his own, far from the border.

Lars was sitting next to Julianna, barely touching his meal. Eddie had decided it would be okay to have the Kezzin with them, so long as he stayed nearby. Surely, the general wouldn't mind that.

"How's your food?" asked Eddie, glancing at the alien.

"I've never had human food," he admitted. "It smells odd."

"Want me to see if Chef can make something more your speed? Maybe he's got a few Kezzin recipes."

"No, please, this is enough," said Lars, trying to smile. He took a spoonful of beans and ate them, chewing slowly. As the taste hit him, he made a strange face.

"Something wrong?" asked Eddie, having little experience with Kezzin reactions.

"Oh, no, it's just—" He paused. "—is this meat or a plant?"

Julianna looked at him, raising her brow. "Beans? Those are plants. Why?"

Lars dropped his spoon and spit the beans out, back onto the plate. He wiped his tongue with his sleeve, trying desperately to get the juice and beans off.

Eddie started to get up, a bit concerned. "Are you okay?!"

Lars was breathing heavily. "Kezzin can't process plants...we'll get sick. We have to have meat."

Eddie breathed a sigh of relief. "Oh, man, I thought you were dying or something."

"We can get you some meat," assured Julianna. She got up and went to the window connecting the dining room to the kitchen, then proceeded to order something new.

"I guess there's a lot I don't know about your species," Eddie said, scratching the back of his neck. "How sick do you get if you have beans?"

"I've never eaten beans before, but when I was young I had some fruit. It gave me a stomach cramp it felt like I might die."

"Seriously? From some fruit?" asked Eddie.

"We're strict carnivores," explained Lars. He opened his mouth and pointed to his sharp teeth. "We can't process anything but meat."

Julianna arrived with a large plate of chicken, turkey, and beef. "There's more back there if you want it. We don't have any meat from Kezza, but I'm sure we can order something. Just tell Chef what you want and he'll get it."

Lars beamed down at the plate with a wide-eyed expression. Eddie didn't have to think too hard about what that meant. The bulking soldier was clearly happy for the gift. "Thank you so much! This is perfect." He tore into the chicken, far more excited than he'd been with the beans.

"Okay, so no more plants. Gotta remember that," said Eddie.

"Unless you want to poison him," corrected Julianna.

Both Lars and Eddie looked at her.

"What? I was only kidding."

"Sometimes it's hard to tell with you," said Eddie.

She smiled. "Good. I prefer to keep people guessing."

Later that night, after having dropped Lars off at his room, Eddie returned to his quarters to rest. He grabbed a cold can of Coke and sat on the small sofa across from the television, taking a long drink and letting out a relaxing sigh. He was glad to be back from the mission, but uncertain about what came next.

With two missions behind him and a ton of new data to sort through, he and his team would soon have their work cut out for them. Even with a weapons cache destroyed and the Ox King dealt with, they still didn't know who was pulling the strings. Maybe Pip and Archangel would be able to find the answer in the newly acquired data they downloaded from the Kezzin Battlebase, or maybe they'd have to search blindly for answers, hoping for the best.

Either way, he was already anticipating the next job. The sooner they could stop the Brotherhood, the better.

There was also the matter of Lars. He had abandoned everything to help Eddie and Julianna escape, putting his family at risk, should the Brotherhood ever discover his betrayal.

Hopefully we can stop them before that happens, thought Eddie, but there was no way of knowing that for sure. It was all a gamble, but they all knew that. To Eddie, it was a risk worth taking, for better or worse.

The comm beeped, indicating a call. It surprised Eddie, since it was so late and he should've been asleep an hour ago, but no matter. He accepted it.

"Captain Teach," said ArchAngel, her face appearing on the television in front of him.

"Yes, what is it?"

"I wanted to let you know, Pip and I have decoded the first segment of data you collected. We have something to share when you're ready."

Eddie sat up. "What did you find?"

"There appears to be a short correspondence between the leader of the outpost you attacked, a man named Commander Orsa, and an anonymous contact located somewhere in the Pal System."

"Anonymous?" asked Eddie. "You don't know who it is?"

"The transmission appears to be partially redacted. Certain information is beyond retrieval, but there's enough here to warrant an investigation."

"It's not much, but it's a start."

"Indeed, sir," agreed ArchAngel. "I've already forwarded this information to General Reynolds, but he asked that I share all my findings with you directly."

"He did?"

"Yes, sir. You are, after all, the acting captain of *the ArchAngel.*"

Eddie nodded. "Right. How long until we arrive at the station?"

"Three hours," answered the A.I. "I suggest you rest until then."

"I will. Thanks."

The screen clicked off and Eddie leaned back, sinking into the couch. He kept forgetting how much responsibility he now carried on his shoulders. He never pictured himself in charge of an entire battleship, but he'd acclimate in time. The general had given him a great responsibility and he would honor that trust with hard work.

He took another swig of the Coke, finishing the can and tossing it into the nearby wastebasket.

Now that ArchAngel and Pip had discovered their next target, it wouldn't be long before Eddie was back in action. One way or another, they'd find the people responsible for the attacks and make them pay for what they'd done.

17

Captain Teach's quarters, *QBS ArchAngel*, Paladin System.

"Captain," said a voice from the intercom. "Captain, are you there?"

Eddie opened his eyes, groggy as hell, but awake. It took him a moment to gather himself. "Who…?"

"Sir, it's Pip. Commander Fregin wanted me to inform you that we have arrived at Onyx Station."

Eddie blinked with burning eyes, twisting in his bed, he threw his legs out. His feet landed on the floor with a thud, and he pulled himself upright and staggered across the room, grabbing a clean towel hanging over a chair nearby. He wiped the sweat from his cheeks. "Tell her I'm coming."

"Yes, sir," said the E.I. "But she's already on her way to your quarters."

He got to his feet and stumbled over to the clean-shower. "Why'd you bother me if she's on her way here?"

"So you could be awake when she arrived."

Eddie turned the knob and started the cleaning process. Unlike the showers he was used to, this one didn't use running water. Instead, it used sonic vibrations to eradicate filth from the body, providing better results than a traditional soap-and-water experience. Eddie wasn't a huge fan, but he accepted that it did the job better, and it was faster, taking only a few seconds. Eddie was a creature of habit, but he could make adjustments when he needed to.

But that didn't mean he had to like it. He enjoyed standing under a hot shower with water raining over his head.

He slipped on a clean shirt and finished getting dressed. Right when he was about to tie his second boot, he heard a knock at the door.

Julianna was framed in the doorway when he opened it, looking pristine and well-rested. Then again, she always looked like that. Maybe it was the genetically modified body or perhaps she'd always been the kind of person who needed less sleep, but she never appeared to be tired or overworked.

A good thing, too, because it meant she'd stay reliable and efficient. Eddie couldn't have asked for a better partner on this assignment.

"Fuck, you look rough," she said when he opened the door.

"I'll be fine when I get some caffeine."

"Here," she said, tossing him a small green pill. "Take this."

"What is it?"

"For energy, but it's not addictive or a crazy drug. It just helps the brain feel like it got enough rest. Totally healthy, unless you take them every day for a month. That's when you get problems."

He tossed the pill back and swallowed. "General Reynolds gave me a pill for hangovers and now you're giving me one for lack of sleep. Does the Federation have a pill for everything? Why haven't I heard of this?"

"That pill was created six months ago in a lab specifically for combat situations where the soldiers had to stay up for days. It's not meant for casual consumption."

"And the hangover pill?"

"They sell those all over the Federation now. You just missed them because you were gone. Stick around and you'll find that we've got the best technology."

Having flown the Q-Ships more than a few times by now, he had to agree. The technology in the Federation was far and away the most advanced available.

The two made their way through the halls towards the docking bay. "Lars and Hatch not coming?" asked Eddie.

"They're already on the station. Hatch said he wanted to spend some time with our new friend and show him around, but I got the impression he wanted to grill him with questions. I told him to bring Lars to the General's office in thirty minutes for the debrief."

"Isn't Reynolds worried about a Kezzin running around the station?" Eddie asked.

"He's got eyes all over Onyx station." They stepped off the loading dock of the *QBS ArchAngel* and onto the ramp leading into the nearby terminal. "In fact, I wouldn't be surprised if the old man wasn't watching us right now."

Eddie raised an eyebrow and looked curiously around the station. "Seriously?"

She laughed, but didn't answer, and then continued walking toward the bustling promenade.

Eddie was surprised to find the General standing outside his office when the two arrived. "Welcome back," said Lance. "And good job to both of you."

"Thank you, sir," said Julianna.

"Before we get on with it, we need to discuss your extra passenger. Teach, what can you tell me?"

"Well, we were placing the bombs around the wall, following the plan, but near the end of it, Lars overheard us. I guess we were making too much noise. Anyway, he managed to—"

"Pip filed a report on the details of your mission, Captain. I know the basics. Tell me why you brought him back with you."

"Oh," muttered Eddie. "Well, sir, he couldn't stay there. He betrayed the Brotherhood to get us out of the base. I couldn't abandon him at that point."

"I understand, but how did you know he wasn't playing you?"

"Sir?"

"How did you know he wasn't pretending to be your ally, only to betray you later?" asked Lance.

"Frankly, sir, a man doesn't shoot his own people, crawl through a sewer full of shit, get shot at, and help destroy a cache of weapons if he's just faking it."

"Could have been an ultra-elaborate ruse to get inside the Federation. At the cost of one weapons cache, and by the way, did you see the weapons actually get destroyed? You still can't be sure, can you?" asked Lance.

"No, sir. I can't, but at a certain point, don't we have to take that risk?"

"What if he betrays you? What if everything he says turns out to be a lie?"

"Then it's something we'll have to live with," answered Eddie. "But I won't live my life expecting the worst in people. I can't."

Lance smiled. "Good. That's very good, Captain."

Eddie raised his brow. "Sir?"

"The Federation was founded on the belief that all people, not just humans, deserve a chance to be happy, to live and let live. If we turned this Lars fellow away just because of where he came from, we'd be fools and liars. My source on Kezza tells me that Lars was speaking the truth before about his family. What he told you about how he was recruited was true, as far as our Kezzin spies tell us."

"You have Kezzin spies working for you?" asked Eddie.

"Of course, I do," said Lance, as though it should be obvious. "Not in the Brotherhood, but I have a few on Kezza."

"Lars took his brother's place?" asked Julianna.

"Indeed, he did," answered Lance. "An honorable sacrifice, if ever I heard one. That's exactly the kind of person I wanted you to find, Teach, and you delivered."

"Thank you, sir," said Edward, still unsure of where the conversation was going. He thought he'd been on trial, but he was getting commended?

"Now, if the two of you are ready, I'd like to discuss our next mission."

"Is this about the information ArchAngel and Pip deciphered when we were en route?"

Lance took out a cigar and lit it, taking a short puff. "That, and a little more. They had most of the puzzle, but—"

"You've got the rest," finished Eddie.

Lance grinned. "Right you are, Captain Teach. It just so happens the Pal system listed in that coded transmission is also home to a prominent merchant known as Val'Doon Sarnack. He's so rich he owns a small fleet of unmanned ships, dozens of which exist solely to protect that system."

"Sounds dangerous," said Julianna.

"Only if you're not prepared," said Lance.

"Which we are," added Eddie. "Right?"

Lance smiled at the two of them. "Oh, yes."

Hatch escorted Lars through the shopping plaza in the promenade while the rest of the team met with Reynolds. Lars had come aboard with nothing but the clothes on his back, so he'd need his share of items if he planned on sticking around. "There's a shop that caters to your kind," Hatch told the tall, red-skinned fellow as they passed a human bathroom.

Lars looked at him. "My kind?"

"Kezzin," explained Hatch. "Or are we ignoring your species for the sake of political correctness?"

Lars grunted. "Fine."

"Reynolds told me you're going to be a member of the team. I hope you're ready to work your ugly ass off."

Lars said nothing.

"Feel free to tell me how ugly you think I am, too. I know you're thinking it."

Lars couldn't deny it. He'd never seen an alien like Hatch, with eight tentacles and a body that inflated and deflated on command. It reminded him of a slimy balloon. "I would never say such a thing."

"Well, I think you've got a face like a scab," said Hatch. "You look like a pile of volcano ash with eyes."

"Excuse me?"

"You heard me, but don't feel ashamed. To most of these people, I resemble a monster. The humans say I look like some kind of animal back on Earth. Something called an octopus."

"Is there a point to all this?" asked Lars.

"Yeah, drop the wall and stop being so damn guarded and polite. I can see it all over your ugly face. You think you're a guest here. You think you're not wanted. But let me tell you, kid. Strangers are polite. People you meet on the street that you'll never trust or care about are polite. But you and me, that's not going to be our thing, buddy. That's not how we're going to do this" Hatch raised his tentacle and stuck it close to Lars' face. "You see the way Julianna and Edward are with each other? How they are with me? If you plan on sticking around, you'd better learn to relax and say what you think."

Lars blinked at the tentacle, surprised by Hatch's frankness. "Why are you telling me this?"

"Because," Hatch went on. "You saved their lives, and

that not only makes you an ally. It makes you a friend. And buddy, I don't let my friends bullshit me. Do you understand?"

"I think so," said Lars. "You're saying I should tell you that you're ugly."

Hatch puffed his cheeks. "That's right, because I know that's what you're thinking, and don't be afraid to say it more often. Be honest with yourself, and be honest with us. If you do, you'll find more than allies here, kid. You'll find friends."

Lars listened to the words with some appreciation. He'd only met a handful of aliens in his lifetime, but never one like Hatch. He was blunt and somehow likeable, despite all the insults and the attitude. Lars couldn't help but respect him, the same way he respected Edward and Julianna.

Could Lars truly find a place among these aliens? He liked to think so, given their determination. "Do you think," began Lars, turning to look at Hatch. "Do you believe Captain Teach will be successful in his mission to stop the Brotherhood?"

"Do you think I'd be here if I didn't?"

"A fair point," acknowledged Lars. "I suppose we'll have to wait and see."

"Yes, we will," agreed Hatch. "But for now, let's find you some new underwear. I'm sure you can use them."

***

Hours later, after a few beers, Eddie returned to the ship with Julianna and the rest of the team. They convened in the conference room near the bridge.

General Reynolds stood beside him, waiting for the others to take their seats.

Once they had, Eddie turned to the screen behind him. "ArchAngel, we're ready when you are."

"Acknowledged," said the A.I., and suddenly the image transformed to show a star system.

"This is our target," Eddie said, motioning to the screen. "The Pal System."

"It is well-guarded," began ArchAngel. "There are three dozen drones patrolling it at any given time. Combined, their firepower is very capable."

"Still, no match for the Q-Ships," said Hatch, confidently.

Eddie nodded. "Not in terms of firepower, but there's one problem."

"What problem?" asked Hatch.

"The base is outfitted with a shield. It allows their ships to pass through, but any unauthorized vessels that come into contact with it are disabled. We can get close, but even with our cloaks raised, we can't pass through."

"A shield?" asked Hatch. "I haven't heard of anything like that."

"That's because we didn't know it existed until last year," interjected Lance.

"Why wasn't I informed?"

"You are now. We had no idea until yesterday that Sarnack was the one responsible for the Brotherhood's attacks on our colonies," explained Lance.

"Who?" asked Hatch.

"I've never heard of such a person," said Lars.

"That's because he's not Kezzin," explained the General.

Lars tilted his head. "The head of the Brotherhood isn't Kezzin? How can that be?"

Eddie shook his head. "We're not sure, exactly, but it's true. The data we pulled from your old workplace pointed here, and the General filled in the rest. This guy's bad news, and it won't be easy to get to him."

"What information do we have about this shield of his?" asked Hatch.

Lance looked at the screen behind them. "ArchAngel, can you send all the data we have about that directly to Dr. Hatcherik?"

"Certainly," agreed the A.I.

Hatch glanced at the pad in his hand, watching as the information appeared before him. A second later, his cheeks puffed. "Ah, well, this is most interesting."

"Does all that make sense to you?" asked Lance. "Feel free to tell the rest of the class."

"The shield has six emitters, it looks like, spread across the six moons surrounding this planet. If we can disable them, we'd have a far easier time of it, but there's a problem, which I'm sure you already know."

Lance nodded. "The generators are inside the field."

"Right, exactly. We'd have to get inside first and disable them."

"How do we do that?" asked Eddie.

Hatch rubbed the side of his cheek with his tentacle. "Well, the only way I can think of is to steal one of their drones, but based on what I'm seeing here, they don't go outside the field unless provoked."

"Which we can't do without setting the entire system on high-alert," said Julianna.

"No, I don't suppose we can," agreed Hatch.

"Anything else?" asked Eddie.

Hatch raised his eyes to the others. "There's one, but I don't want to suggest it."

"Why's that?" asked Lance.

"Because," Hatch explained. "It would mean using one of the Q-Ships, possibly destroying it, and they're too valuable."

"What are you talking about?" asked Eddie.

"The engines use a very specific type of gravitic energy. I could configure them to ignite a feedback surge through the field to disable it, although doing so would fry most of the ship's system."

"We have a few more Q-Ships sitting in storage. I could have them delivered in a few short days," suggested Lance.

"No, that won't do."

"Why the hell not?"

"Because, General, only one of the ships uses the design I mentioned."

"Only one?" asked Eddie. "You don't mean the original, do you?"

"I do, indeed," said Hatch, glancing back at the pad. "The very first one. None of the other engineers who came after me decided to keep my design, which means none of the other Q-Ships are worth a damn."

"What's different about that one? I don't understand," said Eddie.

"The newer models make use of a more constrained gravitic engine. It's the same one used by the rest of the Federation, but I created my own custom design for that first ship. It's unlike anything else." He paused. "It's unique."

Eddie considered his friend's words carefully. "Is there a way to make another machine that can do the same thing as that engine?"

"Of course, but that would take time," answered Hatch.

"How long?" asked Lance.

"If we assume a team of a dozen engineers working around the clock, maybe a month," said Hatch, pausing a moment. "Could be less if everything goes well."

Lance let out a short sigh. "We don't have that long. My intelligence says there's an attack coming within the week. We need to act now."

"All this will do is disable the Q-Ship, right?" asked Julianna. "If we can recover it after the feedback pulse, we can repair the engines."

"Just promise me you won't let my ship get destroyed out there," muttered Hatch.

"We won't let that happen unless there's no other way," assured Eddie.

"Good, because that's the best ship the Federation's ever seen. It would be a shame to lose it. Plus, I'd become a fugitive."

"Say what?" Eddie asked.

"For hunting you down and killing you after you ruined my ship. You need to avoid doing that, for both our sakes."

Eddie nodded. Hatch probably wasn't kidding. Eddie knew full well that the Q-Ship meant more to the old octopus than he let on. Losing it, especially after being separated from it for so long, would be devastating.

"So, it's settled," said Lance. "Hatch will make the modifications to the Q-Ship while the rest of you prepare to move in and assault the enemy stronghold."

Lars, who had until now been largely silent, observing the meeting and taking it all in, leaned forward on the table. He had a determined look on his red face, his yellow eyes narrowed and fierce. "Whatever you need of me, please allow me to help."

Eddie smiled. "Oh, don't worry, pal. You're coming with us. We could use the extra muscle."

"You're allowing me to join the assault team?" asked Lars.

"If you want to."

"I would like nothing more than to assist the ugly humans with punishing the Brotherhood for their tyranny, especially if it is as you say. If there is a man behind the group pulling strings and manipulating my people, he must be made to pay."

"There you have it," said Julianna.

Eddie grinned. "Those bastards won't know what hit them." He glanced sideways at Lars. *Ugly humans, huh? Have you looked in the mirror lately, pal?*

18

Dining Hall 03, *QBS ArchAngel*, Paladin System.

Julianna sat with her pad on one of the tables in the dining hall. There were three other people nearby, talking among themselves. Two women and a young man. They appeared to be from Engineering and Maintenance.

"I heard we're going out again," suggested the man, a red-head with blue eyes.

"Another mission?" asked the first girl, a gorgeous blonde.

The second girl nodded. "No one's saying what it's for. We're supposed to get briefed in a few hours."

"I hope we see more action this time," said the man. "I want to help."

The other two nodded.

"Okay, let's get back to work. See you two later," said the first girl, smiling.

Julianna watched them leave. They were so eager, so ready for war. Did they really know what any of it was for?

Did they understand the importance of what this mission entailed?

You doubt them, came a voice in her head. Pip's voice, always there, listening to her thoughts.

She shook her head. *They're young and stupid. Ready to run into the fight without a second thought.*

I remember when you were the same.

And I remember losing part of myself because of it.

She stared down at the leg she'd lost so long ago, back before the Queen had granted her a new limb. Back before she was given the chance to start again. Before she was placed inside that pod doc and given power and purpose.

Give them time to grow. Time to learn what you understand all too well.

Some will get there, but others won't. They'll die, and there won't be anyone there to save them.

Someone will be there to guide them.

Oh? Last I checked, the Empress is gone. We have to save ourselves now.

You **can help them. You can be for them what Bethany Anne was for you. Look what you did for Edward Teach. He was alone, but you found him. You showed him who he was.**

He did that on his own.

Still, he never would have come this far without you.

She didn't answer. Pip didn't always understand humanity, but he certainly understood her. They'd spent decades together, their voices intertwined, often connected. He saw the world through her eyes as though they were his own. That made them friends, and like any good friend, Pip would always be there for her, always tell her the truth, no matter how hard it was for her to hear it. Right now, he was telling her that she needed to step up and believe in herself while also believing in her fellow soldiers. Maybe she could, but it was so hard not to be afraid for them. So difficult not to worry.

Compared to Julianna, even the older ones were children. Edward Teach included. But as Pip had told her, she was once the same as them, young and eager to make a difference. The same had even been true of the Empress, hard as it was to believe. Perhaps if both of them could learn to live, so, too, could the rest of them.

Captain Teach's Quarters, *QBS ArchAngel*, Paladin System.

Shortly after the meeting, Eddie returned to his room. It wouldn't be long before the mission started, so he wanted to squeeze in a light nap while he could.

He crashed on the couch as soon as he hit it, collapsing on the cushions and sinking into them with ease.

As soon as he opened his eyes, it felt like no time had passed at all.

It had been five hours, but he felt a little better.

Drool had pooled from his mouth, an indication of how hard he'd slept. He must have really needed it.

Before he could orient himself, he heard a knock at the door. Glancing quickly at the monitor, he saw General Reynolds' face.

Eddie pushed himself off the couch and stumbled to the door, touching the wall to open it. When the door slid open, the General looked at him, almost laughing. "Damn, son. You look like you just took a beating."

"Thanks," groaned Eddie.

"If it's a bad time, I can come back later."

"No, please," Eddie assured him, pulling back from the door and motioning for his superior to enter. "I'm glad you're here."

"Good, because I've got a few things I want to talk with you about." Lance entered and the door slid shut behind him. The old man went to the side of the couch and leaned against the armrest. He had the smell of cigar smoke on him.

"Yes, sir," answered Eddie, trying to compose himself.

"You've done a great job, Edward," said Lance, crossing his arms. "Better than I ever imagined, actually."

"Sir?"

"Don't get me wrong. I knew I had the right guy. I was confident about that. Your record and references were the best I'd ever seen. That's why I chose you in the first place, but what I couldn't foresee was how quickly you adapted back into this life. You seem to be made for this."

"I don't know about all that, sir. I just want to do right by you and the rest of our people."

"I know, and it's clear we have the same values. When you brought Lars back here like a stray cat, saying you believed in him, I knew it was time for the next stage in this operation."

"The next stage?" asked Eddie, curiously. Every time he thought he was getting a grip on what they were doing, something new popped up.

"Naming your team, Captain," answered Lance, like it was an obvious thing. "To start with, anyway."

Eddie had wondered about this for a while, but didn't think it was important, considering the classified nature of their outfit. "What did you have in mind, sir?"

"Back on Earth, there were many squads and secret missions all throughout history, and they were all proud of the work they did, but some are less known than others," explained Lance. "One of these was Observational Squadron 67 in the United States Navy. Their missions took place during the Vietnam War and were short-lived. Their job was to fly behind enemy lines above Thailand, listen in on chatter and track enemy supply routes, all while trying not to die in the process. They signed up with little knowledge of what they'd be doing, with an estimated loss rate of about sixty percent, but still they agreed. The missions were largely successful, but over the course of two months, about twenty of them were either killed or went missing."

"I've never heard of them," remarked Eddie.

"I wouldn't expect you to, having grown up so far from our homeworld. But even if you had, the 67th is largely unknown. Their missions were classified for over three decades afterwards." Lance furrowed his brow. "Even if you were in the military like me, you probably didn't know about them."

"I'm sorry, sir, but why are you telling me this?" asked Eddie.

"My point is, son, that sometimes soldiers work in secret to do what needs to be done. Not all of us can return home to parades and celebrations. Not all of us get a medal when we save a life. Those men, brave as they were, and knowing the odds, never expected the rest of their countrymen to give them a pat on the back. They went out there every day in their aircraft, knowing it could be their last, because they believed what they were doing was right. They did it to save lives. They wanted to protect their families."

Eddie smiled. "Sounds familiar."

"The men in that group gave themselves a nickname, the way most units do. They called themselves *Ghost Squadron*." Lance smiled. "A fitting name, don't you think?"

Eddie considered it for a second, letting the name sit with him. "*Ghost Squadron*," he finally muttered. "Yeah, I like that. Thank you, sir."

"You're welcome, son, and good job naming your unit. Now, if you'll excuse me, I need to get back to Onyx. I've got a meeting with a delegate from a neighboring system. They're trying to join the Federation, but they expect us to pay them." Lance laughed. "I don't know what rock they've been living under, but the benefits of being a member outweigh the alternative. We've got free trade and secure borders. Meanwhile, they're in the middle of a civil war. It's pretty obvious they want us to put an end to their issues, which means the Federation taking a side on a planetary issue."

Eddie didn't envy the General. If this was the sort of thing he had to deal with on a regular basis, it sounded incredibly unpleasant. "What will you do?"

Lance sighed. "I haven't decided yet, but we'll probably stay out of it. The Federation isn't an Empire anymore.

We're not looking to interfere in another species' war. Not openly, anyway." He winked. "If you get my meaning."

Eddie nodded. "Yes, sir!"

Lance started walking to the door. "Anyway, I'll leave you to it, Captain. I'm sure you have things to do."

"Oh, sir, wasn't there something else? You said you had a *few* things to talk to me about."

Lance thought for a second before the realization hit him. "Ah, that's right. I was going to tell you something."

"What's that?" asked Eddie.

Lance tapped his chin. "Your callsign."

The term took Eddie by surprise.

Probably seeing his reaction, Lance continued. "We've been so busy getting the job done, no one's thought to do you justice, but every pilot needs it. You can't choose your own, so I figured I'd help you out."

"Oh, sir, you don't have to do that."

Lance fanned a hand at him. "If you think you're getting out of a custom that goes back hundreds of years, you're sadly mistaken."

Eddie gulped.

"I saw in your file that the other boys used to call you *Blackbeard*. Did you think I wouldn't find out?"

It had been years since Eddie heard that callsign. The sound of it took him back. He scratched his head. "I wasn't sure, honestly, since our team's not official."

"It is as far as I'm concerned, Captain," remarked Lance. "And like all other callsigns, yours is for life."

Eddie let out a short laugh. "I guess it is."

"Well, then, *Blackbeard*," said Lance, tapping the side of

the door, opening it. "If you'll excuse me, I've got work to do, and so do you."

"Yes, sir," answered Eddie. "Thank you."

Lance turned when he was outside the door, nodding to Edward. "This ship is now yours, Captain. Don't fuck it up."

The door slid shut, leaving Blackbeard alone with his thoughts.

19

Loading Dock 02, *QBS ArchAngel*, Seolus system.

Hatch worked diligently on the Q-Ship, the first of its kind, attempting to reconfigure the engines to emit a feedback pulse. He'd been at it now for several hours, but he was finally almost done.

"Still here, I see," said a voice.

Hatch swept his whole body around, waddling on his tentacles, to find the Kezzin Lars standing before him. The red-skinned lizard wore an expression that suggested amusement, though Hatch couldn't be certain. He was still having trouble deciphering his new associate's features. "What are you doing here?"

"I wanted to see what you do," answered Lars.

"I'm a mechanic," explained Hatch, keeping his response brief. He could've said he was a doctor and a physicist, but why brag about the little things?

"It appears you're making good progress."

"Oh? You can tell, can you?" asked Hatch.

"I have an eye for ships," Lars told him. "Although, I'll admit, this is beyond my experience. It's advanced."

Hatch puffed his cheeks. "I designed it myself when I worked for the Federation."

"Can you really do what you said? Will we be able to enter the shield?"

"In a few more hours, I'll have everything ready. Trust me. It'll work."

"I do," admitted Lars. "Trust you, that is."

"You sound surprised at yourself."

Lars took a moment, like he was considering this. "Maybe I am, you ugly slimy thing."

"Good. It's important to surprise yourself from time to time. Otherwise, you're just boring, and who wants that?"

Lars chuckled. "You're an interesting mechanic."

"You're just noticing that?" asked Hatch. "I figured you would've learned that when I was giving you shit on the station about your underwear."

"True. Do you need help? I'm not an engineer, but I know enough to get by."

"Hand me that power driver," said Hatch, pointing to the small device near the wall.

Lars did as he asked, retrieving it. "Here you are."

Hatch snagged it with a tentacle and, without looking away from Lars, proceeded to attach and tighten another screw at the base of the ship. "Excellent."

"That's impressive. Do you have another set of eyes on the back of that skull?"

"More like sensor glands on my tentacles. I can see without my eyes, if that makes sense."

Lars nodded. "Strange. Kezzin have nothing like that."

"It's because my species comes from a planet with a vast ocean. We evolved from the depths of the sea, and our ancestors scavenged the bottom, looking for food. They developed these sensors to locate tiny organisms to eat, and to protect us from predators."

"Now you use them to fix starships," added Lars.

Hatch puffed his cheeks. "We've come a long way."

"It seems your planet is very different from mine."

"How's that?"

"We have lakes and oceans, but they're much hotter. Most aliens could never survive, except in remote northern regions. Most organisms develop a tough exterior." He punched his chest and there was a loud, hard thud.

Hatch glanced down at his tentacle, which was soft and easily injured. "We are very different, it seems."

"Yes, we are," agreed Lars. "But as you told me before, we have a common goal. We both want to save people."

Hatch nodded, setting the driver down as he finished. "You're right about that, and soon, I believe we will."

"For my family's sake, I hope you're right," muttered Lars.

"You'll soon learn that I'm rarely wrong about anything," assured Hatch, puffing his cheeks. "Just you wait and see, you ugly red son of a bitch."

Eddie met Julianna on the bridge a few hours after Lance left for Onyx. The General would be watching from a distance, but the bulk of the responsibility of this assignment was now in the two soldiers' hands. For better or worse, it was up to them and the crew of their new ship.

ArchAngel's face appeared on the display. "What are your orders, Captain Teach?"

"Cloak the ship and then set a course for Pal," ordered Eddie.

"Yes, sir," responded the A.I.

Eddie felt a slight vibration beneath his feet, telling him the engines had ignited. It was barely noticeable, but he'd spent enough time on starships to tell.

"Estimated time of arrival is thirty-seven minutes," announced one of the crew.

Eddie looked at Julianna. "Are you ready?"

"We can handle it, easy," she answered, nodding. "The question is, are you?"

He grinned. "Not a problem."

They took the lift to deck seventeen and went quickly to Loading Dock 02, where Hatch was waiting, along with Lars. The tall lizardman was already armed and inside the second Q-Ship, eager to head out.

"The ship is configured," Hatch said as soon as they entered. "I'll operate it remotely from inside the second vessel."

"You mean from here, don't you?" asked Julianna.

"No, the range won't work. I'll need to be onboard yours."

Eddie looked back-and-forth at the two ships. "It'll be dangerous, though. Are you sure?"

"I didn't sign up to be coddled, kid. If you think you can tell me to stay put and leave my beautiful piece of art drifting in space all by its lonesome, you've got another thing coming."

Eddie raised his hands. "Okay, okay. You're coming along."

Hatch waddled over to the second ship and climbed inside.

"Does that ship even have a seat for you?" asked Julianna.

"I installed one today," said Hatch. "And I'll have my flight suit on in a few minutes."

"You mean to change your clothes in front of us?" asked Lars.

"What if I do?" asked Hatch.

"Have you no shame?"

Hatch stared at him for a second, then proceeded to deflate his body and put on the outfit.

Lars gasped, turning around.

"I guess the Kezzin are more modest than I realized," muttered Julianna.

After twenty minutes, once the team had their weapons and gear ready to go, the door to the Q-Ship slid shut, sealing them inside.

"Sir, we've arrived at our destination," said a voice over the com. It was Ensign Trep from the bridge.

"Acknowledged. Keep the lights on for us," returned Eddie.

"Yes, sir!"

He took the controls, lighting the engines and lifting them off the deck of the *QBS ArchAngel*. "This is it," he told the rest of his team. "Hatch, are you good on the other ship?"

"Of course," the octopus answered. "I asked Pip to assist us."

"Pip?" asked Eddie. This was the first he'd heard about the E.I. helping out.

"Yes, sir," a voice said through the com. "I'll be navigating in case of any combat situation."

"I thought Hatch was controlling it from here," responded Eddie.

"I am, but my reflexes aren't as good as Pip's. If we need help before we reach the shield, he'll have our backs."

Eddie nodded. "Good enough for me. Punch it!"

The ship departed through the cargo bay doors, followed by the second one, leaving an invisible ArchAngel behind them.

In the distance, a single star emitted a bright, yellow glow as a small planet passed in front of it. It was the first of six, each one unlivable and devoid of life, except for the second-closest. That was their target, the home of Val'Doon Sarnack. The name meant little to Eddie, but he knew he hated the man. Anyone who could unleash so much death and destruction deserved whatever punishment they received. In this case, a kick in the ass, courtesy of Eddie's boot.

The two cloaked Q-Ships made their way from one planet to the other. When Eddie glanced at his long-range sensor, he saw an icon appear as it moved towards them. "What's this?"

"It could be anything," answered Julianna.

Another one, identical to the last, appeared. "And there's—"

Before he could finish the sentence, several more

popped in, one-at-a-time, until there were dozens of them. At least forty or fifty red dots began moving across the screen from one end to the other. They seemed chaotic at first, almost directionless, but after a moment, several turned around, headed back in a loop. Yes, they were moving together.

They had purpose.

"Is that an asteroid belt?" asked Lars.

"Pip? Do you have anything?" asked Julianna.

"Oh, my," the E.I. answered. "I believe those are—"

"Fucking robots," interrupted Eddie.

"Drones, if we're being precise," corrected Pip.

"Shall we annihilate them?" Lars asked, an eagerness in his voice.

Hatch raised a tentacle. "Let's stay on mission. We've got a shield to bring down, don't we?"

"Right," affirmed Eddie. "How's the second ship looking?"

"Cloaked and steady," answered Hatch.

"Good. I want it down as soon as possible. We'll sneak through afterwards."

The two cloaked ships continued on their present course towards the field. As they did, a small group of drones came within firing distance. As the viewscreen in front of Eddie zoomed in, the objects filled the image.

They appeared to be small, about five meters long, too cramped for a pilot, but that was the beauty of unmanned weaponry. Unlike a real ship, these didn't need the extra space for pilots or soldiers, which meant there was no need for bulky environmental systems. Instead, they could remain small, which meant more space for weapons and fuel.

Great idea if you could afford it, but there were problems with drones. They couldn't go very far, for starters, being largely limited to staying within signal distance. It was very likely that most were being controlled from the facility on the nearby planet, probably with repeater hardware scattered throughout the system on each of the neighboring moons and asteroids, adding to the range.

The solution for dealing with these was simple: take down the base and you eliminate the swarm.

That would be step two, once the shield dropped.

"How far is this shield?" asked Eddie, staring out through the glass. "I'm not seeing—"

"Stop!" barked Hatch.

The ship came to an abrupt standstill. "Acknowledged," said Pip.

"What the fuck was that about?" asked Julianna.

Hatch pointed a tentacle to the empty space in front of them. "The field is less than fifty kilometers ahead of us. Any further and we would have slammed straight into it!"

"Oh, shit," muttered Eddie. "Pip, why didn't you say something?"

"I was planning on getting us as close as possible," explained the E.I. "The goal was within half of a kilometer."

"Too dangerous," said Hatch. "Someone needs to teach you that there's more to life than numbers, Pip."

Eddie checked the radar. "Looks like we've got a swarm of drones coming back around. Let's wait until they pass before we do this."

Lars sat in the back, saying nothing. Eddie couldn't help

but wonder what the lizardman was thinking. He seemed to be staring off, his mind elsewhere. Was he preparing himself for combat? Was he reflecting on his family, wherever they were? "Lars, are you ready to kick some ass?" asked Eddie, after a moment.

Lars blinked at the sound of his name. "Ah," he muttered, coming out of his thoughts. "Yes, Captain."

"You don't sound very enthusiastic," Eddie grinned. "I need you to get excited! We're about to rush into a supposedly impenetrable base and take down the man responsible for the Brotherhood. Tell me you want this, Lars!"

The alien nodded. "I'm ready, Captain."

Julianna laughed. "I don't think he's going to yell the way you want, Teach."

"I'll still take it," said Eddie, chuckling.

"There goes the swarm!" announced Hatch.

Eddie checked the radar, but as he did, a dozen ships passed overhead. They came exceptionally close, so much that for a second Eddie thought one of them might—

The Q-Ship shook as an enemy drone struck its side. "What the fuck!" snapped Eddie.

"Oh, dear," said Pip.

"What happened?" asked Julianna.

"It appears one of the drones changed course at the last second, away from the swarm," explained Pip.

"Did the others notice anything?"

Eddie stared at the radar, watching the red lights as they moved. Each one continued forward for a few brief moments, but then slowed into a full stop. Slowly, they turned towards the Q-Ship, and then started moving.

"Fuck," muttered Eddie.

"I'm on the gun!" barked Julianna. She took the controls and aimed the cannons at the oncoming swarm.

Eddie turned in his seat. "It's now or never, Hatch! Get that ship to the field and do what you came here to do!"

"I'm on it," said the mechanic. Using the pad in his tentacle, he started moving the other ship into place. It was still cloaked, and the swarm didn't appear to notice it. Their attention was, instead, focused on the spot where the other drone had been destroyed.

Julianna pulled the triggers and a barrage of shots left the Q-Ship, colliding with the oncoming fleet. The bullets grazed several of them, splitting their sides apart. At the same time, the drones returned fire, unleashing their own ammunition on the Q-Ship.

Hundreds of enemy bullets struck the ship at once, rattling it. "Status!" yelled Eddie.

"Our hull is holding," returned Pip.

"Of course it is," said Hatch. "These ships aren't made of cardboard like the rest of the Federation's fleet."

Eddie hoped the old octopus was right. He'd never put one of these ships through the ringer, not yet, but if it could withstand these drones, then maybe they could pull off the rest of this mission.

Julianna continued laying down fire on the swarm. Four of the drones exploded, colliding into one another as they lost control. Several were set adrift, floating in the void like dead fish in a lake, lifeless and still. The rest continued forward. "Time to hit the big gun," muttered Julianna, flipping the nearby switch and taking aim at the center of the remaining ships.

"No, wait!" commanded Hatch. "A blast that close will risk both our ships!"

Julianna withdrew her thumb from the trigger. "Oops."

The drones came closer, and suddenly Eddie took the controls, yanking the Q-Ship so as to avoid them. He pulled the ship away, tilting the ship as it moved out of the way. In seconds, Eddie had them positioned so that the cannons were facing the swarm again. "Let them have it, Jules!"

The Commander grinned and pulled the triggers. Bullets tore through the remaining drones, shredding them like paper. She moved from one to the next as Eddie kept the Q-Ship away, dodging whatever firepower the enemy ships sent their way. In a matter of seconds, Julianna released the controls, all the drones destroyed.

There was nothing left but dust and floating metal.

"Hatch, how's the other ship looking?" asked Eddie, without missing a beat.

"In position," answered Hatch. "Overloading the gravitic engines now. Prepare to move in five…four…"

Eddie gripped the control stick and leaned forward.

"…three…two…one…!"

A light emitted from the distance, revealing the other Q-Ship as it lost its cloak and all its onboard power.

Hatch looked up from his pad. "The field is down!"

"Time to move!" yelled Eddie, and suddenly they were off. They passed the second Q-Ship, entering the place where the shield had been. On the other side, more drones appeared on the radar. More than Eddie expected.

"Julianna!"

"I'm on it!"

The ship flew quickly towards the nearest moon, two dozen drones in pursuit. As the ship entered gravitational orbit, Eddie swung them around so that the cannons were facing their pursuers. With the help of the moon's pull, they continued forward while Julianna unloaded on the swarm.

"Six ships have been destroyed," informed Pip. "Excellent work, Commander."

"Save the compliments!" ordered Julianna, striking another drone in its engine and causing it to spin out of control, striking another nearby.

The two drones tore each other apart, destroying themselves.

Four more followed, firing at the Q-Ship, but before they could do much damage, Julianna sent them careening towards the moon's surface. There, they struck the dirt, bouncing like rubber balls along the crater-filled exterior before finally coming to a stop, their parts scattered like breadcrumbs.

"All pursuing units have been destroyed," Pip told them.

"Let's get to that base while we can," suggested Eddie.

"I'm ready when you are," said Julianna.

The Q-Ship tore through a few more drones near the outer orbit of the planet. They never stood a chance, as Julianna struck them before they managed to react. These machines might be more efficient than regular ships or soldiers, but someone was still flying them remotely, and no one had the reaction speed of an enhanced super soldier like Julianna.

Eddie flipped the ship back around and, using the pull

of the moon's orbit, slingshot the ship towards the nearby planet. "Any signs of more drones?"

"Several are ahead, lifting off from the surface," said Pip.

"Get ready for another firefight!" barked Eddie.

The Q-Ship entered the atmosphere right when seven drones appeared from the other side of a storm cloud.

Julianna targeted them immediately as Eddie maneuvered the ship. The planet's gravity made the ride a little bumpier than before, and Eddie felt the pressure in his body as the ship continued forward and sideways.

Hatch was in the back, puffing his cheeks. He wore his flight suit, which helped stifle his body's reaction to the ship's intense vibrations, but it clearly wasn't easy for him, even with the suit on. "Are you okay?" asked Lars, staring at him. "You seem distressed."

"I'm fine!" answered Hatch. "Worry about your own hide."

"Hatch's species doesn't react well to this sort of thing!" yelled Julianna as she fired another fifty rounds into the pursuing ships. "He just needs a minute!"

Eddie performed a horizontal roll, spinning the Q-Ship as it entered a thunderstorm. The drones came in after them.

"What are you doing, Captain?" asked Hatch, flailing his tentacles.

Eddie didn't answer, but instead dove straight down and curved back up. The drones followed, diving with him before ascending. Eddie turned around as the ship ascended through the gray clouds, slowing at the zenith of the climb, and pausing.

In that instant, the drones broke through the cloud, rising up after them. "Now, Julianna!"

As the Q-Ship began to fall back toward the planet, the cannons fired into the mob of ships, killing them with ease. The Q-Ship plowed straight through them, knocking several away, sending them toward the planet.

Eddie held the controls steady, and the ship tore through the thundering storm, vibrating like it was about to rip itself apart. "Initializing stabilizers," informed Pip.

The ship calmed instantly as it broke through the lowest layer of clouds. They entered the rain, which softly beat against the glass of the cockpit windows.

Eddie watched the radar for drone activity, but saw nothing. No more dots, neither in pursuit nor ahead of them. "Looks like we're clear!"

"It's about damn time!" Hatch snapped.

"Pip, initialize the cloak," ordered Eddie. "Now that we're in, it's time for the real mission to begin."

Northern Continent, Pal III, Pal system.

"Mind the thorns," said Eddie, having just stepped off the Q-Ship and onto a patch of prickly blue grass. "Scratched my boots to hell."

"Poor you," teased Julianna. She followed him, leaping off the ship and onto the field. They were right outside the stronghold, no sign of pursuit.

"Hey, I paid good money for these, I'll have you know."

"Liar. You got them for free. We both did."

"That's not the point," scoffed Eddie.

She snickered, then cocked her rifle. "Ready to head inside?"

Eddie peered back at the ship. "How about it, guys?"

Lars poked his head out, stepping down to join them. "By your side, Captain."

"To hell with that," called Hatch, who was still in his seat. He tapped his pad and suddenly the door to the ship slid closed. The comm inside Eddie's ear clicked on, and Hatch continued. "I'm a mechanic, not a soldier."

"Come on, Hatch," teased Eddie. "Live a little."

"Have you seen how fat I am? I'd be an easy target for even the worst ugly-ass Kezzin marksman. Fuck that."

"Suit yourself," said Eddie before glancing at his two companions. "Ready?"

They both nodded.

"All right, Hatch, wait here for us. We'll be back in two shakes of a Lindil's tentacle."

"Hurry up, if you can. I get bored if I'm not busy. Oh, and one more thing, Captain," added Hatch.

"What is it?"

"Try not to get yourselves caught this time. I doubt you'll find somone like Lars to help you out like before."

Eddie smiled, glancing at the reptile next to him. "No, he's one of a kind."

Eddie motioned for Julianna and Lars to start moving.

The nearest building looked to be roughly twenty stories tall. It had no outer walls to protect it, nor any towers for defense. The only reason Eddie could figure was that the man in charge probably thought he'd be safe inside the shield surrounding the planet. It felt a bit short-sighted, now that he thought about it, especially for a man as conniving as Val'Doon Sarnack, the guy who supposedly ruled the Brotherhood.

It also felt wrong. There was no way the building was unprotected.

For all Eddie knew, there were traps all around this place, even if he couldn't see them. After all, he'd flown here in a cloaked ship with enough firepower to wipe out a small armada. If they weren't trying to capture Sarnack alive, they could've wasted this entire compound with nothing but the cannons on their ship.

Luckily for Sarnack, that wasn't the plan.

"It's eerily quiet here, don't you think?" asked Julianna as they drew closer.

"It does seem that way," muttered Lars.

"Keep your guard up," cautioned Eddie, tipping his chin to the Kezzin, while holding his rifle at the ready.

They edged toward the building. It was old, almost archaic, like it didn't belong here. Rather, it seemed like something you'd find in the middle of a large cityscape. Yet here, stowed between fields and forests, it stood as tall as the sky. On each of its four sides, a smaller tower stood, each with blacked-out windows. The combination of structures made Eddie uneasy, though he couldn't figure out why.

He opened his mouth to ask if his companions saw anything, but before he could get the first word out, a sound erupted from somewhere nearby.

Eddie's eyes widened and he clutched the rifle, holding it tightly. "What the fuck was that?"

Before anyone could answer, the doors at the base of the centermost building opened and a dozen soldiers appeared. To Eddie's surprise, there were more than Kezzin in their ranks. Strangely enough, he spotted Kezzin, Trids, and...humans.

Each of the guards were heavily armed and spreading out into the field.

"Incoming!" barked Julianna.

The three of them separated, heading in different

directions.

Eddie threw himself behind a large tree, peeking out with his rifle and taking aim at the approaching squad. He fired, shooting one of the Trids, the shark species, in the neck. A clean shot, straight through. The alien fell, clutching his throat with both hands, gasping as the blood poured out.

At the same time, Julianna slid forward, shredding grass as she unloaded her weapon on two separate Kezzin soldiers. She hit one in the shoulder, knocking him back, while managing to one-shot the second, right in the forehead.

Lars charged ahead, shaking the ground as he went. He took out a small device, strapping it to his chest and tapping a button. When he did, a large sheet of metal extended from it, covering his torso. The guards tried to attack him, but their bullets bounced from the metal shield. Before they could make a second attempt, the Kezzin collided with them, knocking them to the ground. He reached for one of the humans' necks, raising him above his head, then squeezed until the man went still.

The other, a Trid, scrambled to get away, but it was no use. Eddie targeted him and fired, piercing the guard's leg and shattering his bone. The Trid screamed, but was quickly silenced by another shot to the side of his head.

In seconds, the field was silent once again.

"Inside, quickly!" ordered Eddie.

"Why are there humans here?" asked Julianna as the team ran into the tower.

"We'll worry about that later! Get inside, now!"

The three of them reached the doors as they were closing. Lars threw himself between the sliding metal and held the doors open, extending both his hands, letting his friends inside. He jumped in as he let go, and the doors slammed shut.

"Thanks," said Julianna.

The Kezzin nodded. "Let us move."

"Pip," said Eddie, tapping the comm in his ear. "Do we know the layout here?"

"I'm afraid not," answered the E.I.

"We'll have to press on, make it up as we go," said Julianna.

"Business as usual, then," added Eddie, looking at each of them. He trotted to the nearby staircase. "Time to climb."

———

The Q-Ship was quiet. Hatch didn't like that.

He hated waiting around like a scared little child, but there wasn't much he could do, except watch. That was the problem with being the only engineer in a team of soldiers.

"Is there anything I can do for you while you wait, Doctor Hatcherik?" asked Pip.

Hatch turned in his seat. "Not really."

In addition to worrying about his friends, Hatch's mind was on the other Q-Ship, his most prized creation. It was out there, floating in space, dead and lifeless. Any of those drones could kill it, wipe out all his hard work. *Jules, why did I ever let you talk me into this nonsense,* he thought, twirling his tentacles.

He let out a long sigh.

"What's wrong?" asked the E.I.

"Nothing," lied Hatch.

"I can tell by scanning you that something is bothering you."

"Don't scan me, unless you feel like being reprogrammed," warned Hatch.

"Understood, but could you tell me the truth of your distress first, before you go through all the trouble?"

"Why are you so curious?"

"Part of my programming requires me to look after the well-being of my crewmates."

"Oh?" muttered Hatch. "Well, don't concern yourself with me. The mission is what matters."

"To me, they are one and the same, sir."

"Well, I don't know what to tell you, friend. When I'm alone, I think too much. It's what I do."

"Are you worried about the other Q-Ship?" asked Pip.

The question surprised him. "What?"

"You keep looking out the window, towards the sky. The only reason I can deduce is that your mind is on something else. Something not on this planet. Given your history, both designing and piloting the other ship, it seemed the highest calculated option."

Hatch scoffed. "Aren't you the little detective? Yes, if you gotta know, I was wondering how it's doing up there, all by its lonesome. You have any idea how long I spent building that glorious machine?"

"Six years, according to my records."

"Was that all?" asked Hatch, genuinely surprised by the answer. "I thought it was seven."

"Is that why you came along today?" asked Pip. "Because you were worried about your ship?"

"Don't be ridiculous," said Hatch, fanning a tentacle. "I had to be here."

"I could have piloted the ship in your stead," suggested Pip.

Hatch didn't answer, maybe because what Pip said felt true. The more he thought about it, the less necessary his coming along seemed. He'd known this beforehand, but instead of accepting it, he'd convinced himself that the best chance was doing it himself. Had he really done all this because he was afraid of losing his ship? Afraid of letting someone else handle things?

"I don't know what will happen to your ship. I can't detect it from here, due to both our distance and its lack of power," explained Pip. "However, what I can tell you is that I will make salvaging it a priority."

"You sure are being friendly," muttered Hatch.

"I've been told that before."

"Oh? You do this a lot, huh?"

"I spend a great deal of time inside Commander Fregin's head."

"That must be annoying," mused Hatch.

"I rather like it, actually."

"I didn't know E.I.s could like anything."

There was a long pause.

"Pip?"

"Apologies, Doctor. What were we talking about?"

"Wait! They're coming up the—" A blast struck the soldier in his chest, sending him to the floor.

Eddie leapt up the stairs, kicking off the wall as he came around the corner, pressing his rifle out and firing two shots into the nearest soldier. The bullets tore through the alien's chest, spraying blood as the guard collapsed. Three others stood behind him, watching with fear in their eyes, unable to move.

Before they could shake their trepidation, Julianna was already on them, knocking the first one in the jaw with the butt of her rifle, then kicking him in the temple, knocking him out, and removing him from the fight.

Lars took two more, a human and Trid, one in each hand, and threw them against the nearest wall. The blunt force knocked the human out cold, but the Trid struggled, flailing his arms. Lars dropped them both, taking the rifle from the Trid, expecting him to stop moving and surrender, but instead, the alien began to spasm.

"What the fuck is wrong with him?" asked Eddie.

The Trid grabbed at his waist, grasping at a device on his hip. It was a small box. A moment later, the Trid's face started turning blue, like he was suffocating, and then he stopped moving.

"That device," said Julianna, pointing at it. "It helps them breathe, doesn't it?"

"Oh, that's right," muttered Eddie. "They can't breathe oxygen normally without it, can they?"

"Why?" asked Lars.

Eddie went to the Trid's side, examining the device. "Their natural habitat is in the ocean. Saltwater, you know?"

"I've never seen an alien like this before," said Lars.

"Never?" repeated Eddie.

Lars shook his head. "They're not common on Kezza, nor were they stationed where you found me. I haven't visited many worlds."

"Curious that they should be here," said Julianna.

"Not to mention the humans," added Eddie. "We're looking at something different here. A new collaboration."

Footsteps echoed down the nearby stairs. Eddie stood, readying his rifle, then motioned for the others to get into position.

Eddie, Julianna, and Lars leaned against the side of the wall adjacent to the stairs, and took aim.

Any second now.

A human rounded the corner, revealing a head of ginger hair. A woman with blue eyes. She stopped in her tracks, turning to look at the three of them, blinking with a stunned expression on her face.

Eddie cocked his eyebrow, but kept his barrel on her. "Don't move!"

She stared directly at the rifle. "Um."

"Who are you and what are you doing here? Where's the guy in charge?"

"I, um," she stuttered. "Don't shoot!"

"We won't hurt you if you just tell us who you are," said Julianna.

"Margo," said the woman.

"Margo?" asked Eddie.

"You want to tell us why you're here, Margo?" asked Julianna.

"I was on a colony," she whispered, remaining still with her hands in the air.

"A colony?" asked Eddie, looking at Julianna. "Think she means the Federation colonies?"

"Yes, that's right," said Margo, pulling Eddie's eyes back. "They took me away from my home. They killed my brother."

"They abducted you?" asked Julianna. "Wait a second, are there others here with you? Did they bring prisoners here?"

Margo nodded. "Most are under us."

"Under us?" repeated Eddie. He dropped his eyes to the floor. "Oh, fuck."

"What is it?" asked Lars.

Eddie lowered his rifle. "Margo, I need you to listen very carefully to me, okay? Will you show us how to find the rest of your people? Can you do that?"

The girl nodded. "Um, okay."

"Captain, shouldn't we look for the one in command before going after those prisoners?" asked Lars.

He was right, of course. Eddie knew there wouldn't be time for both. If they took off underground, the enemy would either flee or reorganize their forces. He'd have to make a decision and prioritize. "We'll have to split up and do both at the same time. It's the only way."

Julianna nodded. "We'll have less firepower, should we encounter more guards, but you're right."

"Understood," agreed Lars. "I'll help however I can."

Julianna stepped forward. "I'll go with Margo to find the rest of them. You two head to the top and secure this facility."

Eddie didn't bother asking if she could handle this. He knew full well she could. Julianna was a badass with at least two hundred years of experience and a genetically engineered body that doubled as an extreme weapon of death. She'd be fine. "Do your thing and save those people. We'll take care of the asshole above us."

"Right," confirmed Julianna. She waved at Margo to lower her hands and pointed at the stairs. "After you, Margo."

21

Northern Continent, Pal III, Pal system

The basement of the alien stronghold was like a labyrinth. Julianna had little indication of where to go, other than the vague guidance of her new escort, the human female Margo. The girl was quiet, timid, and looked like she hadn't eaten much in weeks. Depending on the number of colonists on this rock, getting them out of here would be a feat in and of itself.

They went slowly through the corridors, with Julianna leaving a trail of soldiers in her wake as she found them, dropping the bodies like stones.

"This way, quickly," said Margo as they reached an intersection. "The cells are ahead."

"What's that way?" asked Julianna, nodding in the other direction.

The girl seemed to tense up as she stared down the other hall. Whatever was there, she obviously didn't like it.

"Forget it," Julianna told her. "Let's keep going. Show me where your friends are."

The girl nodded. "R-Right."

The hall continued until, but at last they came upon a door. Light streamed through the cracks, in addition to the sound of voices. "I was thinking I'd get some food. Want anything?" asked a man on the other side.

"Like what?" asked the other.

"They got some steak, I heard, over in the mess hall."

"Anything else? I ain't in the mood for meat."

"Ain't in the mood?" asked the first. He laughed at the thought of it. "I don't get you humans. Shows how weak you are, you have to mix your meat with grass."

"We're not carnivores," said the man. "We eat both."

"No wonder you're only half as strong as me. You eat half grass, you only grow half size."

The man said nothing, but Julianna could hear him sigh, probably biting his tongue.

She heard footsteps approaching the door, and, taking Margo by the hand, brought her close to the wall beside it.

The door opened, and out walked a large Trid soldier, wearing armor and wielding two pistols at his sides.

As he turned to shut the door, Julianna reacted, lunging forward, going for his gills.

His eyes widened and he pulled back, nearly dodging her, though she still managed to strike him in the neck.

The soldier wheezed, but didn't stifle. Instead, he went for his guns, pulling them from their holsters and shooting them both from the hip.

In an instant, Julianna threw Margo to the floor, a meter beside them, and dodged the two shots, letting them hit the wall behind her. She struck one of the pistols with her rifle, knocking it free, and it slid away.

The Trid clutched the second gun in his hand, pulling it up and firing at her chest. She raised the butt of her rifle in time to deflect the bullet, sending it away. She recoiled from the shock of the point-blank discharge.

The alien was about to fire again when another shot erupted from nearby. A hole went clean through the Trid's hand, forcing him to drop the gun. Julianna looked and saw the girl, her escort, holding the other pistol with both hands, trembling. It wasn't surprising. She couldn't have been more than nineteen.

Without another thought, Julianna took out her knife and stabbed the alien in the gills of his neck, then kicked him away. He staggered backwards, blood oozing from his flesh, making an awful shriek as he fell to the stone floor.

The man on the other side of the door appeared, running with his weapon. Seeing Julianna and the dying Trid, he paused, mouth hanging wide open. "Holy fucking shit!"

"You're next," muttered Julianna, stepping towards him.

"No, wait!" he begged, dropping the gun and raising his hands. "Please, I didn't do anything!"

Julianna leapt at him, taking him by the throat. Her eyes sparked wild with rage as she hoisted the man above her head like a doll. "Liar!"

He tried to speak, but couldn't, her hand was so tightly bound against his flesh. Tears filled his eyes and spit came from his mouth.

"Please, wait!" called Margo.

The girl's voice brought Julianna back, snapping her out

of it. She looked at Margo and saw her worried face. There was genuine concern there, not fear or a need for revenge. "What is it? He's the enemy! He imprisoned your people."

"No, it's not like that!" said Margo. "He's being forced!"

"Forced?" Julianna looked at the soldier. She lowered him to his feet so that he could speak. "Is that true?"

The man coughed, trying to gasp for air. "O-Only for some of us."

"Some of you?"

"The men upstairs…they…they're like you said…traitors…"

"And you?" she asked.

"My wife…they took her. They said if I didn't guard the rest, they'd kill her. I have to do like they said. I have to…"

"Is this true?" Julianna asked Margo, glancing back at her.

The girl nodded. "They use us against each other. They find out who we care about, then they take them away."

"Who did they take from you?" asked the man, looking at Margo.

"My Dad," she said, looking like she was about to cry.

Julianna glared at the soldier. "And you're telling me that they have these people, like your wife, somewhere else inside this facility?"

He nodded.

"Where?"

"If I knew, I would've tried to rescue her by now. No one knows where they keep our people, except the Kezzin and the Trids."

There was no way Julianna was going to trust the word of two people she'd only just met, but she wanted to believe them. "Show me the cells, but don't try anything. I'm here to get you all home, but I'll put you down in a heartbeat if it comes to it. Do you understand?"

"I do," he answered, quickly. "I promise. I just want my wife back."

Did you get all that, Pip?

I did. Would you like me to relay all of this to the others?

If you wouldn't mind.

What are you going to do?

Rescue a fuckton of people and kill whoever stands in my way.

A fuckton? You're beginning to sound like him, you know.

You're talking about Teach, aren't you? Do you think I sound so brash?

It isn't such a bad thing, I think.

No, she thought, a slight smile forming on her face. *No, I don't suppose it is, Pip.*

A few minutes later, beneath the surface.

Julianna stood before a long stretch of hall, cells along each side. There had to be dozens of them, if not more, and each seemed to have someone inside. Nearby, three enemy soldiers were unconscious on the floor, fresh victims of Julianna's wrath.

"Help!" shouted one of the residents. It was a young girl, roughly sixteen. She had brown eyes and short blonde hair. "Please, help us!"

"It's okay," calmed Julianna. "We'll get you all out."

"The release switch is here," said the human guard who had shown her the way. He pointed to a small monitor display on the wall.

Julianna touched the screen, bringing it to life. A password screen appeared, stopping her immediately. *Pip, can you get through this?*

I'm already doing it.

Hurry. We don't have much—

The cells began to open, two at a time, filling the corridor with a series of loud clanks. The prisoners piled out of their cells, scrambling to leave.

You were saying?

You're so dramatic, she thought, but couldn't hold back her smile. Then, with a thunderous voice, she yelled, "Everyone, please calm down! Does anyone know where the rest of your people are being kept?"

The crowd began to talk back, but their voices overlapped one another. Still, she managed to piece together several responses, most of which were questions, rather than answers. Only a few attempted to provide any information. "We don't know!" shouted one. Another yelled back, "They took them away!"

Commander, I believe I have some data that may prove useful.

What was that, Pip? You found something?

Correct. Now that I've been granted access to the local network, I can see the entire layout of this facility, including another set of cells to the east. They appear to be nearby.

Julianna regarded the crowd. "Everyone, listen up!" she barked. "We're going to get the rest of your people! Your husbands, wives, daughters, and sons! We're going to take you home! Do you hear me, people? We're going to get you the fuck off this godforsaken rock!"

The people cheered. "Thank the heavens!" "We're finally free!" "The Federation has finally come!"

Pip, let's move. Where do I go?

Back the way we came, then north through a short passage. You'll encounter four locked doors, but I can handle those. There's a guard there, but nothing you can't manage, I'm certain.

"Everyone, head to the surface!" shouted Julianna. She turned to Margo and the human guard. "Except you two. Come on."

"Are we going to rescue my wife?" asked the man, a wide-eyed expression on his face.

"I promise you, if she's alive, I'll find her," assured Julianna. "What's your name?"

"Jeffrey," the man said.

"Okay, Jeffrey. Both of you stick close to me." She motioned for him to follow, and together the three of them took off down the long underground hallway.

Elsewhere, near the top of the tower.

Eddie downed three Trid soldiers as he and Lars entered the highest floor of the building. At the same time, Lars came head-to-head with another Kezzin, locking with him, both their arms wrapped around each other.

The other Kezzin struggled to break free, but Lars would not oblige him. Instead, he pushed the alien's hand away and then slammed his fist into his side, jabbing his stomach and forcing the Kezzin to yelp. Then, Lars pulled back and, using the heel of his palm, jammed the Kezzin's nose up and into his skull.

The enemy staggered, a confused and disoriented look on his face. He opened his mouth like he was about to say something, but then collapsed, hitting the floor with a loud thud.

Eddie looked at Lars, cocking his brow. "Damn, Lars. You aren't playing around, huh?"

"What?" asked Lars. "We have little time to waste, do we not?"

Eddie nodded. "Right, let's go!"

Together, they kicked the double doors open. The metal creaked and snapped the hinges as the entrance opened into a large, egg-shaped room.

A fist slammed into Eddie's chest immediately, knocking him back and into the foyer. He wheezed, gasping for air. "Fuck," he muttered.

Two guards were there, running at him, both of them Trids. They must have been waiting to take them by surprise.

Eddie leapt to his feet, shaking off the pain, and then raised his rifle.

But before he could fire, the Trid came at him, grabbed the gun and tried to pull it away. Eddie fired, but the bullet only hit the glass windows along the nearby wall, shattering them and letting in the outside light.

A strong wind suddenly entered the floor, filling the area with the scent of wet grass.

Lars tackled the second Trid, kicking him in the neck and causing the alien to scream. Before he could get to

Eddie, the Trid grabbed at his feet, pulling him to the floor. The two of them wrestled together while Eddie continued fighting with the other one.

The Trid pushed Eddie back, almost to the staircase, but Eddie stopped him there, holding his ground. He wouldn't be taken down so easily, not by some grunt.

Eddie shoved his leg around the back of the Trid, forcing him to turn. As he did, the alien tripped over Eddie's foot, falling forward.

Eddie quickly stepped aside, letting the Trid fall, but the alien would not release the rifle, and he took it with him, forcing Eddie to let go.

The soldier tumbled down the stairs, breaking bones as he hit the steps, one after the next. As Eddie watched him fall, Lars called out for him. "Captain!"

Eddie turned and saw a Trid's arm around his friend's throat. "Lars!"

He ran at him, seizing and pulling the Trid's hand away from Lars' neck. Eddie wrapped the alien's arm around his back so Lars could squeeze out from under him. Once he was free, Lars took his gun and slammed it into the Trid's forehead, knocking him out.

Eddie let go, standing back up. "Well, fuck," he muttered, breathing a little heavily.

"Where's your weapon?" asked Lars.

Eddie nodded at the staircase. "Lost it, but I can go get—"

A shout rang out from the other side of the doorway. "Hurry! They're here!"

"Who the fuck was that?" asked Eddie.

Lars blinked, pausing. "I...I recognize that voice." He took a step forward. "Quickly, Captain!"

Lars ran into the room with Eddie close behind him.

There, straight ahead, Eddie saw two men near the farthest window, a pad in one of their hands. One was a Kezzin, while the other was a Trid. Eddie wasn't good with alien faces, but he was pretty sure he'd seen the Kezzin before.

Somewhere.

"You!" shouted the Trid individual as Eddie and Lars came running.

"Who the fuck are these two?" asked Eddie.

Lars's eyes widened as he stared at the other Kezzin. "Commander Orsa!"

"Lars Malseen?" Orsa stepped forward, surprised. "Is that you? What are you doing here?"

"I could ask you the same question," demanded Lars.

"Are you with this human?"

"What does it look like?" asked Eddie.

Orsa examined Eddie. "You're the one who escaped our facility."

"You're goddamn right I am."

"I suspected you had help, but I never believed the one who captured you would be the one to free you. When Lars went missing, I assumed he'd been killed." Orsa shook his head. "Lars, how could you betray the Brotherhood, after all we've done for you?"

"You've done nothing for me!" barked Lars. "I only joined your organization because you threatened to take my brother away."

"Such disrespect!" scoffed Orsa. "The Brotherhood has

kept the Kezzin race safe and secure from the human invaders for nearly twenty years. If it weren't for us, these despicable aliens would have killed us all by now."

"The humans aren't the problem with Kezza. You are," said Lars. "The Brotherhood kills its own people. It enslaves children. It destroys families. You've proven yourselves the enemy of our people, not the humans."

"I will admit, Lars, that sometimes we must burn the field to regrow the crop, but only because it is necessary."

"Is that why you attacked those human colonies?" asked Eddie. "To regrow your crops?"

Orsa nodded. "The universe must be purged of all who would threaten the Kezzin people. We were a dwindling species before the Brotherhood took charge, but since then, we've expanded our worlds and seized what is rightfully ours. We have become strong!"

"At the cost of your soul," said Eddie.

"He is right," agreed Lars. "Kezza was once a place of beauty. We prided ourselves on our ability to reason, to discover. We were scientists, painters, and farmers, but now—"

"Now, we are strong!" snapped Orsa. "What good are painters when the armies of other worlds are seizing our territory? What good are farmers when the galaxy is shrinking?"

"Shrinking?" asked Eddie.

"The universe is only so big, human. There aren't enough worlds for everyone. Imagine the Kezzin's surprise when we discovered how much of the galaxy was already discovered and owned by others. You left us with nowhere to go! You left us to wither away and die!"

"So you kill colonists and take their land," finished Eddie.

Orsa nodded. "For the good of my people! We did what had to be done."

"You did nothing for Kezza," interjected Lars. "You did it for power, for yourself! We had eight thriving worlds when the Brotherhood seized control. Now, our population starves and fights among itself, all because of what you have done."

"Quiet!" barked Orsa. "Silence yourself right now, traitorous filth!"

"Enough," shouted the Trid, standing beside him. "I grow tired of this exchange. Really, Orsa, you waste your time on them. I thought more of you."

Orsa stifled. "I-I'm sorry, General Vas."

"Vas?" asked Lars. "Commander Orsa, who is this person?"

"None of your concern!" snapped Orsa.

"I think it is our concern," corrected Eddie. "In fact, if you don't tell us right now, I can promise it won't be good for you."

"Threaten all you want, but we aren't telling you anything," said Vas.

"You don't have to," said Eddie. "We'll just toss you in a cell and wait. I'm sure you'll want to tell us something after you haven't seen daylight for a few months."

Vas laughed.

"You think that's funny?" asked Eddie.

"I think you don't know what you're talking about, boy."

Lars raised his gun and aimed it at the two aliens. "You heard him. The two of you are coming with us."

Eddie heard a click in his ear. "Captain, I'm sorry to interrupt, but Commander Fregin wanted me to relay a message to you."

"What is it, Pip?" asked Eddie.

"She's found the prisoners beneath this facility. There appears to be several hundred of them, based on my estimates, but there are more located somewhere else in the compound."

"That's great, but I'm a little busy right now." Eddie glanced at Orsa and Vas. "I'm looking at the two guys responsible for everything."

"Understood," confirmed Pip. "I'll let her know. Please update me with any further progress you make. Try not to kill them, if you can help it."

"I'll use a soft touch," agreed Eddie, staring at Orsa. The comm clicked off and he raised his voice again. "Now, put your hands where we can see them and move your asses out from behind that desk."

Vas looked at Orsa and muttered something that Eddie couldn't hear.

"Hey, no whispering over there. I told you, if you try anything, we'll—"

Vas laughed. "I'm afraid I have some bad news for you, Captain."

"Oh? Did you wet yourself while I was kicking your guards' asses? It's okay. I won't hold it against you. You seem like the cowardly sort."

"Ah, not quite," said Vas. "But I'm sorry to say, we can't do as you requested."

"How's that now?"

"We're unable to walk over to you."

"You, what?" asked Eddie. "He took a step towards them. "Look, buddy. If you don't stop with this bullshit, I'm going to do something rash, like break a rib. You don't want that to happen."

"I'm sure you're right, Captain, but unfortunately, the issue has more to do with physically moving. You see—" Vas raised both his hands, and suddenly he flickered, disappearing briefly. "—We're not actually here."

Eddie's eyes went wide as he finally understood. "Oh, fuck."

"That's right." Vas smiled.

Lars snarled, then charged into the two holograms, passing straight through them. The images flickered again before coming back together. "While you've been storming the castle, so to speak, we've been on a ship in orbit, sitting behind a moon."

Eddie clenched his teeth.

"Like an idiot, you let us talk while we broke orbit," said Orsa. "Now, we'll be free to—"

Lars crushed a small box sitting against the window and suddenly the two aliens disappeared. He screamed in rage, full of anger.

Eddie tried to think for a second, to try and find a solution. Those two were the key to understanding all of this. The key to stopping the Brotherhood once and for all. If they got away, the entire search would have to begin again.

And Eddie had talked with them. The conversation raced back through his mind. What had he given away? He couldn't remember. Fuck!

"Bastards!" snapped Lars.

The word jolted Eddie. He looked at his angered friend, a man who had given up everything for this mission. He deserved something out of all this. He deserved his revenge. His justice. Eddie wouldn't let all his sacrifice be in vain, nor would he allow these people to just walk away from this. "Fuck this," he muttered. "Pip, are you hearing me?"

"I am, sir," said the E.I.

"Put me through to the Q-Ship, now!"

A short pause, followed by a click, and then, "Hello?"

"Hatch, are you hearing me?" asked Eddie.

"Is everything okay, Captain? Did you—"

Eddie motioned at Lars to follow him, and he started running out of the room. "Listen carefully, Hatch. I need you to get that ship over here to pick us up right away. We've been tricked!"

"Oh, I, uh, okay," answered Hatch, trying to process what he was hearing. "I'll be right there."

The comm clicked off right as Eddie reached the stairs. He leapt down nine steps, then jumped to the following floor. "Pip, patch me through to *the ArchAngel!*"

"Yes, sir," responded Pip. "I'll have to use the Q-Ship's long-range communicator, but it won't take long."

Eddie reached the next floor, racing down as fast as his body would let him, continuing onto the next section. As he took another leap, a Kezzin guard appeared, a surprised look on his face. Eddie twisted in the air, kicking off the wall of the stairwell and slamming his foot into the alien's face, knocking him several meters back. The Kezzin dropped to the floor like a sack of bricks.

"Sir, I have ArchAngel on the line," interrupted Pip.

"Captain?" asked ArchAngel. "I do hope everything is going well for you down there."

"Listen up, Arch," said Eddie. "I need you to get your giant metal ass over here. We've got a runner."

"A what?" asked the A.I.

"The fucking aliens in charge of this whole debacle are trying to run and I need you to stop them. Can you do it?"

Without so much as a pause, she said, "You can count on me, Captain. I'm on the way."

"They just broke orbit. Use your sensors to find them and keep them targeted, but don't engage. We don't want to kill them. Not yet."

"Understood," answered ArchAngel.

The line clicked off again as Eddie reached the next floor. He glanced behind to see Lars coming right behind him. *Almost there*, he thought as they continued down the stairwell.

22

Northern Continent, Pal III, Pal system

Seven large cells, which were really more like cattle pens, unlocked and slid open as Julianna entered the massive prison room. Dozens of thin, filthy, and deprived people walked past the bars, staring at the woman who had just rescued them.

"Olivia!" yelled Jeffrey. He ran and wrapped his arms around a young woman. She was dirty and bruised, and he dropped to his knees, wrapping his arms around her waist.

She stared down at him, looking shocked, but after a moment, she seemed to understand. "J-Jeffrey? Is it truly you?"

He clutched her and buried his face in her thigh, wailing like a small child. "You're here! You're here!"

She knelt to him and embraced his whole body. "Oh, my sweet man!"

They cried together, and so did several others as they watched.

Margo looked for her father, rushing through the crowd. "Have you seen Jeremy?" she asked each of them. "Jeremy Holistar?"

"Margo!" called a bearded man near the back of the room. "My girl, is that you?"

She ran to him. "Father!"

Julianna watched all of this, relieved at the sight. She'd been worried that these people might be dead and that the guards were using their memory as an incentive to keep the rest in line. Thankfully, this had only been partially true. They were alive, although only barely. She had to get them back to ArchAngel, and quickly. They all looked like they were on the verge of death.

Pip, how's the rest of the colonists? Did you direct them topside?

They're arriving there now. I told them to wait in the field to the north of this complex. They...

There was a short pause. *Pip? Pip, are you there?*

Apologies, but it appears Captain Teach is requesting your presence above-ground. It seems the enemy has fled.

They ran?

Archangel is on her way, but I suggest we move quickly. Doctor Hatcherik is coming with the Q-Ship to retrieve the team.

It seemed these people would have to wait until the mission was over, unfortunately. "Everyone, please follow Margo and Jeffrey. They'll take you to the surface," she told them.

"Are you leaving?" called Margo, running up to her.

"I have a job to finish," Julianna responded. "Think you

can handle the rest on your own? I promise I'll join you soon."

The girl nodded. "Of course. Thank you so much for your help. You're a godsend, Commander Fregin!"

Julianna shook her head. "You showed me the way. If it hadn't been for you, Margo, none of these people would be walking out of here."

Margo smiled, a tear in her eye. She ran back to her father, telling him what was about to happen. A second later, she raised her hand to get the attention of the rest of the prisoners. "Everyone, we need to get going! Help carry anyone who can't walk, okay? We have to leave together."

Looks like she can handle this. Okay, Pip, time to go!

The Q-Ship is about to arrive. I suggest you get going.

Julianna took Pip's advice and started running, exploding into a mad dash through the hallways. Without the prisoners to slow her down, she moved with lightning speed, able to unleash her full abilities. In under a minute, she was back at the stairwell, ascending to the ground floor, ready to find the one responsible for the unforgivable atrocities she had found.

Whoever it was, they were about to pay.

Eddie and Lars boarded the Q-Ship as soon as it landed. "Welcome back, you two," greeted Hatch, waving a tentacle at them. "Where's Julie?"

"On her way," answered Eddie, strapping himself in. "Pip, where's ArchAngel?"

"Arriving in less than thirty seconds," said Pip.

Lars took his seat. "We need to go after them now, before they get away."

"Not without Julianna," ordered Eddie. "She's—"

Just then, Julianna came running through the doors of the tower, barely stopping long enough to spot the ship.

"And there she is," said Eddie, grinning.

The Commander moved like she was possessed, leaping from the ground and into the ship with more than her share of urgency. "Sorry I'm late!"

The second she was in, the door slammed shut and the engines roared, lifting them off the ground. "No need to apologize, Jules," assured Eddie. "We're only going after the most dangerous criminals in twelve systems."

"Is that all?" she asked, taking her place next to him.

The ship broke quickly into the upper atmosphere as the stabilizers kicked in, settling the inside of the ship to a soft, calming hum.

The ship rocketed through the clouds, breaking through and pulling trails of white into the clear sky beyond. In an instant, the blue world faded, replaced by stars and darkness.

"Pip, activate long range scans and run a sweep for any outgoing ships. Not drones," ordered Eddie.

"Already working," responded Pip. "I'm detecting two, each on the opposite side of the third moon."

"Activate gravitic thrusters," said Eddie.

"Anyone want to tell me exactly what's going on?" asked Hatch.

"You don't know?" asked Lars.

"All Pip told me was to bring the ship in," answered the mechanic. "I've gathered since then that we're after someone, but if you wanna fill me in on the rest, I'm all—"

"There he is!" snapped Eddie, pointing to the radar on the dash. It showed the two vessels, though one was significantly closer. He clutched the controls. "We need to reach him before he leaves!"

"Pip mentioned a couple of holograms," said Julianna. "I take it they were decoys for these two?"

"You're right as usual," answered Eddie. "They thought they could run, but we won't let them."

She nodded with a smirk. "No, we damn sure won't."

Hatch looked back at Lars. "Are you following all this?"

"It's as they say. We were tricked by Commander Orsa and a Trid named Vas inside the building. They used a hologram to make us believe they were there while the two of them escaped."

"Oh, is that all?" asked Hatch, rather sarcastically. "I swear, nothing's ever simple with you people, is it?"

"We like to keep things interesting," Eddie told him, then ignited the second set of thrusters, allowing him to break planetary orbit.

He brought their ship to the edge of the moon, passing through its light gravitation pull, setting his sights on the enemy vessel. "Pip, open a channel to whoever that is."

"The line is ready," said the E.I.

"This is Captain Teach. Enemy vessel, respond. We know who you are. I strongly suggest you comply."

"Captain Teach, you say?" asked a voice on the other end. "You certainly waste no time."

"Surrender your ship and prepare to be towed."

"You have me, sir. I'll comply."

Eddie glanced at Julianna, who gave him a slow nod. She paused, her eyes going a little distant, and then she said, "Pip muted us. Do you think it's a trap?"

"I'd bet money on it," answered Eddie. "Pip, are his engines dead?"

"They appear to be, but—" The Q-Ship rattled, shaking suddenly. "—it seems his weapons systems are active."

"Activate the cannons but don't destroy the ship!" snapped Eddie. He clutched the controls and took the Q-Ship forward, dodging the incoming fire.

"Sir, the ship is activating its engines," reported Pip.

"Guess we spoke too soon!" Eddie avoided another spread of firepower, performing a horizontal roll and moving away from the moon's surface.

"Sir, there's one more thing," added Pip.

Eddie aimed and fired a light shot across the hull of the other ship as it attempted to leave. "What is it now?!"

"The second vessel is departing."

"Tell ArchAngel to move her heavy ass and stop that fucker!" Eddie fired again, this time landing several bullets against the side of the ship. It dipped in the moon's gravity, nearly falling, but then righted itself and ascended.

At that moment, several dots appeared on the radar. They were small, the same as the drones they'd encountered upon their arrival, except now there were more of them. "Shit!" shouted Eddie. "Looks like we have more company!"

Julianna took the controls. "Focus on flying and I'll handle the guns!"

"Right," affirmed Eddie.

"Captain," began Pip as the ship dodged several

oncoming shots from the swarm. "Might I make a suggestion?"

"What is it, Pip?" snapped Eddie.

"Now might be a good time to deploy the Q-Ship's Combat Assault Mode."

Eddie's eyes widened at the suggestion. He'd completely forgotten about the second mode. Activating it would release the outer shell of the ship, which meant added firepower and maneuverability, but it also meant losing the ship's cloak. Considering the situation, that seemed like a fair trade. "Do it, Pip! Activate the CAM!"

A red light illuminated the interior of the Q-Ship as it released clamps on both sides, snapping off large chunks of the exterior hull. The entire ship vibrated as huge metal slabs released themselves, revealing a thinner, rougher interior design. The ship lost its smooth, elegant skin in favor of several more guns and thrusters. In less than a few seconds, the ship had changed into something totally different, and several new options appeared on the dash.

"Combat Assault Mode has been activated," informed Pip.

Multiple drones appeared from the other side of the moon, joining the rest. They flew together like a swarm of insects, so intensely thick that it was impossible to tell their numbers or even differentiate the individual ones from the mob. They fired wildly on the Q-Ship, and it shook violently.

"Hold on!" barked Eddie, taking the controls.

The drones came together like a massive wave. Julianna took aim and fired armor-piercing rounds, hitting multiple drones, but hardly making a dent in the mob. "Pip, prime the cannons!" she yelled.

"Acknowledged," responded Pip.

Another blast struck the Q-Ship, knocking them off course for a brief second, until Eddie regained control.

A switch lit up on the panel, creating a soft yellow glow on the dash. Julianna flipped it, readying the cannon, leaning forward. "Hold on!"

The Q-Ship unleashed a blast so bright it illuminated the surface of the moon. It tore through the mob of drones, destroying so many that it left a wide gap in their ranks, sending several dozen of them crashing into the cratered moon.

As the drones reformed their ranks, Eddie brought the ship around and avoided their incoming fire. "There sure are a lot of them!" he yelled.

"Too many to count," observed Lars.

"I'm not sure if we can keep this up!"

Julianna unloaded a few hundred rounds into the swarm, knocking down another dozen drones in a matter of seconds. "We'll be okay! Just keep going!"

Just then, a blast of white light, very much like the one from the Q-Ship's cannon, erupted from nearby, hitting many of the drones. The destruction took Eddie by surprise, forcing him to quickly move the ship out of the way. "What the fuck was that!"

"*The ArchAngel?*" asked Julianna.

"Hardly," said Hatch, who was busy on his pad.

Eddie scanned the area, searching for the cause of the chaos, only to see the other Q-Ship floating in the distance, no longer immobilized. "Well I'll be damned," he muttered.

"Is that the other Q-Ship?" asked Julianna.

Hatch nodded. "I set it to reboot the system after a certain amount of time. When we were close enough, I took control again. Good thing, too, considering how terrible you both are at killing the enemy."

A drone came flying directly towards them, only for Julianna to respond with due force. Several rounds broke through the metal and sent the tiny vessel careening away. She looked back and smirked. "Speak for yourself, Octopus."

Hatch's cheeks puffed. "Shall we proceed?"

"Don't mind if I do!" answered Eddie, gripping the controls.

The two Q-Ships pulled away from the moon. Julianna continued firing on the remaining drones, picking them off one-by-one.

As the enemy ship came into view, Eddie activated the com. "Attention: this is your final warning. Surrender and prepare to be taken into custody."

"Go to hell!" returned the voice on the other line.

Eddie glanced at Julianna, giving her a nod. "Care to give him a nudge?"

"Knock-knock," she whispered, sending a spray of shots against the ship's hull.

"Enemy vessel has taken damage," announced Pip. "Engines are disabled. I'm also detecting atmospheric leaks. Suggest extraction."

"You heard him," Eddie said into the com. "Give it up now or you'll end up suffocating."

A few seconds passed without a response. "You win," the voice finally answered. "I'm giving up. This is General

Vas, surrendering myself to your control."

Eddie muted the line, then looked at Julianna. "Looks like we got the boss. Now, let's see about the second guy, Orsa. Pip, where's he at?"

"The ship appears to be—"

The Q-Ship shook as a blast struck its side. "What the fuck was that!" barked Eddie.

"As I was saying, the enemy is upon us," finished Pip.

"Goddammit, Pip!" snapped Julianna. She twisted the control stick in her hand, searching for the source of the firepower. "Where the hell is this guy?"

"There!" said Hatch, examining his pad. "He's in the crater!"

Eddie scanned the moon, quickly rotating the ship. There, just as Hatch had said, a small craft was positioned inside an opening on the moon. "Julianna, take care of that asshole, would you?"

"Right!" she answered, and immediately returned fire.

The shots rained down on the enemy vessel, bombarding the surface of the moon with great prejudice.

The bombs fell and the ship fled, avoiding the crumbling structure around it. "Stay on him!" shouted Julianna.

Eddie looked at the other ship. "We can't chase after him without leaving the other one alone. Hatch, can you—"

"Already on it," the mechanic responded. In an instant, Hatch had the second Q-Ship moving after the fleeing vessel. He hit the command to start firing, sending shots after the ship. "I'll try to knock out his engines!"

Eddie glanced back at the first ship. He couldn't just sit here, could he? "Wait a second," he muttered, entering a command on the dash. "Pip, I'm going to try something. See if you can help me out."

"I think I understand, sir," responded the E.I.

Julianna watched as Eddie played with the controls. "What are you—"

But before she could go on, the Q-Ship released a grapple, hooking the enemy ship. "Now, for the other part," Eddie went on. "Pip, let's anchor this asshole."

"Understood," answered Pip.

The Q-Ship released the tug, shooting the other end of the wire into the surface of the moon. As soon as it was inside the rock, the anchor extended, like roots in the ground, taking hold.

"Ship is secured," informed Pip.

"Good," muttered Eddie, and he pressed the controls forward, heading after the second ship.

It was already on the move, though, and nearing the next planet, with Hatch controlling the second Q-Ship right behind.

In moments, Eddie caught up to them both, and started firing across Orsa's hull, the same as he did with the last one. "Orsa, surrender your ship and prepare to—"

"I don't think so, Captain," he answered.

Orsa's ship turned quickly to face them, and he let loose a burst of missiles. Eddie reacted quickly, pulling back and avoiding the first few, then releasing a stream of flares to ignite the bombs.

Julianna held her seat tightly with one hand while keeping the other firmly on the controls. "Want me to blow him up?" she asked. "Just give me the fucking word!"

"No, we need his ass alive," responded Eddie.

The ship settled, once the missiles were gone. Before Eddie could do anything, however, Orsa sent his ship directly at them, firing wildly.

A spread of bullets hit the side of the Q-Ship as the vessel came forward, no sign of moving out of the way. Eddie had to swerve sideways to avoid a head-on collision. "Is this fucker crazy?!"

"He must not care if he dies," said Lars.

"Well, I care if I die," quipped Eddie. "We need to find a way to stop him before—"

The ship came back at them again, taking Eddie by surprise. He reached for the controls, trying to get out of the way, but it was going to be a close one. He might not be able to—

The remote controlled Q-Ship slammed headfirst into the side of the enemy vessel, partially piercing the hull. Both ships continued sideways. "Holy shit!" snapped Eddie.

Orsa's shuttle started firing, but without the ability to properly aim, thanks to the Q-Ship's nose buried inside its center, the bullets careened into deep space. "That's what he gets for trying to kill us," said Hatch.

"Release me at once!" yelled the voice on the other end.

"Sorry, but you'll need to speak up," answered Eddie. "Maybe if you surrender, we'll be able to understand you better."

There was a short pause, and then a laugh. "You idiots!"

Eddie and Julianna glanced at one another, curiously. Who did this guy think he was? His ship was disabled. His facility was destroyed. His boss was captured. "Look, Orsa. You can either surrender yourself willingly or not. It doesn't matter. We're taking you in for questioning. That's your new reality."

"I'll show you a new reality," muttered Orsa. "You humans think you're so perfect. You think the universe is yours to control. You think the rest of us are beneath you. Well, look how smart you are now! I'm not even on this ship." He laughed. "And this is hardly an escape shuttle. In fact, it's something else altogether."

"Did he just say he's not on that ship?" asked Lars.

"Sir, if I might interject," said Pip.

"What is it?" asked Eddie.

"That shuttle's engine is beginning to overload. I believe the operator is doing it intentionally with the hope of creating a large-scale explosion."

"You mean that ship's about to blow?"

"Quite so, yes."

"Fuck!" snapped Eddie. He took the controls, backing the Q-Ship away, turning around in a single motion as it continued in the opposite direction.

"You can try to escape, but this ship is using a Federation-style gravitic engine," said Orsa. "You're about to die from your own technology! You humans are so—"

Eddie cut the line. "Shut that guy up already," he said, accelerating the engines. It would take a few seconds to prime the gate. "I could use some options here, people!"

"I'll try to move him back with the other ship!" responded Hatch. He tapped the pad, sending the enemy vessel forward. "If I can just maneuver him towards that planet, we can contain the explosion."

"I should inform you," began Pip. "A gravitic explosion

of this nature is enough to obliterate a quarter of a star system."

"Thanks for the details, Pip!" snapped Eddie. "Goddammit!"

The ship ignited in a white flash of blinding light, filling the dark space so much it resembled a new sun. The Q-Ship accelerated towards the moon where Vas's ship was planted, attempting to reach the opposite side. With any luck, perhaps the rock itself would be enough to block the explosion and keep them from harm.

"It should be noted," Pip continued, "that even if we escape the blast, there's still the problem of—"

Eddie swerved the ship around right to the other side of the moon, right near Vas's ship, when a sudden burst struck them. The lights inside flickered and the controls went dead, no sign of power.

Julianna tried to bring the dash online, but there was no response. "What just happened?"

"Pip? Are you there?" asked Eddie.

"He says the ship's power is out," answered Julianna.

"I don't hear him," said Lars.

She pointed to her temple. "He's still here, but the lack of power on the ship means he can't speak through the computer system."

"Ask him why we lost power," finished Eddie.

She nodded. "He says there's a secondary EMP wave whenever a gravitic engine explodes."

Eddie leaned in closer to her, shouting, "Thanks for telling us in advance, Pip! You fucktard!"

23

The ArchAngel picked the Q-Ship up as soon as it arrived, saving the squad from what would surely prove a horrible death. The atmosphere inside could only last eight hours, so it was a good thing the dreadnaught starship was close enough to reel them in.

"Send whatever ships we have to retrieve the civilians," ordered Julianna as soon as the team was back aboard *the ArchAngel*.

"Automated shuttles are inbound," returned Pip, only a few moments later.

While the rescue took place, the crew worked on retrieving the enemy shuttle, maneuvering it into one of the cargo bays. Julianna, Lars, and Eddie, along with several security officers, stood outside the little ship, waiting for ArchAngel and Pip to override the system and open the door. As soon as they did, Eddie planned on taking this Vas fellow directly to a holding cell and deliver him to General Reynolds as soon as possible. All their hard work was about to pay off.

"Override complete," announced Pip. "Opening airlock."

The door cracked open, releasing internal atmosphere into the bay. It slid down, beneath the shuttle, transforming into a small staircase and revealing the pilot inside.

But it wasn't the one they expected.

"You've gotta be kidding me," muttered Julianna.

The alien standing there was none other than Commander Orsa himself, rather than General Vas.

Lars darted towards the shuttle, leaping over the stairs and grabbing Orsa by the throat. "What is this?!" barked Lars, pressing his pistol against the Kezzin's face. "What are you doing here?"

Orsa smiled through the pressure of Lars' fist, staring up at him across the barrel of the gun. "Good to see you again, traitor."

Eddie took a step towards the shuttle. "I gotta say, Lars has a point. If you're here then where is Vas?"

Orsa laughed, wheezing as Lars tightened his grip. "We tricked you. I've been controlling the other shuttle from this one, using it as a weapon. And General Vas was already gone before you—"

"Don't you see the destruction you've caused?" raged Lars.

"You're the one who's turned your back on your people!"

"I've done no such thing!" he yelled.

"You're a traitor," insulted Orsa.

"I betrayed you for the sake of our people. You're a danger to all Kezzin! You would have us murder and pillage, all for the sake of your own ego. What comes next, Commander? What happens when the Federation responds with due force? What would you do under the full assault of their wrath? You would awaken a sleeping giant with open arms, all to satisfy your own desire for power?" Lars scowled at his former master. "You're the traitor, Commander. You sold our people to Vas without a thought to our future."

"I did it to save us!"

"No," said Lars, letting him go. Orsa staggered back, clutching the place on his neck where Lars had held him. "You did everything for yourself."

Lars turned away from the Commander, a look of sadness on his face.

"You bastard!" shouted Orsa, withdrawing a knife from his backside lunging forward.

Eddie and Julianna reacted instantly, each of them rushing to stop the knife. Before it touched Lars, both their hands snagged Orsa's wrist, and together they threw him back and onto the floor of the shuttle. "I don't fucking think so!" shouted Eddie.

The knife left Orsa's hand and slid along the metal grate beneath the nearest seat.

Julianna punched the Commander in the jaw. "Fuck you and the horse you rode in on."

Orsa trembled, trying to pull away.

She pulled him to his feet and wrapped his hands behind his back, securing him. "Let's go!" she barked, pushing him out of the ship.

Eddie and Lars watched her leave with the new prisoner, several security officers following behind the pair.

———

Hatch sat alone in the second cargo bay, staring at the spot where he had previously worked on the Q-Ship. That one had been designed after he'd left the Federation, a mere replica of his original design. His actual creation was now destroyed, lost in the self-destructive blast of a madman. All that time developing it, modifying, tweaking. All of that was lost.

He reached to the floor and picked up a wrench with his tentacle, examining it. "Goddammit," he muttered.

"What is it, Doctor?" asked Pip, his voice coming over the nearby speaker.

Hatch started to look, but stopped, realizing that the E.I. had no face or presence. He was everywhere, in all parts of the ship. "It's nothing," said Hatch, tossing the wrench on the floor. It clanked and rattled. "I was just thinking."

"About what?"

"My poor life decisions."

"Could you be more specific?" asked the E.I.

"Why do you want to know?"

"You do not seem like yourself, so I am curious."

Hatch sighed. He knew he shouldn't feel this way about a piece of technology, even one he'd spent so long developing, but it was difficult. He couldn't help himself. "I guess I'm just pissed that they blew up my fucking ship, Pip."

"You mean the Q-Ship, correct?"

"Yeah," confirmed the mechanic.

"Is it difficult to lose something you created?" asked Pip.

"It is," replied Hatch, a somber tone in his voice.

"I am sorry," the E.I. responded. "I have lost things. I have lost friends."

"You've had friends?" asked Hatch, surprised at the E.I.'s use of the term.

"I believe so," answered Pip. "But perhaps my assessment of the word is incorrect. I have known individuals with whom I have shared time and discourse. They are no longer alive, nor can I speak with them again. They are gone forever, and knowing this fills me with…"

"With what?"

"I don't know," Pip admitted, after a moment. "I would like to call it loss, but it is difficult to define with any true precision. Is that wrong? Am I incorrect?"

"No," said Hatch. "I think that's probably right."

"Do you ever think about people in such terms?"

"Sometimes," admitted Hatch. "It's one of the things that reminds us that we're alive."

"But I'm not alive," said Pip. "Not like the rest of you."

Hatch didn't answer.

"What will you do now, Doctor?" asked Pip.

The mechanic glanced at the place where the ship had been, not long ago, drenched in oil stains and covered in tools and parts. "Now?" he echoed, thinking about it for the first time. "I suppose my job is still what it was, to maintain the Q-Ships."

"Is that your only purpose?" asked Pip.

"My only purpose?" muttered Hatch. "No, Pip. I don't

think any of us has a single purpose. Not when you consider how vast our experiences are and the breadth of our lives."

"I have many protocols and functions," replied the E.I.

"Ain't that the truth," said Hatch. "You're an impressive creature, that's for sure."

"Do you truly think so?"

Hatch laughed. "I do, Pip. In fact, I'd like to have a closer look at your software, if that's okay."

"Why would you want to do that?" asked Pip.

Hatch turned around and faced the other side of the bay. "I figure, maybe I can make some upgrades. You know, help you grow a bit more."

"Grow?" asked Pip. "You think I can expand my programming?"

"I don't see why not," said Hatch.

"Would such modifications allow me to better assist the team?"

"Is that what you want?" asked Hatch.

"Very much so, yes," answered Pip, and for a moment Hatch thought he heard a touch of enthusiasm in the E.I.'s voice.

"Then, let's see what we can do, my little friend."

"Whatever I can do to assist, I am willing," answered Pip.

Hatch smiled, waddling over to the nearby wall, cracking open the interface board. He retrieved a small pad and plugged it into the jack. "Okay, Pip. Let's see what makes you who you are."

Back in the cargo bay, Eddie and Lars were finally alone, all the security officers and personnel finally having left. Lars was quiet, he noticed. Almost isolated in thought. "Are you good?" asked Eddie, looking at his friend. Despite only knowing the Kezzin for a short time, he could tell something was wrong.

Lars nodded, slowly. "I am. Thank you." A moment later, he walked over to the wall and stared out through the large glass window, towards the system they'd just come from.

Eddie waited, briefly, letting the mood settle. "You know, the shit Orsa said to you…it's not true. In fact, it's grade-A bullshit."

"I know," said Lars, not sounding convinced. "He's a coward and a liar."

"But you're not," Eddie told him, walking to his side.

"Aren't I?" muttered Lars, his eyes distant and cold. "Everything he said to me was true. I betrayed them. I left the Brotherhood. Perhaps I truly am a coward."

"You stood up for what you believed in, Lars. My people call that bravery. We call it having values. Just because your leaders give an order, it doesn't make it right. You saw that and you acted. You stood up for your family and refused to be a tool of destruction. People like Orsa only want power for themselves. You're not like that, Lars. You're a good man."

"Thank you," said Lars, smiling a little. "Your words mean a great deal to me, Edward Teach, even though you are an ugly one."

Eddie shook his head. "Same to you, Lars Malseen," he replied, and it was the truth. He did appreciate him, the same way he did the rest of his team. Julianna, Hatch, Pip, and ArchAngel. All the people on this ship. Even General Reynolds. Each of them had given him something, a gift of trust, long before he came here. Long before he proved himself.

They saw a lost man, wandering the galaxy without purpose. They believed in him, and that was more than anyone had ever done. More than anything Eddie could've asked for, to be given purpose again, to be told he was useful.

He was a soldier, through every fiber of his flesh and his soul, every shred of his being. He was a man of service. To lose that status had been the greatest tragedy of his life, and yet, somehow, for whatever reason, General Reynolds and Julianna had found him and brought him home. They saved him from oblivion, from himself.

Now, he was back, and with a new family. To whatever end the journey took him, at least he would be with the people he had come to trust. At least he would have them beside him, giving him purpose.

Standing there in the cargo bay, neither Lars nor Eddie spoke again for quite some time. Instead, they stared out into the twinkling sea of light beyond the darkness, watching the universe together, contemplating how they had come to be here.

And together, they remembered.

EPILOGUE

Vas sat patiently in a room with no windows, waiting for the man he was supposed to meet. He'd come a long way to get here, escaping the attack on his facility, losing many soldiers in the process. The last few weeks had been staggering to his network, with repeated losses to both his finances and military forces. Without any assistance, he could be looking at a complete collapse of his entire infrastructure.

He touched the small hydration device on his hip, meant to keep his body from drying out. The Trid had not evolved to live on land for extended periods of time. In order to travel off planet, technology was built to accommodate their needs, including devices such as this. Without it, he would dehydrate and die. It was a risk worth taking, however, once the Trid achieved the power they so desperately deserved.

If only Vas had been allowed to continue his work, his victory would have been assured.

But instead, the Federation had found him, despite his careful planning and attempts at staying hidden. Still, if he could remain off their radar for a while, he might be able to recoup his losses.

But such an outcome was reliant on the present meeting. If it went poorly, there would not be a second chance.

The door opened across the room, and an individual in dark blue clothing entered, a human with a wide-brimmed hat.

Even after a year of taking orders, Vas still did not know his name.

Vas got to his feet, nervously. "Thank you for coming."

"I came because you couldn't do the job," said the man, taking a seat across the table, staring at Vas with dark eyes.

Vas sat back down. "I apologize," he told the man with the wide-brimmed hat. "We had no way of predicting that the Federation would attack us."

"How do you know it was the Federation?"

Vas hesitated. The truth was, he didn't know. Not at all. The only evidence he had for it was that a few of the soldiers were human, which wasn't enough to lay the blame on the Federation as a whole. After all, humans were all over the galaxy. There was even one sitting across from him now. "Their weapons were advanced. They were highly trained. Who else could it be?"

"So, you don't actually know," said the man. "Typical. I demand answers and you give me speculation."

"I-I'm sorry."

"Save your apologies. I want answers. I want the truth. Who were these people that killed all your men? How did they find you? How did they get through the defense network that I loaned you?"

Vas said nothing. He had no answers to give.

"As I expected."

"Please, give me a second chance at defending our movement," begged Vas. "I promise you, this will not happen again. I still have an army of Trid and Kezzin soldiers waiting for orders."

"An army that could just as easily be led by someone else," cautioned the man. "I could kill you now and no one would miss you. No one would care."

Vas swallowed.

The man tapped his chin. "But I won't do that. Not yet. It would be troublesome to train a new pet to do this work."

"Y-You mean I can continue to serve?" asked Vas, rather surprised.

"For now, yes," answered the man. "But fail again and you will suffer the full wrath of the New Empire. Do you understand me, Vas?"

Vas nodded. "Yes, sir."

The man rose to his feet and started to leave. "As always, I will send you encoded instructions on your next target. Don't do anything until you hear from me. Do you understand?"

"I do."

"Good."

The human left, closing the door behind him, leaving Vas to himself. The remaining silence was deafening, and for a brief moment, Vas felt a shiver of fear creep down his backside. If he failed again, he was done. The man with the wide-brimmed hat would kill him.

But the risk was worth it. The Brotherhood would rise again, and those humans, whoever they truly were, would not stand in the way.

General Vas would see to that.

FINIS

You know those conversations that change your life, but you don't realize you're having them until afterwards? I have those conversations often when talking with Michael Anderle, my cowriter for this series.

Anyway, I remember the day we discussed this series. I wished I could say I was plastered when I agreed to take on yet another series in the Anderle machine, knowing how demanding the deadlines are to keep the voracious readers happy. The truth was it was late morning, so I was mostly sober. I kid. You'll get used to it. Actually, some say that most people can't tell when I'm joking. Apparently I spent way too much of my youth watching Jack Benny. Before you wonder if I'm gray-haired making such a reference, please know that I usually only watch programming if it's British or old. I'm a weird snob like that. Remind me later to tell you about Red Dwarf.

Okay, back to that autumn morning when I decided I hated free time and wanted to take on another series. I had this harebrained idea that since I was in between projects that I should take on Ghost Squadron. Did it make sense at the time? No. Did it intimidate the hell out of me? Yes. Did my instinct say, "DO THIS"? Yes. And so, I did.

Has it been a challenge to write military space opera? Well, some of you might have read my other works, so you know this isn't my usual genre. I hope that's not a surprise. When MA asked me if I could do it I said, "You just replace the wand with a gun, right?" You're wondering if I'm kidding again... I'm not. I'm writing the Soul Stone Mage Series in the Oriceran universe for LMBPN. I also have five other NA and YA fantasy series. So I get asking the question about my comfortability writing space opera. When asked the question I answered with, "I've watched every episode of Red Dwarf." I told you it had to be British and/or old for me to watch it. And as hard as it is to believe I've watched Red Dwarf as a child and consequentially never watched a Disney movie until I was an adult. My point isn't that I was strangely sheltered. It's that I knew I could do anything I decided to. So I said yes to Michael. And I was incredibly relieved when Craig read my first space opera and said, "I think you've been writing space opera all along and never realized it."

ACKNOWLEDGMENTS

SARAH NOFFKE

Thank you to Michael Anderle for taking my calls and allowing me to play in this universe. It's been a blast since the beginning.

Thank you to Craig Martelle for cheering for me. I've learned so much working with you. This wild ride just keeps going and going.

Thank you to Jen, Tim, Steve, Andrew and Jeff for all the work on the books, covers and championing so much of the publishing.

Thank you to our beta team. I can't believe how fast you all can turn around books. The JIT team sometimes scares me, but usually just with how impressively knowledgeable they are.

Thank you to our amazing readers. I asked myself a question the other day and it had a strange answer. I asked if I would still write if trapped on a desert island and no one would ever read the books. The answer was yes, but the feeling connected to it was different. It wouldn't be as much fun to write if there wasn't awesome readers to share it with. Thank you.

Thank you to my friends and family for all the support and love.

AUTHOR NOTES - MICHAEL ANDERLE

WRITTEN NOVEMBER 13, 2017

First, let me say THANK YOU for not only reading all the way to the end of the story, but reading these author notes as well!

For you romantics, I hope you caught the hints in the author notes.

It's 3:32 AM and I'm now back at home in Las Vegas after a conference on Sunday in Austin, Texas. We went to go eat at Chin-Chin in the NY NY Hotel and found out Chin-Chin closed at 12:00 at night.

That was a complete bummer.

I had some rather so-so pizza at the pizza place, and my wife and I listened to music coming out of the piano bar place. Afterwards, we might have stopped to play a couple of machines before heading back to the car to come back home.

I get ready to take a shower (get rid of that smoke) and think to myself "is anything coming out tomorrow?"

I check on SLACK and Steve lets me know this book is

to be released in the morning and he needs my author notes.

At the aforementioned 3:32AM in the morning.

Screw my life.

I could have written them earlier, but I had been working all day speaking with a small handful of people in Austin and didn't check Slack, so didn't know about the notes needing to be done in about one hour from now.

<Sigh.>

I remember our first conversations about this series, working on the characters, and setting up how the members of the military must feel at this point in the Federation negotiations.

It feels VERY nice to be releasing this book, so many months after those first conversations.

ANOTHER BABY IS BORN!

On my side, I'm just now writing the book that will be feeding into this series (Capture Death). A bit out of order – but I hope it will all make sense when I finish book 20 and 21 in the very near future.

In six months, none of these missed books will mean anything as we seal up the holes in the timelines and answer the questions that you, the readers, have been asking.

In a few hours, I will change the pricing on TKG 01 / 02 and Leira Chronicles 01 and 02 back to their regular pricing and our first weekend collector's sale will be over. It has been a successful and appreciated effort and we (the authors) appreciate you supporting us as we work to bring you stories that will entertain you for years to come.

I'm sorry these author notes are so short – but my head

is dropping down to my chest and Stephen Campbell needs me to finish these up and get them to him.

For those who are wondering, I have the beats for Capture Death completed, and the first 1,000 words written (and the last 1,000 for that matter) in the book.

I'm super happy to have Sarah Noffke working with us in the this Universe. It will be interesting to see what happens going forward when she replaces wands with laser pistols ;-)

Ad Aeternitatem,

Michael

SNEAK PEEK OF EXPLORATION

Turn the page for an excerpt from
Exploration
(The Ghost Squadron, Book #2)

General Lance Reynolds' Office, Onyx Station, Paladin System.

"Chief? You there?" asked General Reynolds.

"I'm here. Comms out here aren't secure, but I don't have to tell you that," said Chief Jack Renfro.

"I'll keep it brief," said General Reynolds. He stubbed his stogie out, a slight smile on his face. He'd taken to Jack early on. There were very few you could trust when everyone was out to serve themselves or have the Federation serve them. However, Jack Renfro didn't do something to get something. He'd passed up many promotions because they didn't make sense for his real ambition. This was a man who wanted to serve in the right position, not the one that got him a better title and more money. At the core, he had always been a servant to the cause.

"I've got a job for you," said Lance.

"When and where do I need to be?" asked Jack.

"You haven't even heard the details yet." Lance laughed.

"When did that ever matter between the two of us? If you need my help, then I'm there."

"I wouldn't normally ask, but I have a squadron that needs some oversight. I was taking care of it, but I've been pulled away for more...pressing matters. I'm sure you know why and by whom," said Lance.

"I believe I do," responded Jack.

The cloud of smoke Lance blew out filled his office, making it appear gray. "Anyway, I wouldn't trust anyone but you to handle this group. They have an incredibly important mission, and I've handpicked them myself. I'm sending over the details of the team right now, along with their previous mission assignments. You'll find that they've been quite busy."

"The report is just coming through. Give me a sec," said Jack, a shuffling sounding over the comms. "Holy shit, Lance. You can't be serious?"

Lance chuckled. "I'm completely serious. See, I thought you'd have fun with this."

"Those two working together?" he asked. "I'm impressed, boss."

A familiar pride filled Lance's chest. "I'm glad you think so."

"And you've given them the *ArchAngel*?" asked Jack.

"They have an important mission," said Lance.

"Damn, and you even brought back Hatcherick, I see. Damn impressive, sir. Haven't seen a team like this since... well, you know. It's been a *long* time."

"Just wait and see who else I have lined up for this crew," said Lance.

"Don't leave me hanging, boss. Send over the report."

"Does that mean you'll oversee them?" asked Lance.

"I already told you I was committed, and that was before you gave me the details," said Jack.

"I knew I could count on you, Chief," said Lance. "Sending you the rest of the report now. Good luck, Jack."

"Thank you, sir," said Chief Jack Renfro. "It's always an honor to serve."

CHAPTER 1

Harbor District. Trinidad City, Axiom 03, Axiom System.

The warehouse was filled with dust and age, the scent of industry still lingering in the air. That was the case with many of the old buildings in this city, ever since the Alegro Corporation packed up its bags and left the system for better financial opportunities. Less money meant less security, which meant more opportunity for criminals.

Captain Edward Teach stood quietly in the middle of the warehouse, waiting for the Trids to unload the merchandise.

"Here you are," said the Trid named Doka. He set a crate down in front of Eddie and stepped back.

Eddie looked to his left at Lars Maldeen, a massive Kezzin in full body armor. "Check it."

Lars nodded, bending down to the crate and popping the lock. He opened it, revealing a set of rifles, and took one out to examine it. "Looks good."

"What about the grenades?" asked Eddie, glancing back at Doka.

"All here, all here," Doka assured him. He waved at his associates, who brought three smaller boxes.

Lars checked those, too, and gave Eddie the clear.

"Good," said Eddie. "Mind if I ask where you got these?"

"What do you care?" asked the Trid.

"I just like to know where my guns come from."

"From me. That's all you need to know."

"Is it?" asked Eddie. "Because you're the middle man, last I checked."

Doka tapped the small device on his hip, a piece of tech that kept his body hydrated. Trids evolved on an ocean planet and required a very specific chemical to prevent them from drying out. If they went too long without it, they'd die. The device was essential for this reason, as it monitored their vitals and injected the chemical whenever it was needed. "You insult me," Doka finally said. "That isn't wise."

Eddie chuckled. "Maybe you're right. Sorry, I was just messing around."

"Are you satisfied with these weapons?" asked Doka, who was ready to end this meeting and move on.

"Just about," said Eddie, looking around. "My associate should be here soon to help me square this."

"Your associate?" asked Doka. "You never mentioned—"

"I know, I know. I thought she'd be here by now. I don't know what's taking her so long."

"Maybe she was held up," suggested Lars.

Eddie nodded. "Could be. I guess I could call."

Doka looked at both of them. "What are you talking about? Which one of you has the money?"

Eddie ignored him. "You know, she always does this. I bet she and Hatch are at a bar right now. Probably forgot all about this job."

"I don't think she'd do that," said Lars. "But Hatch might."

"Hey!" barked Doka. "Are you even listening to me?"

Eddie felt his stomach growl. "Speaking of bars, remind me after we're done here to stop and get some grub. I'm fucking starving."

"Me too. I could use a good slab of meat," said Lars, almost drooling at the thought.

Zoka snarled, taking a step closer to Eddie. "If you don't tell me right this second what exactly is going on, I'm going to kill both of you and strap your guts to the side of my fucking ship! Are you listening to—"

The door in the back of the warehouse flung open, and an athletic-looking brunette walked in carrying what could only be described as a big fucking gun. She hoisted it up, cocking the rifle, which must have been half her size, with little effort. "Afternoon, boys. What did I miss?"

Don't Miss Book 2 in the Ghost Squadron Series!

THE GHOST SQUADRON

by Sarah Noffke and Michael Anderle

WANT MORE?

ENTER

THE KURTHERIAN GAMBIT UNIVERSE

A desperate move by a dying alien race transforms the unknown world into an ever-expanding, paranormal, intergalactic force.

The Kurtherian Gambit Universe contains more than 100 titles in series created by Michael Anderle and many talented co-authors. For a complete list of books in this phenomenal marriage of paranormal and science fiction, go to:

http://kurtherianbooks.com/timeline-kurtherian/

ABOUT SARAH NOFFKE

Sarah Noffke, an Amazon Best Seller, writes YA and NA sci-fi fantasy, paranormal and urban fantasy. She is the author of the Lucidites, Reverians, Ren, Vagabond Circus, Olento Research and Soul Stone Mage series. Noffke holds a Masters of Management and teaches college business courses. Most of her students have no idea that she toils away her hours crafting fictional characters. Noffke's books are top rated and best-sellers on Kindle. Currently, she has eighteen novels published. Her books are available in paperback, audio and in Spanish, Portuguese and Italian.

SARAH NOFFKE SOCIAL

Website: http://www.sarahnoffke.com
Facebook: https://www.facebook.com/officialsarahnoffke
Amazon: http://amzn.to/1JGQjRn

BOOKS BY SARAH NOFFKE

THE SOUL STONE MAGE SERIES

House of Enchanted #1

The Kingdom of Virgo has lived in peace for thousands of years…until now.

The humans from Terran have always been real assholes to the witches of Virgo. Now a silent war is brewing, and the timing couldn't be worse. Princess Azure will soon be crowned queen of the Kingdom of Virgo.

In the Dark Forest a powerful potion-maker has been murdered.

Charmsgood was the only wizard who could stop a deadly virus plaguing Virgo. He also knew about the devastation the people from Terran had done to the forest.

Azure must protect her people. Mend the Dark Forest. Create alliances with savage beasts. No biggie, right?

But on coronation day everything changes. Princess Azure isn't who she thought she was and that's a big freaking problem.

Welcome to The Revelations of Oriceran.

The Dark Forest #2

Mountain of Truth #3

Land of Terran #4

New Egypt #5

Lancothy #6

Awoken, #1:

Around the world humans are hallucinating after sleepless nights. In a sterile, underground institute the forecasters keep reporting the same events. And in the backwoods of Texas, a sixteen-year-old girl is about to be caught up in a fierce, ethereal battle.

Meet Roya Stark. She drowns every night in her dreams, spends her hours reading classic literature to avoid her family's ridicule, and is prone to premonitions—which are becoming more frequent. And now her dreams are filled with strangers offering to reveal what she has always wanted to know: Who is she? That's the question that haunts her, and she's about to find out. But will Roya live to regret learning the truth?

Stunned, #2

Revived, #3

THE REVERIANS SERIES

Defects, #1

In the happy, clean community of Austin Valley, everything appears to be perfect. Seventeen-year-old Em Fuller, however, fears something is askew. Em is one of the new generation of Dream Travelers. For some reason, the gods have not seen fit to gift all of them with their expected special abilities. Em is a Defect—one of the unfortunate Dream Travelers not gifted with a psychic power. Desperate to do whatever it takes to earn her gift, she endures painful daily injections along with commands from her overbearing, loveless father. One of the few bright spots in her life is the return of a friend she had thought dead—but with his return comes the knowledge of a shocking, unforgivable truth. The society Em thought was protecting her has actually been betraying her, but she has no idea how to break away from its authority without hurting everyone she loves.

<u>Rebels, #2</u>

<u>Warriors, #3</u>

VAGABOND CIRCUS SERIES

<u>Suspended, #1</u>

When a stranger joins the cast of Vagabond Circus—a circus that is run by Dream Travelers and features real magic—mysterious events start happening. The once orderly grounds of the circus become riddled with hidden threats. And the ringmaster realizes not only are his circus and its magic at risk, but also his very life.

Vagabond Circus caters to the skeptics. Without skeptics, it would close its doors. This is because Vagabond Circus runs for two reasons and only two reasons: first and foremost to provide the lost and lonely Dream Travelers a place to be illustrious. And secondly, to show the nonbelievers that there's still magic in the world. If they believe, then they care, and if they care, then they don't destroy. They stop the small abuse that day-by-day breaks down humanity's spirit. If Vagabond Circus makes one skeptic believe in magic, then they halt the cycle, just a little bit. They allow a little more love into this world. That's Dr. Dave Raydon's mission. And that's why this ringmaster recruits. That's why he directs. That's why he puts on a show that makes people question their beliefs. He wants the world to believe in magic once again.

Paralyzed, #2

Released, #3

Ren: The Man Behind the Monster, #1

Born with the power to control minds, hypnotize others, and read thoughts, Ren Lewis, is certain of one thing: God made a mistake. No one should be born with so much power. A monster awoke in him the same year he received his gifts. At ten years old. A prepubescent boy with the ability to control others might merely abuse his powers, but Ren allowed it to corrupt him. And since he can have and do anything he wants, Ren should be happy. However, his journey teaches him that harboring so much power doesn't bring happiness, it steals it. Once this realization sets in, Ren makes up his mind to do the one thing that can bring his tortured soul some peace. He must kill the monster.

Note This book is NA and has strong language, violence and sexual references.

Ren: God's Little Monster, #2

Ren: The Monster Inside the Monster, #3

Ren: The Monster's Adventure, #3.5

Ren: The Monster's Death, #4

Alpha Wolf, #1:

Twelve men went missing.

Six months later they awake from drug-induced stupors to find themselves locked in a lab.

And on the night of a new moon, eleven of those men, possessed by new—and inhuman—powers, break out of their prison and race through the streets of Los Angeles until they disappear one by one into the night.

Olento Research wants its experiments back. Its CEO, Mika Lenna, will tear every city apart until he has his werewolves imprisoned once again. He didn't undertake a huge risk just to lose his would-be assassins.

However, the Lucidite Institute's main mission is to save the world from injustices. Now, it's Adelaide's job to find these mutated men and protect them and society, and fast. Already around the nation, wolflike men are being spotted. Attacks on innocent women are happening. And then, Adelaide realizes what her next step must be: She has to find the alpha wolf first. Only once she's located him can she stop whoever is behind this experiment to create wild beasts out of human beings.

Lone Wolf, #2

Rabid Wolf, #3

Bad Wolf, #4